shift

shift

EM BAILEY

EGMONT

USA

NEW YORK

EGMONT
We bring stories to life

First published in Australia by Hardie Grant Egmont, 2011
First published in the United States of America by Egmont USA, 2012
443 Park Avenue South, Suite 806
New York, NY 10016

1 3 5 7 9 8 6 4 2

www.egmontusa.com

Library of Congress Cataloging-in-Publication Data

Bailey, Em.
Shift / Em Bailey.
p. cm.
Summary: Olive, having recently suffered mental problems, is unsure whether to trust
her instincts when a new student, rumored to have killed her parents, develops a parasitic
relationship with Olive's former best friend, Jubilee Park High School's "Queen Bee."
ISBN 978-1-60684-358-1 (hardcover) -- ISBN 978-1-60684-359-8 (ebook)
[1. Interpersonal relations--Fiction. 2. Popularity--Fiction. 3. Mental illness--Fiction.
4. High schools--Fiction. 5. Schools--Fiction. 6. Orphans--Fiction.] I. Title.
PZ7.B15135Shi 2012
[Fic]--dc23
2011034349

Book design by Ektavo

Printed in the United States of America

For Jim and Julie.

ONE

There were two things everyone knew about Miranda Vaile before she'd even started at our school. The first was that she had no parents – they were dead. And the second? They were dead because Miranda had killed them.

When these rumours started spreading, people got all steamed up about it, saying it was disgusting that she was allowed to come here and, you know, mix with us nice, non-murderous types.

Not everyone felt like that, though. Personally, I couldn't wait to meet her. As I said to Ami, what kind of wonk *wouldn't* want to meet someone who sounded halfway interesting? Of course, maybe that just showed I didn't belong at our school either.

o

One night, my little brother Toby woke up screaming in the darkness. He hadn't done that for weeks, and somehow that made it worse. I'd been stupid enough to think that maybe Toby was finally accepting that Dad had gone. I thought maybe the nightmares had finished for good. After the screaming, Toby cried. Cried like a baby. I sat beside him feeling like I might sink into the sadness of it and never escape.

Mum appeared in Toby's room moments after I did, the hallway light shining behind her. Standing there in her baggy T-shirt, she looked even more like Toby than usual. Small and delicate, with these big, grey-blue eyes and that fine, fair sort of hair that always sits smoothly, even when you've been woken in the middle of the night.

It used to bother me that I didn't look like anyone else in my family and I'd examine photos, searching for similarities. A nose, ears, the curve of a jaw. Anything that resembled me. But there was never anything. In the end I quit looking.

'It's OK,' I said to Mum. 'You go back to bed. I'm good at calming him.' That was true. But there was another reason I wanted to stay. It was my duty. Because it was my fault Tobes was in this state in the first place.

I snuggled up next to him, our heads side by side on his pillow like two pupils in the one eye socket. He finally drifted off. But there was no chance of me doing the same – I was way too keyed up. So I just lay there, looking at the model solar system he'd made in grade two. Waiting out the night, and thinking about all the things that had happened.

o

I don't remember much about the next morning. Not Showering or Having Breakfast or Taking My Meds or any of that stuff which must have happened because that's what mornings were about. You Did Something, then you Did Something Else. I was supposed to congratulate myself for every little accomplishment. *Good job getting out of your PJs! Eaten all your toast? Nice work, you!*

Baby steps, Dr Richter called them. But people seemed to forget that babies fall over all the freakin time.

But I do remember the rush of relief when I got to school and found Ami waiting for me. Ami, who I *did* look like – even though we weren't related. We had the same black eyes and freakishly long lashes. The same short, mussy dark hair, although hers looked like it was meant to be mussy and mine looked like I'd slept on it funny. We had our differences too, of course. Her skin was blemish-free and her uniform didn't strain and bulge the way mine did. But the biggest differences were things you couldn't see. I mean, if I'd been alone like that in front of the lockers, I would've looked like a complete loser. Not Ami. She was standing there, calmly watching everyone swarm around her with this big grin – like the whole thing was some special event put on for her amusement. The group of non-stop chatterers. The panicked last-minute homework-finishers. The tracksuit-wearing cretins who'd nicked some poor kid's bag and were chucking it around. The smoochy year nine couple weaving their way down the hall, stopping every few seconds to exchange saliva.

As I came up, Ami inhaled deeply. 'Smell that?' she said. 'The *shtink* of Monday morning. What's in it? Sweat, of course. Smoke. Hair products. But there's something else …'

The smoochy couple from the year below walked right into me. It's hard to walk straight when your lips are fused to someone else's. The guy's elbow dug into my arm. 'Sorry,' he said, laughing. 'We weren't –'

When he realised who he'd jabbed, he edged away like he might catch something. 'Oh,' he muttered. 'I'm –'

His girlfriend tugged his arm. 'Come *on*.'

Ami turned to me as they hurried off. '*Pheromones*,' she said. 'That's the other smell.'

I let my bag slide off my shoulder and fall to the ground. I rested my head against the wall. 'I can't smell anything,' I said. My nose was blocked. My lungs too. I was drowning in myself. I felt Ami examine my washed-out face. My hair sticking out in dark, wilted quills. The smears of black beneath my eyes.

'Bad night, huh?'

'You could say that.' I bent down and unzipped my bag.

Ami sat down beside me. 'Toby?'

I put my hands up to my face, palms together like I was praying. Or sneezing. *Keep it together.* 'Shouldn't it be easier by now?' I said. 'It's been six months. Almost seven.'

'Olive,' said Ami, steady and firm as a heartbeat. 'It'll get better. Easier. I can promise you that. I've been through it too, remember.'

I wanted to believe her.

Ami took my hand, her fingers folding around mine. The smooth, perfect nails at the end of each long, elegant finger made my hands look even more stumpy and chewed-on. 'Hey,' she said. 'If I can make it, why wouldn't you?'

There were about a thousand reasons why. Ami was a coper for one thing. She adapted and evolved. She could shift her mind so she didn't just focus on the bad stuff. Not exactly my strengths. Then there was the other thing. Yes, Ami's dad had left, just like mine had. But it hadn't been Ami's fault.

'How about we chuck school for the day?' said Ami suddenly. 'Go down to the beach. Hang out. Talk.'

I shook my head. I'd made some promises to Mum and Dr Richter, the first one being that I wouldn't cut school anymore. Besides, Ami and I had already spent a lot of time talking about our dads. That was to be expected at first – it was the main reason we became friends after I'd been discharged. I could vent stuff with Ami because she understood what I was going through. But there was more to our friendship now. At least, I hoped there was.

Ami's mouth twitched. Mischievously. 'Yeah, I figured you'd want to hang around,' she said. 'The new girl and all.'

That was something else Ami was good at – dragging my mood out of the swamp and sending it towards the rainforest canopy. 'Oh my *god*. The parent-murderer!' I said. 'I can't believe I forgot.'

'Olive!' Ami laughed, pretending to look shocked. 'She's not a murderer.'

'Probably not,' I said, grabbing some books from my bag and shoving the rest in my locker. 'But I can hope, can't I? Come on.'

Now I was in a rush to get to class. We headed off down the corridor and straight through the middle of everyone – the starers, the pointers and the whisperers stepping aside as we came through, before falling back into place behind us.

'Do you really think they'd let a murderer into the school?' said Ami. 'Around *here*? Anyway, if it was even a tiny bit true it'd be all over the news.'

'Maybe there's been a big cover-up,' I said. 'Maybe Mrs Deane was given a heap of cash to take her on. They're not exactly picky, are they? I mean, they took me back after my little Incident.'

A group of year seven stupidos rushed by, yelling like they were still on a footy oval somewhere. One of them squirted the others with the fire extinguisher, bubbles flying everywhere.

Ami stepped over a little foam mountain in the middle of the floor. 'Just don't get your hopes up,' she said. 'It might be like when that year twelve girl was preg-not.'

'That could still be true, Ames,' I protested.

Ami did an eye roll. 'Admit it. She's just putting on weight.'

I sighed, über dramatically. 'You're so freakin logical and … *sensible*. Remind me. Why are we even friends?'

'Who said we *were* friends?' Ami's smile was cheeky. 'As far as I'm concerned, you're my science experiment.'

'Funny. Let's get a move on. That was the first bell.'

'Don't you think it's weird that everyone's so obsessed

with her?' said Ami as we neared our classroom door. 'When that new guy started last week no-one acted like this.'

A new guy? For a moment I couldn't picture who she was talking about. And then I remembered. He was just more of the same. Sunny and bland and hard to distinguish. You know, one more piece of sky in the jigsaw puzzle of our school.

'That's my point,' I said. 'All this hype. It must mean something.'

Ami frowned. 'She can't be a child genius *and* a model *and* a drug dealer all at once.'

'Of course she can,' I laughed. 'Or she might be just one of those things.'

'Come on, Olive. We both know where the rumours probably started.'

'Katie.' I pushed a sprig of hair behind my ear. Instantly it sprung back out. 'I dunno, Ames. Is she capable of making up stuff quite that interesting?'

'Let's ask her,' Ami murmured, looking ahead. 'Here they come.'

Sure enough, Katie and the others were walking towards us. I found myself searching for some kind of emergency exit. Preferably one that led directly into a parallel universe.

'I am so not in the mood for this,' I muttered.

Katie and the others arranged themselves in front of me like a thin-lipped smile. I could just about feel the gleam of Katie's teeth, so radiant it was probably causing skin cancers on my face. Katie was staring at me, seemingly transfixed with horror.

7

Her eyes moved over me, noting my gnawed-on nails and my uniform straining in ways it never used to before. Along with pimples, my medication had given me a brand new body. *Softer,* Mum kept saying. *Curvy.*

Katie stopped at my hair. 'God, Olive. When are you going to let your hair grow back?'

Justine and Paige shook their heads, obviously too overcome to speak. Katie touched her own hair then – blonde and super-smooth. The sort of hair that stayed tucked behind your ear if you put it there. The dark pink thread she wore around her slender wrist slipped slightly.

Sometimes I almost enjoyed these encounters with Katie. Ami called it *Rate with Kate,* because Katie always made you feel like she was mentally giving you a score out of ten. Ami pointed out that if I no longer wanted to be the person I was before – all skinny-jeaned and long-haired and whatever – then I may as well have some fun being different. And when I was in the right mood, it *was* fun seeing the confusion on Katie's face as she tried to figure out what had changed. But that day I just wasn't into it.

'Thanks for the feedback, Katie,' I said, 'but I have to go.'

'I'm only doing this because we used to be friends,' Katie shot at me. 'Do you *want* to end up a road accident?'

'Oh please,' I said. 'Not this again.'

Katie's expression changed. It's amazing how a face can shift from pretty to ugly just by tightening a few facial muscles. 'The old you would've died rather than look like this,' she said.

The metallic, medicinal taste was in my mouth again. 'The

old me *did* die,' I snapped.

Ami's hand was on my arm. 'Calm down,' she whispered. 'Don't be pissed off by someone who is still bragging about winning the Sweetest Smile on the Beach competition. You should be glad she doesn't like how you look.'

Ami was right, of course. It was a long time since I'd wanted Katie's approval. A long time since I'd been on the other side of this type of conversation, making a fat chick's life miserable. My anger began to loosen and slip away. Not completely, but enough.

'Go on then,' called Katie as we walked away. 'But don't forget, once you're a road accident, that's it. No going back.'

We were opening the classroom door when my ears did this *thing*.

Ami caught my expression. 'One of your headaches?'

'It feels different this time,' I said, giving my head a shake. 'There's a noise. Buzzy, like static. Can you hear it?'

Ami stood still for a moment. 'Nope.'

I rubbed my ear, wincing.

'Maybe you should go home, Olive.'

I snorted. 'Yeah right. You know what my mum's like when I'm sick. Anyway, I want to see the new girl.'

I could see Ami trying to work out if it was worth arguing. She decided against it, as I knew she would. In her own way, Ami needed me around too.

'No blaming me if your head explodes,' she said.

'OK,' I said. 'But if it does can you make sure it stays off the school blog?' I'd been on that thing way too much already.

Miss Falippi was standing up the front when we arrived, dressed in her unstructured layered clothes and jangling, dangling jewellery. One hand held her usual mug of foul-smelling herbal tea and the other fiddled with her locket. I used to look at that silver disc all the time, wondering what little secret was tucked away inside it. A photo of her hippie boyfriend? A lock of hair from a child she'd been forced to give up at birth? A stash of weed to get her through the day? That would explain why she sometimes zoned out, gazing off into the distance like she'd forgotten we were there.

After I'd returned from the clinic, though, I lost interest. The locket was probably just a necklace.

'People,' said Miss Falippi. 'Sit down, please.'

Ami and I sat at the back these days. The front was occupied by the students with *focus* issues – either too much or not enough. The middle rows belonged to Katie. That's where everyone wanted to sit, and the closer to Katie the better. Paige sat on one side of her, and Cameron Glover – naturally – sat on the other. It was where I used to sit too, and occasionally I still stopped there. Habit, I guess. Forgetting for a moment how things had changed. Who I was now.

Usually I kept my eyes fixed on the posters on the back wall as I walked to my seat. The posters depicted insect life cycles from pupae to adult. I'd learnt a lot about this fascinating subject since I'd moved seats.

But that day something surprising pulled my eyes away from the posters. The flash of a smile from an unfamiliar face. The new guy's. New Guy was what my mum would call a looker – all broad-shouldered and dark, tousled hair. He looked like he'd been incorrectly shelved, sitting two rows away from Katie. But it wouldn't be long before he moved. Katie would match him up with one of her buds and soon New Guy would be sitting where he belonged. I turned to see who the smile was intended for.

There was no-one behind me. When I looked back, New Guy's eyes were waiting and his smile twitched a little. Then I understood. He'd heard about what happened from Katie – like everyone else had – and the smile was a mocking one. It showed that he'd already begun his journey up, up and away from the likes of me. I turned my head and stalked the rest of the way to my seat.

Miss Falippi shut the door and put the mug on her desk half-way between a tin of pencils and her Greek mythology textbook. 'People,' she said, raising her hand for silence. 'I'm sure you've heard there's a new student joining us today. Miranda Vaile.'

'The chick who knocked off her parents?' someone called. Cameron, I think. There was muchos sniggering.

Miss Falippi sighed. Clearly she'd heard the stories too. 'OK, it's time to sort a few things out here. It's very sad, but Miranda *is* an orphan.'

'Rumour confirmed!' I said to Ami a little smugly.

Half of the row in front turned to stare. Oops. The buzzing was making it hard to judge how loudly I was speaking.

Miss Falippi twirled a finger in the air. 'But let me make this very clear. Miranda Vaile is *not* a murderer. Her parents died in a car accident when she was just a baby.'

Now it was Ami's turn to look smug. 'Rumour squashed,' she said. 'Unless you think she cut the brake cable with her little baby hands?'

Miss Falippi was swinging her locket like a pendulum. 'Miranda has spent most of her life overseas,' she said. 'This will be a big change for her, leaving the vibrancy and excitement of Europe to live in our quiet little suburb. We'll need to be very understanding. It might take her a little while to fit in.'

'She should've just stayed over there,' said Katie, cleaning a fingernail with Paige's pen lid. 'If it was so *vibrant* and *exciting*.' Somehow Katie could say this shit and not get into trouble.

'Miranda is moving here to live with her great-aunt,' Miss Falippi said over the giggling, trying to keep control of the discussion. 'Some of you might know her. Oona Delaunay.'

More snickering. Loony Oona the germ freak? Yeah, we knew her.

'Hard to picture Oona taking care of someone,' I said to Ami. 'She looks like she struggles to take care of herself.'

Katie turned around, her face screwed up. 'Can you *stop* doing that?'

'Doing what?'

'*Muttering*,' she said. 'It's really disturbing.'

This was so typical. It was OK for Katie to blather away as

much as she wanted, but when I said something it was somehow disturbing.

Miss Falippi's bangles clashed together as she clapped. 'People! Enough.'

The buzz in my ears grew louder. *Maybe there's something* in *there. A little bug, crawling around.* The thought made me shudder. As I tilted my head to one side and shook it again, I caught a glimpse of something out the window. Two figures were heading across the quadrangle towards our classroom. I recognised Mrs Deane straight away, of course – solid and dark in her principal's suit, heels click-clacking across the concrete. The other figure I hadn't seen before. *That must be her. Miranda Vaile.*

I don't know what I thought a possible parent-murderer would look like, but it certainly wasn't this thin, pale creature trailing along behind Mrs Deane. I leant closer to the window, wanting a clearer view. As the two figures disappeared from sight, I turned to Ami, my heart skittering.

Ami looked up. 'What is it?'

'I saw her,' I whispered. 'The new girl.'

Ami's eyes widened. 'What did she look like?'

I struggled for a minute, trying to find a way to describe what I'd just seen. 'She looked ... blurry.'

Ami sighed. 'Stupid dirty windows.'

I didn't reply. Mrs Deane hadn't looked blurry – just the new girl. She seemed out of focus, like she'd moved at the last minute when someone took a photo. But I knew how dumb that would sound, especially to super-sensible Ami. So I stayed quiet, watching the classroom door. Waiting.

o

Everything about Mrs Deane was efficient. The way she knocked. The way she spoke. How she stepped into rooms. It was like she had devised some mathematical formula to ensure there was no wastage in anything she did. 'Miss Falippi. Class. This is Miranda Vaile.'

Twenty-two pairs of eyes locked onto the girl standing beside Mrs Deane. Took in the chalky skin. The rain-grey hair that dripped down from her head and drizzled across her hunched, old-woman shoulders. Miranda's uniform hung in sheets, like there was barely enough of her to hold it up.

I examined her as closely as everyone else. Strange. She didn't look blurry now, of course. *It must have been the windows after all. Or my eyes playing tricks on me.* But there was definitely something about Miranda that made her hard to focus on. She was so nothingy that you found your eyes sliding off her to fix on something else more solid nearby. She would have blended in with the background, except that the background was more interesting.

Katie's nose wrinkled and she made her call. The one that would determine how everyone treated this new arrival. 'Just what we need,' she said in her quiet-but-loud voice. 'Another road accident.'

'Welcome to Jubilee Park!' said Miss Falippi, stretching out a hand for Miranda to shake. Miranda stared at it blankly. The hand faltered and then fled back to where it belonged, on the locket.

'There's a spare seat down the back, Miranda,' Miss Falippi said, clearly flustered. 'Next to Olive.' Then she kind of whooshed Miranda down the aisle towards me, like she was pushing smoke away.

I looked down, fiddling around with my books and pens. Why was I so edgy? *It's my headache,* I told myself. *The buzzing.* When I knew Miranda would be really close I looked up, unable to resist any longer. She was almost directly in front of me and I found myself staring into her eyes. Instantly, the buzzing in my head rose to a crescendo, loud and insistent as an alarm. *Oh my god …*

o

Memory is such a weird thing. There are some things, like songs, that I literally only need to hear once and they are permanently locked into my brain. Other things, like algebraic formulas, can pass through my mind multiple times without leaving a trace. But sometimes you remember stuff even when you don't want to. Some things you know will stay with you, in perfect detail, for the rest of your life.

This moment was like that, when I first made eye contact with Miranda, and I recoiled like I'd been stung. I'd never seen eyes like hers before. The pupils seemed to be made of metal, hard and brightly polished. Reflected in them I could see my own face, staring back.

TWO

Outside the rain was falling hard, but the cinema foyer was warm and dark. Everything about the Mercury was old. The carpets. The wallpaper. The movies. The popcorn. The damp-damaged pictures of mulleted movie stars behind the snack bar. Above the photos was a giant plastic ice-cream that whined and pulsed with light when I switched it on.

I liked working at the Mercury. It smelled of my childhood.

Ami was leaning against the snack bar, watching as I set up for the evening. *'Mirrored* eyes?' she said. 'Are you sure?'

I wiped down the sign announcing our latest attraction. *Gremlins.* Part of that year's Retro Horror Film-Fest. Toby was waiting for Mum on his usual stool at the end of the counter, face glowing green from the laptop in front of him.

I began wiping the counter. I was regretting telling Ami about Miranda's eyes. It sounded stupid now.

Toby lifted his drink can so I could wipe underneath. His

forehead was creased. 'Do you have a carrot?' he asked. 'Mum might smell the sugar on my breath.'

'She'll be an hour at least,' I said. 'Don't worry.'

'Maybe Miranda's some kind of alien,' Ami mused. 'Here to take over the world, starting with the bustling suburb of Jubilee Park.'

The projectionist's door opened and Noah appeared. He strolled over to the snack bar openly checking me out. 'Hey! How's my favourite employee going? Love your get-up – you look even more luscious that usual.'

I ignored that last bit, even though I was kind of proud of my outfit. I'd put it together myself for the film-fest, including a bloodied axe-on-a-headband for full effect.

I began refilling the straw dispenser. 'Technically, your *dad* employs me,' I pointed out. 'You know, that guy who owns this place? Works upstairs in the projectionist's booth. The one who'd probably be pretty interested if I told him you were harassing me. *Again.*'

Noah chuckled. 'I like your fire.'

He was like a cockroach, Noah. Small. Slick. Hard to squash.

I plugged my iPod into the stereo and turned up the music. Instantly Noah frowned. 'What's this?' he said. 'Not the official Mercury music, that's for sure.'

I showed him the album artwork I'd made in Photoshop.

'Who's that guy?' he asked, pointing to the beauteous face on the screen.

'That,' I said, 'is Dallas Kaye.'

Dallas Kaye. Even saying his name made me feel good. When I'd first come out of the clinic – before I found Ami – things were pretty dark. I'd thrown out my old clothes (which no longer fitted anyway) and most of my possessions too. I'd taken a pair of scissors to my hair, giving it jagged lines that mapped my interior state. When I'd discovered Dallas and his band Luxe, his songs filled some of the empty spaces in my newly cleaned-out life. I holed up in my bedroom and fantasised my way into his life. Luckily when Ami came along, she totally got it and we often sat around listening to Luxe together. And she didn't even mock me when I told her I knew I'd meet him one day.

Noah put the iPod down. 'I suppose you think that guy's hot,' he said. 'But you're wrong. He's a total fake.'

I snorted. 'Right, and you're a hotness expert?'

'I know it takes more than what *that* guy's got,' Noah said. 'It's got to be ... genuine.' He tapped his chest. 'Something that comes from here.' Then he looked at me through the filter of his lashes. '*You're* hot.'

'That would be flattering,' I said, 'if you didn't think every girl you met was hot.'

'I'm just being honest,' said Noah. 'You *are* hot. I've always had a thing for ... unusual girls.'

'Have you actually *seen* what I'm wearing tonight?' I said, gesturing at my axe.

'I did wonder if you'd overdone the blood a little,' said Noah. 'But that's the thing. You still look amazing.' He sat up suddenly.

'Hey! Tomorrow we're showing *An American Werewolf in London*. You could dress like a wolf. A *sexy* one.'

'Ew!' I said, piffing cups at him. 'Piss off, Noah. Go back into your little booth and learn to project something other than your creepy fantasies.'

The cups clattered to the ground. 'I need a beverage first,' Noah said. 'Only that and the image of your sweet face will see me through the long evening alone.'

'With your dad,' I pointed out. 'The projectionist.'

'With my dad,' agreed Noah. 'But otherwise totally alone. Hey … is your brother using the Mercury's laptop? That's against the –'

There was a muffled thud as something hit the front window. Through the blackness I could just make out the shape of an old woman, struggling with an inside-out umbrella. As I watched, the wind flung Loony Oona's umbrella against the window again and then ripped it from her grasp and sent it whirling down the street. She was wearing long white gloves and large wraparound sunglasses, even though it was completely dark.

It was a moment or two before I noticed the other person beside her. Someone who was also in danger of being inverted by the wind. Her face was in darkness but I knew at once who it had to be.

I slid off my seat. 'I'm going out there.'

Do something that scares you every day, Dr Richter told me once. *Do it because it scares you.*

Ami shook her head. 'Don't,' she said. 'It'll look so weird.'

'I'm just delivering this,' I said, grabbing an umbrella. 'Oona's has blown inside out.'

Ami sighed. 'Hang on. I'll come too. If she turns out to be some freaky laser-eyed alien, you'll need back-up.'

I grinned and held open the door for her.

'Who is going to sell snacks?' demanded Noah.

'I was thinking you,' I said, as the door swung shut behind me.

o

The rain was even heavier than before. The wind was strong too. But at least the sound covered the humming noise that had started up again in my head. Oona was standing at the edge of the tattered awning that trimmed the cinema roof, peering up at the sky. The broken umbrella blew in circles on the footpath behind her, scratching against the concrete. Miranda was leaning against the Mercury's wall, still as a poster. Her eyes were closed.

'Oh dear,' Oona said, twisting the fingers of her gloves. 'When will it stop?'

'Miss Delaunay?' I said, holding up the umbrella. 'Take this.'

Oona shrank back. Like she could *see* the germs crawling on me. I smiled as gently as I could. Made my voice soft and coaxing. 'Go on. Take it.'

Finally, she nodded. 'Very kind of you. It's for my great-niece. She loathes getting wet.'

That didn't surprise me. A direct hit from a raindrop would probably knock Miranda unconscious.

But before Oona could grasp the umbrella, Miranda spoke.

'I'll take it.' It was the first time I'd heard her speak and her voice matched the rest of her – flat and featureless. If there was an accent I couldn't hear it.

'But you have no gloves on, my dear,' quavered Oona. 'Remember what we discussed? What we agreed? I'll take it, then I'll pass it straight to you.'

'No,' said Miranda. She glided out of the shadows, hand outstretched. 'Give it to me.'

I could see her quite clearly now. Her eyes weren't mirrored. Not anymore, at least. But their expression was familiar. It was the same way Katie checked people out while she *rated* them. There was a difference though. With Katie I could always tell what my score was.

The blood sang in my ears. Dr Richter had told me that when things started to get too much, I needed to focus my thoughts and control my breathing so that the fear never had a chance of taking hold. I tried to do this, but sometimes an old reflex of mine would kick in and I'd find myself babbling.

'Don't worry about giving it back,' I said. My voice went all high and weird when I babbled. 'It's from the Mercury's lost property. I work there. It's only a tiny cinema – probably way smaller than anything you went to in Europe. That's if you even went to the cinema. You were probably too busy going to the opera or the theatre or whatever you do over there –'

Ami looked at me warningly and I managed to shut up. Then, stepping forward, I proffered the umbrella, holding it out like it was a bouquet. Or a shield.

'That's close enough!' snapped Oona, her voice suddenly shrill. She was making me jumpy. *What exactly does she think I'm going to do to her precious great-niece?*

'Miranda, please. Just take the umbrella. Quickly.'

Miranda reached out and her fingers wrapped around the handle, just below my own hand. The muscles of her arm strained, as if holding the umbrella required all her strength.

Something's wrong with her, I thought. *She's sick.*

The wind whipped round and splattered raindrops across Miranda's arm. A car went by and her arm was suddenly lit up. I stared. The skin where the water had touched wasn't the same shade as the rest of her arm. Like the skin of a totally different person.

The water beaded and rolled away, leaving a white-ish streak. *Make-up. That's all it is.* But who wore foundation on their arm?

With a sudden movement, Oona darted a glove out and tugged Miranda's coat sleeve down. 'Come *along*, Miranda,' she said nervously, and gripped her arm. 'We're heading home. Now.'

Miranda's mouth curved up at each end. Perhaps it was meant to be a smile. Then she turned and floated off along behind her great-aunt, pushed along by the wind, umbrella held high.

THREE

There was a post on the Jubilee Park High School blog the following week with photos of the new students. I'd promised myself that I'd never look at that load of *merde* again, but I did take a quick peek to see if it had any new information about Miranda. But it just said the same old stuff. *Lived overseas. New to our community.* There was a photo but it was so low-res that if it hadn't had her name at the bottom, I wouldn't have known it was her.

There was a photo of New Guy too. The one with the mocking smile. The one I'd been careful not to look at ever since that first time. I didn't bother reading what was written about him, but I couldn't help seeing his name. Lachlan Ford.

By that stage, everyone else had completely lost interest in Miranda. The rumours, the suspicion, all that build-up surrounding her arrival – everything had been forgotten. By everyone except me and Ami, that is. We watched Oona drive up in her funny little bug-like car every morning, just before the bell went. We watched Miranda drift like a cloud to our classroom. During classes she sat down the back, near me. Totally silent and still. Miss Falippi never called on her to answer questions. She would look over at Miranda sometimes, but an unsure expression would pass over her face and she'd look away again.

And we watched Miranda during breaks as she sat on the bench near the back fence. Eyes half-closed. Palms together in her lap. Was she praying? Photosynthesising, maybe? I never saw her eat.

'Go and talk to her,' Ami urged me sometimes. 'She's so alone.'

I always found an excuse. *I think she'd rather be alone. She's not much of a talker.*

'She's just new,' said Ami. 'It's shitty being new.'

But I wanted to observe Miranda, to try to work her out, and you have to stay back if you want to do that. The only thing was that sometimes I felt like she was the one observing me.

Then one lunchtime, Miranda wasn't on her bench. I felt the same dizzy confusion I'd had when the portable classroom was moved to the back of the oval. I knew it could move. I just wasn't expecting it to.

For the rest of the break I felt jumpy. My skull had begun to throb when Ami nudged me. 'Miranda's behind us,' she murmured.

I turned, as subtly as I could. Sure enough, Miranda was there, blending in with the shadows. I couldn't see her face, but I didn't need to. I knew what she was doing. She was watching me.

An ice-spider scuttled down my back. 'Let's start walking,' I whispered. 'See if she follows.'

We walked along casually, and we were nearing the corner of the library when Katie etc. came around it. Katie was in full rant mode. She swished by and plonked herself down on a bench. Paige and Justine sat on either side of her. Paige was holding a massive bottle of water, her hands interlocked around it like someone might attempt to steal it. Katie reached out and tugged it from her hands. She took a swig, then handed it back, without even looking. Cameron was a little way off, joking around with someone. New Guy. No surprises there. Two puzzle-pieces of sky, clicking together.

Katie's rant continued. I assumed it was the usual stuff. The stuff I'd heard a thousand times when we were friends. Her agent wasn't getting her enough work. The jobs she was getting weren't good enough. She deserved more. Like, *everyone* said so. Paige and Justine nodded in all the right places. Made the appropriate shocked noises. No butting in. No advice. No contradicting.

She's just as bad as ever, I was about to mutter to Ami. But that wasn't true. She was worse. No-one told her when she'd gone too far anymore. No-one pulled her up on anything.

I suddenly remembered Miranda and looked around. She wasn't far from Katie etc. Her head was to one side, forehead creased with concentration.

'She's eavesdropping,' I whispered.

Ami shook her head. 'She's not close enough, is she?'

When the bell rang, Katie stood up and moved off, still talking. Justine and Paige followed.

Ami turned. 'We'd better go too.'

We started towards our next class. But after a few steps I steered the other way, pulling Ami with me. Ami looked at me curiously. 'It's a test,' I said. 'To see what Miranda does.' A few seconds passed before I risked a look behind to see if Miranda was following us. I admit I was surprised when I turned and she wasn't there, lurking in the distance. It took me a moment to spot her, trailing behind Katie.

When Katie reached the door she stopped. Miranda, a few metres behind, stopped too. Katie smoothed her hair and adjusted her skirt. Miranda stood still and watched. Two seconds passed. Three. Then slowly Miranda raised her hand to her head and smoothed her hair, just as Katie had done. Then she tugged at her skirt, making it perfectly straight. Just like Katie.

I turned to make some comment to Ami, but the look on her face silenced me. Ami, my ever-calm, logical friend, looked disconcerted.

'What?' I said.

'There's something –' Ami broke off and I could see the rational part of her struggling to come to terms with what she was about to say. 'There's something not quite right about that girl.'

The pain in my head grew suddenly stronger.

o

By that afternoon, my headache was so bad that I let Ami convince me to go home. The idea of curling up in the darkness of my room for a couple of hours, maybe with Luxe playing very softly in the background, was too appealing to resist. I wobbled off home on my bike, the afternoon light playing weird tricks on my aching eyes.

When I'd come home from the clinic, I did some major redecorating. I stripped my bedroom of all the girly, princessy elements that Katie and I had loved, and I considered leaving it like that – bare and stark and ugly – but in the end it was too much like my room at the clinic. What I needed was something I could escape into. Once the idea of a fortune-teller's tent struck, I became obsessed. I suppose it was something to think about other than my mess of a life. I sourced some lush red velvet curtains and nailed them to the ceiling and the walls so they made a basic tent shape. I moved my bed so that it was in the middle and arranged a whole lot of cushions around the room, as well as a Persian rug that I'd relocated from the hallway. I kept my Magic 8 Ball on top of the ancient – but still excellent – ottoman I found in the neighbours' hard rubbish.

Riding home that afternoon, I focused on how good it would feel once I was in my room with the curtains down and it was that thought alone that kept my feet turning the pedals.

Dad used to describe our place as a *weathered*-board house, which is the kind of bad joke he was fond of making and that Mum laughed at every single time. Or used to. The thing was that neither of them meant it – the beaten-up-ness of our house was one of the things they loved best about it. Most of the damage had been caused by the wind blowing in off the bay and as far as Mum was concerned, the sea air was something magical. If it thought we needed fewer roof tiles, then so be it. The other thing Dad joked about was what he called our free-range garden, i.e. the weed paradise. I swear that things evicted from other people's gardens would turn up in ours. Every time we wanted to have a barbecue, Dad had to mow down a path to it. He'd lift up the things he unearthed along the way – buckets, shoes – pretending they were treasures. When he moved out he took the gags with him, but left the mower and the barbecue set. The grass grew longer and longer anyway.

As I walked up our creaky steps the front door flung open and two hopeful faces greeted me.

'You're home!' said Toby. He was grinning, but looked pale. Paler than usual, that is.

Mum stroked his hair. 'Tobes came home at lunchtime,' she said. Her voice was cheerful, but I heard the concern beneath it, flickering like a pilot light. Then a third face squeezed between Mum and Toby and began enthusiastically licking my hand.

'Hi, Ralphy,' I said, giving his head a scratch.

'How about you three stay outside for a while?' said Mum, eyeing me. 'A bunch of orders came through at lunchtime. I'd love to get them out.' She worked for a health-food company, selling vitamins over the internet.

I could see the door to my room from the hallway. Beyond that door was my fortune-teller's tent and the promise of peace.

Then I looked back at Toby and Mum. *You owe them*, I reminded myself. *Big time.*

'No problem,' I said, slinging my bag down on the porch. It was probably best if Mum didn't know about the headache. It felt a little better now I was home, anyway.

'Mum bought a watermelon,' Toby said. 'Want to help me kill it?'

I rolled my eyes. 'I can't believe you're even asking. Go and grab the smashing sticks. I'll meet you down the back.'

'Awesome!' yelled Toby, running off. Ralph ran behind him, doing a crazy dog dance of joy.

I shook my head. 'Is it possible to die from overexcitement?'

Mum laughed. 'You were exactly the same at seven,' she said. 'Maybe worse. I used to hide on the couch whimpering and praying that we'd both survive until your dad came home.'

She gave one of those fragile smiles. The sort I hated because it meant she was remembering the life we'd had before. The life I'd wrecked. Her eyes glistened. I hugged her – fierce and tight. Trying to squeeze the sadness and worry out of her. Or the guilt out of myself.

'You know,' I said, 'Ami says it gets easier.'

Instantly Mum stiffened.

I usually avoided mentioning Ami to Mum. Talking about her always seemed to lead to more worry and hassle. For some reason, though, I didn't feel like hiding our friendship today.

'Jeez, Mum,' I said. 'It's not like she'll give away any family secrets.'

Mum made a weird noise – a snorting sort of laugh. 'Well, I know *that*,' she said.

I pulled away, feeling the old irritation rise. 'I need someone to talk to about it with. A *friend*,' I added quickly, before Mum inevitably said that I could talk to her. Then immediately, I felt bad. I had no right to get cross. Not after what I'd done.

I buried my face into her shoulder like I used to. 'I'm sorry.'

Mum stroked my hair. 'Oh, Liv,' she murmured. 'Don't be.'

'Olive!' Toby's voice rang up from somewhere down the back of our yard. 'Come *on*.'

I gulped in some air. Counted to three. 'Coming!' Then I put my hands on Mum's shoulders and swivelled her around so she was facing the house.

'Go and work,' I commanded. 'The vitamin-deficient citizens of the world need you.'

'You're a love,' said my mum. She stooped and picked up a shopping bag that was tucked behind the front door. Inside the bag was a large watermelon. Mum gave it a pat as she handed it over. 'May your death be swift, brave fruit,' she intoned. 'And your suffering short.'

Kill-the-watermelon was my idea. I invented it shortly after I'd finished constructing the fortune-teller's tent. Around the time I first met Ami. I wasn't feeling great myself, but Toby was in total shut-down mode. He used to spend hours on his own in the backyard, just sitting there in a chair like an old man. And I guess I felt responsible – because he was upset about Dad, and Dad would never have left if it hadn't been for me. So one day I went to our fridge and took out the biggest thing I could find. A watermelon. Then we took it down to the back fence and smashed it to a pulp with sticks. Not the most complicated game. And yeah, totally wasteful.

Mum had freaked when she'd seen what we were doing. Had we lost our minds? Did we have any idea how much organic watermelons cost? So many people in the world were starving! But Toby suddenly burst out laughing and it was, I swear, like the sound of the sun shining. I remember how Mum stood there, staring at him like she was mesmerised. Then, without saying a word, she jumped in the car and drove off, returning shortly with four more watermelons. Non-organic ones this time.

We hadn't played kill-the-watermelon for a while, but after Toby's recent bad night Mum must've figured it was time to place another melon on the sacrificial altar.

When I got down the back, Toby was waiting with the two smashing sticks in his hands. He held one out to me. I took it, and we tapped the sticks together three times. Then a bow.

'Let the smashing begin,' I said. 'You first.'

FOUR

Everyone knew that I no longer did the monthly Friday swim, but I was still expected to turn up at the pool. I suspected that Dr Richter had something to do with that arrangement, but I didn't complain. Being near the pool didn't bother me half as much as being near the ocean did. I was happy to be in the complex, hanging out up the back of the seats, listening to music or talking with Ami.

Generally no-one bothered me. But that particular Friday, Miss Falippi waved me over as I walked into the swim centre.

'You're a timer today,' she said, looping a stopwatch around my neck. I considered arguing, but Miss Falippi had her determined face on. 'The other timers are already at the end of the pool,' she said. 'Go and join them, please.'

Jade and Lavinia were deep in conversation, their backs to me as I came over. The third timer was Miranda. It wasn't surprising. She didn't exactly seem the athletic sort and I couldn't picture her in bathers. It was hard to imagine that she had any body at all inside that baggy uniform. She was surely just bones.

Miranda was standing not far from the edge of the pool, apparently absorbed in watching the reflections on the surface. But as I came closer her eyes lifted. They still made me shiver, just a little, those pale pupils – even though they didn't have that mirrored effect I'd seen on the first day.

'Is your friend here today?' she asked. Her voice wasn't so flat and boring this time. She sounded curious.

'What friend?' I said.

'You know,' said Miranda. 'The one you're always talking to. What's her name again?'

It was none of her business, of course, but I found myself answering anyway. Maybe I was thrown by her speaking to me directly.

'Ami.'

Miranda nodded, like she'd already known. 'So,' she said, finger on her chin. 'These days you're friends with Ami. But you used to be friends with Katie Clarke.'

'Who told you that?' I said sharply.

'No-one. It's obvious if you pay attention,' said Miranda. 'You hate each other now though, that's pretty clear. But you don't seem to care. Funny. I'm not sure if that makes you strong or pathetic.'

I felt a sudden flare of annoyance – bright and hot. Who the hell did she think she was, asking such personal questions? Passing judgement like that? Then I imagined Dr Richter waggling her finger at me. *Control that temper, Olive.*

So – a deep breath, and a quick change of topic. 'Not swimming today?'

For a moment I thought she might ignore the question. But eventually her lips parted. 'I suffer from dermatitis.'

I had a flash of how strange her skin had looked flecked with rain the other night. Like she'd slathered it all with a heavy foundation. Today she was wearing her jumper, even though the swim centre was stiflingly hot. But I could see her hands. They looked papery and dry. Flaky.

As I was looking, Miranda tugged up her jumper sleeve and I saw that she'd tied a thread around her wrist – just like the one Katie wore. Katie and I had started wearing them years ago, when we were little, and I could hardly believe Katie still had hers. Why Miranda would want to copy Katie was beyond me, but I knew it was a thin, pink death sentence.

'You'd better get rid of that,' I said.

Miranda shook her wrist, making the thread even more visible. 'Why?' she said. Her voice sounded different. Like someone who wanted to be heard.

'Because,' I explained, 'if Katie sees you wearing it, she'll probably remove both the thread and your throat with her teeth.'

Miranda shook her hair. It had a shine to it that I hadn't noticed before. 'Do I look like I care?' she said scornfully. 'I mean, seriously!'

I shrugged. Turned away. Miranda could make her own mistakes.

The first race was called – boys' 100-metres freestyle – and the competitors began shedding trackpants and lining up at the end of the pool. We timers stood at the end of a lane each. Miranda was in front of lane one. I was next to her. People up in the stands started calling out. Cheering. Whistling.

Ami had turned up by then. 'So who's going to win?' she said. 'Or don't you do that anymore?'

'I still do it,' I said, turning slightly so that Miranda wouldn't see me talking. She already knew too much about me. I scanned the row of swimmers, stretching and wind-milling their arms on the blocks. 'Well, Joshua Bauer won't win,' I said. 'Obviously. And not Aaron either.'

'How about Cameron?' asked Ami. 'He's pretty fast.'

'True. But he has no focus,' I said. 'Look at him. He's way too busy showing off his hot bod to Katie to win. And Tyler is always slow off the blocks. So that just leaves the guy in my lane.'

'That's Lachlan Ford,' said Ami. 'Don't pretend you haven't noticed him.'

I summoned up the haughtiness of a queen. 'What does that freakin well mean?' The haughtiness of a queen, but maybe not the vocabulary.

Ami's eyeballs did an exaggerated loop. 'Come off it. Every girl at school has noticed him.'

The memory of his smile flashed into my mind. A beautiful smile, even though I'd sensed the cruelty behind it. 'He's going to win,' I said. 'He's got winner hands.'

'Which are …?'

'The sort that like to hold up trophies and punch the air.'

We watched as Lachlan casually bent his arms behind his head, interlocking his fingers and stretching. Next he pressed each leg, one by one, up to his chest. A streak of light fell across his shoulders, making his hair and face glow.

'He's lush,' murmured Ami. 'Admit it.'

But I wasn't admitting to anything. Especially not the fluttering in my stomach. 'He looks like someone who likes winking,' I said. 'And you know how I feel about winkers.'

Ami studied my face for a moment. Then she smiled with just one corner of her mouth.

'What?' I said.

'I've just realised,' said Ami. 'You're scared of guys.'

I laughed loudly. 'Ah ... I have a brother, remember?'

'That's different,' said Ami. 'You find something wrong with every boy I've ever pointed out to you.'

'That's not because I'm scared,' I said quickly. 'It's because your taste is so *shtinky*.'

Ami folded her arms. 'OK then, oh Glorious Princess of the Alternative. You tell me who *you* think is lush.'

Easy. I'd worked on this list a lot. 'Dallas from Luxe. Kurt Cobain, Jeff Buckley, Holden Caulfield.'

I stopped when I saw the look on Ami's face. Oh yeah. Two of my crushes were dead. One was fictitious. And the only guy who was both alive and real was someone I realistically had no chance of meeting, no matter what I secretly, desperately hoped. Because why would Luxe ever come to a dump like Jubilee Park?

'On your marks …'

I clicked my stopwatch just as the starter pistol fired. As the swimmers began churning their way down the pool, the yelling and cheering ramped up. By the time they were shooting towards the timers on their last lap, the screaming had reached deafening levels.

I stood there with my thumb poised over the stopwatch. Lachlan won easily. As he climbed out and reached for his towel, I had an idea. A way of proving Ami wrong. I glanced meaningfully at her before marching over to Lachlan and sticking out my hand.

'Nice work,' I said.

He looked surprised, but he took my hand. Shook it.

'Best time so far,' I continued.

'Thanks. But that was the first trial.'

'True,' I said. 'But still. I get the feeling you've done this before.'

Lachlan laughed. I'd expected him to have one of those meaty, fake laughs that boys like Lachlan usually have. But his laugh wasn't too bad. For a sports-crazed *dummkopf.* Then he went and spoke.

'Once or twice,' he said. 'I'm a lifesaver.'

I opened my eyes wide. 'Really?' I said. 'How very not predictable.'

By then I figured I'd proven my point to Ami, and turned to walk off. But Lachlan kept talking. 'I don't think we've met yet,' he said. 'Not properly at least. I mean, I know who you are.

38

You're Olive Corbett.' He was speaking quickly – tripping a bit on his words – and his face had gone a little red.

He's probably on steroids or something, I thought. 'Well, now we've met,' I said. 'Properly. So. I've got to go.' I showed him my stopwatch. 'Official timing duties to perform.'

'Hang on,' he said. 'There's a few minutes before the next race. I just want to know a bit about you. About who you are.'

Of course I instantly knew what was going on. He'd been put up to this. Dared – probably by Cameron Glover, who obviously still hadn't forgiven me.

'Why don't you ask someone, then?' I said. 'I'm sure anyone at Jubilee Park High would be more than happy to tell you everything you'd like to know about me.' I said it loudly, hoping it would reach the ears of whoever was hiding nearby, listening and laughing.

Lachlan shook his head. 'I don't want to hear someone else's version of you,' he said. 'I want to hear yours.'

The funny thing was it seemed like he meant it. I wasn't fooled though, no matter how genuine he managed to sound. I crossed my arms. 'Why?' I said. 'Why the hell would *you* want to know about *me*?' I stood there, waiting for the whole stupid charade to fall apart.

'I don't know,' said Lachlan, shrugging. 'You're so … mysterious. Different. To everyone else here, I mean.'

I snorted. Talk about stating the obvious. 'So, you're a detective as well as a lifesaver then?'

Lachlan didn't seem to notice my sarcasm. 'You keep to

yourself a lot,' he continued. 'But you didn't always, did you? I've seen the school blog – you used to be on it almost every day. You and Katie Clarke.'

'You should stay away from that blog,' I said, grimacing. 'It'll rot your brain.'

'I didn't recognise you at first,' said Lachlan. 'You look so different now. Your hair, I guess. But you're also much more …' His eyes swept across me and it was suddenly like I was standing there in bathers, not him. I felt horribly exposed. Actually, I just felt horrible.

Lachlan coughed and looked away – like I was too hideous to look at anymore. 'I guess I'm curious,' he said. 'What happened?'

I felt a burn of irritation. All these personal questions. First Miranda. Now this guy. All this snooping around, pulling up stuff I wanted to forget. I fixed Lachlan with the sort of look that in ancient Greece would've turned him instantly to stone.

'I guess I got more picky about who I mix with,' I said frostily.

Lachlan stepped back, like he was steadying himself after a push. *Good*, I thought, pleased that I'd caused him at least one moment of discomfort. Except a second later I realised it wasn't me that had made him react that way. He was looking at someone over my shoulder.

'Oh no,' he muttered. 'Not her again.'

I turned to see who he meant and started laughing. 'No guy has ever said *not her again* about Katie Courtney Clarke!' I said. 'Especially not when she's swishing her way towards them in her bathers.'

Drips of pool-water ran down Lachlan's face. 'She's trying to set me up with one of her friends.'

'Ooh,' I said, clasping my hands together. 'You *are* lucky.'

Lachlan wore the same panicked expression I'd seen on Ralph when he thought I'd forgotten about his walk. 'I have trouble telling those girls apart,' he said. 'They all look the same.'

'That's awkward,' I said sympathetically.

'Hey, Lachie,' Katie said, positioning herself in front of him and blocking me out completely.

'Your back certainly is lovely,' I said.

Katie didn't seem to hear. 'Come and sit with us,' she said to Lachlan. 'Paige has saved you a space.'

'Ah,' said Lachlan, retying his towel like that would somehow protect him. 'I –'

'He's busy helping me with something,' I heard myself say. Not to help out Lachlan, though. It was strictly a Katie-tease.

Katie turned slowly. 'Helping you with what, exactly?'

I took off the stopwatch and dropped it on the concrete floor. The screen shattered. 'Busted stopwatch,' I said.

Lachlan's shoulders started doing these uppy-downy movements and I realised that he was trying not to laugh. He bent down and picked up the watch, shaking his head. 'This thing is *really* stuffed,' he said.

'Especially as I'm such a weirdo,' I pointed out. 'It takes me forever to fix stuff.'

Katie glared. 'I never said you were a weirdo.'

'Not out *loud* maybe.'

Katie exhaled rapidly through her nose. As our friendship had crumbled, she'd made that noise more and more. 'Why are you *like* this, Olive?'

A voice boomed through the PA. 'Competitors in the girls' 100-metres backstroke, please take your positions.'

Katie adjusted the straps of her bathers and they cracked like whips against her back. 'Pathetic,' she flung at me as she headed off. 'Just pathetic.'

The words seemed to echo, bouncing off the tiled walls of the pool complex. *Pathetic. Just pathetic.* I heard a movement nearby and realised with a start that Miranda was standing right near us. She was paying no attention to me, though – her head turned to follow Katie and I saw that her mouth was moving, forming silent words. Almost like she was practising her lines.

As Katie stepped up on her block, Miranda moved – surprisingly quickly – to the end of Katie's lane, stopwatch raised.

'Hey!' said Lavinia. 'I'm doing this lane.'

But Miranda clearly had no intention of budging and after a moment, Lavinia huffed and went over to where Miranda was supposed to be.

With no stopwatch, I couldn't time the girl in my lane. Not that it mattered. From the moment the race began, Katie was so far in front that no-one else had a chance. On it went until the predictable ending. Katie pulled herself neatly out of the pool, took off her swimming cap and shook out her hair. She took the towel that Paige was holding out to her and the praise everyone else was offering in exactly the same way.

'What was my time?' she called to no-one in particular. That was the kind of relationship Katie had with the world. She asked it for things and they appeared, as if by magic.

'A minute twenty-four,' said Miranda.

Katie nodded. Totally unsurprised. 'My best time yet.'

'Your best time yet.' Miranda copied Katie's inflection perfectly.

Katie's forehead folded. 'Are you imitating me?'

Miranda frowned too. 'Are you imitating me?' Her voice rang with the exact same note of disbelief.

Katie's eyes narrowed and began a slow and thorough scan of Miranda. It didn't take long for her to spot the pink thread poking out from the sleeve of Miranda's jumper.

Katie's hand shot out and yanked up Miranda's sleeve. The thin pink thread was fully revealed, bright and sharp as a razor-slash.

'Why are you wearing that?' said Katie.

A few girls from the race had formed a ring around Katie and Miranda. You could feel everyone tense up, waiting to see how the hell Miranda was going to get out of this. I had no idea why either of them cared about stupid pink threads but I still found myself holding my breath. I don't think anyone was expecting her to say what she did. The truth.

'Because *you* are.'

A new word would be needed to describe the look on Katie's face. Angry isn't strong enough. She was *thrombtipic* with rage. *Murashable.*

'Take. It. Off.'

Miranda paused for a moment – mulling it over. Then she shook her head. 'No. I like wearing it.'

I felt uneasy then, knowing that Katie was capable of tearing someone to shreds when she was truly enraged. Where were the *responsible adults*? I glanced around. Miss Falippi was standing on the other side of the pool, chatting with another teacher, oblivious. My ears began to ring. *Maybe I should do something.* I used to be able to calm Katie down – often the only one who could. But things moved so fast then I couldn't have gotten involved, even if I'd wanted to.

Katie grabbed Miranda's wrist so tightly her knuckles blanched. But Miranda didn't even flinch. In fact, she *smiled*, which of course sent Katie off into the stratosphere of fury.

'Who do think you are? Trying to be like me? You're a no-one, don't you get that? Nothing but a pathetic, tragic *road accident.*' With her free hand, Katie hooked her fingers under the thread and yanked.

A few of the girls nearby actually cheered when the thread broke. Like Katie had done something heroic. It made me want to puke. Yeah, I know Miranda was stupid to turn up wearing that thread. But the fact Katie cared was stupid too.

From across the pool, Miss Falippi glanced over and smiled. Who knows what she thought was going on. Maybe that there was some *spontaneous school spirit* being displayed.

Katie let go of Miranda's arm and it fell heavily to her side. Boneless. Miranda stood there as Katie marched over to the pool and flicked the thread in. There was this almost peaceful

44

moment as the thread floated, turning gently, before disappearing into a filter.

When Katie turned back, she had an ugly, triumphant look on her face. 'I hope you enjoyed trying to be like me for five minutes,' she said to Miranda. 'Because that's the closest you'll ever get.'

Katie walked off then – doing her victory walk – with Paige and Justine trotting along behind. Gradually everyone else just drifted away too until I realised with a jolt that it was just me and Lachlan left standing there. Even Ami had disappeared. Somehow during the whole Katie-Miranda chaos we'd ended up right next to each other – so close that his arm brushed mine, soft and cool. I moved away quickly, my heart beating out some crazy rhythm and my skin suddenly covered in tiny bumps. Lachlan had gone a bit red. Probably from the shock of touching me.

'Katie is such a freakin wonk,' I said. It came out way louder than I'd intended.

Lachlan's head tilted. 'What's a *wonk*?'

I could've kicked myself for blurting that out. 'It's just a word I came up with,' I told him. 'Because so far I haven't come across one word in any language that does the same job.'

Lachlan nodded – not laughing as I'd been expecting. 'What about the new girl? Miranda. Is she a wonk too?'

'No.' That was one thing I was sure of.

'So what is she then?'

'I'm not sure,' I admitted. Which was true. I hadn't yet figured out what Miranda really was.

Lachlan looked at the stopwatch in my hand. A piece of it clattered to the ground. 'Do you really want help with this?'

'Nah, it's OK,' I laughed. 'I'll figure out an explanation for Miss Falippi. I'm good at making stuff up.'

Lachlan raised an eyebrow and grinned. 'You mean, for a weirdo?'

He was teasing of course, but not in an awful way. In a pretty freakin cute way, actually. I had to admit he was funnier than I'd expected. Smarter too. And I could see how other people might find Lachlan quite attractive. You know, if you like that perfect, god-like look. The old Olive probably would have thought he was. Scrub that. She *definitely* would've thought he was. She would've gotten all giggly and simpering over Lachlan Ford. But the new Olive – me – wasn't interested in boys, especially not ones like him. Which was lucky, because he wouldn't have found the new Olive attractive either.

What happened next took me off-guard. Lachlan raised his hand, like he was saying goodbye. He even said something about seeing me in class. I stood there, waiting for him to go. But he didn't. Instead he shuffled his feet around and drew wet lines on the tiles with his big toe. His words finally slid out. 'Isn't there a formal coming up?'

'You tell me,' I said. 'You're the one who reads the school blog.' I mean, obviously I knew there was a formal, but since coming back from the clinic I'd prided myself on not knowing the details.

Lachlan did a few more tortured movements, and just as I

was about to ask if he was having a fit, he said, 'Do you … think you'll go?'

In my peripheral vision I became aware of someone dancing around frantically. Ami, of course, looking like she was about to explode. I knew what she was thinking – that Lachlan was about to ask me to the formal. But that was impossible. You don't smile mockingly at someone one week and then ask them out the next. But all the same, I felt a little dizzy. Must have been the chlorine fumes. Lachlan was looking at me expectantly. Like my answer mattered to him. Despite the sweltering heat, I shivered.

'Um … well …' I grasped around for something that would jettison me from this weird situation. 'Yenope.'

I heard the faint sound of Ami groaning.

Lachlan regarded me in silence. 'I like the way,' he said after a moment, 'you made "no" *almost* sound like a "yes".'

'It's my speech impediment,' I said. 'Thanks for drawing attention to it. Look, I'll probably be working at the Mercury anyway. On the night of the dance, I mean.'

Lachlan dipped his head slightly. It was almost a bow. 'Understood,' he said. He raised one of those winner's hands in a goodbye gesture. '*Adios*, Olive. And thanks. You know. For saving me from the – the –'

'Wonk?' I said. 'No problem.'

As he turned to walk off his words replayed in my head. *Olive.* It was nice the way he'd said my name. He'd said it as though he liked dark, salty, intense little things – not like someone who picked them off their pizza.

o

I was fully expecting Ami to let me have it once Lachlan had left. But she was staring at something behind me.

'She's still there,' she murmured.

Miranda was standing in the same place she'd stood during the fight with Katie, one arm cradling the other. Her jumper sleeve had been pushed back and, even from where I stood, I could see red marks from where Katie had gripped her – almost like burns against her pale skin.

'Most people would be curled up in the foetal position after the public humiliation she's been through,' Ami muttered.

But Miranda didn't seem upset. She was smiling to herself, like everything had gone exactly how she'd hoped. It made me uneasy, that smile.

When the next race was called over the PA system, Miranda seemed to wake up. She adjusted her sleeve and walked off.

It was strange. Her walk seemed different. Bouncier. A victory walk.

When Miranda was out of view, Ami looked at me. The furrow between her eyebrows had deepened.

'So,' I joked. 'Your Miranda-is-an-alien theory looks good.'

Ami didn't laugh. 'Let's get on a computer,' she said seriously. 'I want to find out what's going on.'

FIVE

Ames and I ditched the rest of the swimming and headed for the computer lab. It was a Friday anyway, so school was basically out for the week. Technically, I decided, it wasn't breaking any promises. And anyway, I was desperate to do something that would stop me replaying the conversation with Lachlan in my mind.

The lab was down in the basement of the old wing. It was stuffy and reportedly haunted, so no-one was likely to disturb us. Even the computer tech guy avoided the place.

Ami and I pulled up chairs. Out of habit I almost logged onto Facebook and then remembered I'd deleted my account. It was tempting to check Pitchfork to see if there were any new band reviews posted, but that wasn't what we were there for. I opened Google instead.

Mirror eyes, I typed in. *Weird skin. Alien?*

I started feeling excited when several thousand results came up. Maybe there was some neat, simple explanation for what the hell was going on with Miranda. Who better to help me than a whole community of people out there who saw things differently from the mainstream? People like me and Ami.

I shot Ami a grin and clicked on the first link. But the moment the site loaded, my hope dried up. It's hard to take a site seriously when it's covered in flashing banner ads.

The site was called Shifter World and the homepage featured pictures of celebrities – mostly actors and politicians. Below were words in red. *Beware! These people are all shifters. That's why they're so successful.*

'Shifters, huh?' said Ami, leaning in. 'Scroll down a bit.'

There was a link to a quiz – *Find out your shifter percentage –* and a list of things to do if you meet one:

1. Avoid them!!

2. Don't let them touch you!!

3. Don't give them your shit!!

The forums section seemed to be mostly arguments about which famous people were definitely shapeshifters (just about every famous person, living or dead, seemed to be mentioned), and how you could tell.

'Seriously, Ami,' I said, pushing away from the desk. 'This is pointless rubbish. Let's go.'

But Ami – who usually had no time for this sort of stuff – hunched forward. 'Not yet. Try the FAQs.'

I clicked and pulled up a list of twenty questions. The first one was: *Isn't 'shapeshifter' just another word for werewolf?*

Another click and the answer appeared. *Shifters vary from country to country. Werewolves are just the most well-known type. There are also legends from around the world about people changing into panthers, reptiles, dolphins, birds and even insects.*

There are also humanoid shifters. *They don't transform into animals but take on the characteristics of other humans. Humanoid shifters 'latch' on to people (generally those with strong personalities) and slowly drain them of their vitality and spirit. Gradually the shifter adapts to the physical attributes and mannerisms of the host until they can be difficult to tell apart. The shifter* becomes *the person they've latched onto.*

Once the host is dry, the shifter rids themselves of the host (or what's left of them) and enters a search phase. *This is when they 'fade into the background' – presumably to be better disguised as they hunt for a new host. It is common in this phase for their eyes to become reflective, like mirrors.*

The computer lab noises started up then, the slow clicking of the pipes expanding and contracting that some idiots said proved the place was haunted. There were also the website sounds, a loop of music playing over and over. *La la di dah. La la di dah.* So cheesy and tinny, and yet also somehow creepy. My head began to hurt.

'It's just a weird fantasy site,' I said, pushing back from the desk. 'It's not the real world.'

This was Ami's cue to grin and make some joke about how I actually looked like I was falling for this crap. But she didn't.

'I guess so,' she said slowly. 'But it sure would explain a lot.'

o

The next day was Saturday, and date night at the Mercury – busy and super-stressy. Lots of couples would turn up, buy crap food and tickets to crap movies and try like crazy to impress each other. I was supposed to turn up fifteen minutes earlier on Saturdays but somehow I was always late instead. Maybe it was subconsciously deliberate. Date night was pretty depressing.

How come none of them realised their relationships were doomed? It seemed so obvious to me that they didn't match. Not just physically either. One of the pair would always be way more into the relationship than the other. Or they just had nothing in common. At first I made a little game of it – predicting how many more date nights each relationship would last. I stopped after a while. My accuracy was getting me down.

That particular date night, I'd just served my tenth jumbo tub of stale popcorn when Katie and Cameron came in. He had his arm around Katie and she was leaning into him. They were both laughing. I mean, if you were picking perfect couples in a magazine, the picture of Katie and Cam is the one most people would circle. They looked like a match. But they didn't fool me. I happened to know that before they got together Cam had been chasing after another girl. Me. The old me, that is. I'd had fun stringing him along for a while, making him think I was interested while treating him like shit. Because that's what I was like back then. It wasn't until I hooked up with someone else at a party in front of him that he went after Katie.

Still, I had to admit they'd been putting in a regular appearance at date night for a few months now. Longer than I'd thought they'd last. They bought their tickets from Noah, then came over to my counter where I had their stuff already waiting for them. Water and large salted popcorn for Cam. Diet coke and choc-top for Katie. The choc-top was Katie's weekly treat in an otherwise super-strict diet. Having the snacks set up and ready to go was my way of minimising our interaction, which was – from my perspective at least – leg-amputationally painful.

Cameron always gave me these patronisingly sympathetic looks, like I'd totally missed out when I rejected him. Although knowing Cam, he probably turned the whole thing around so it was *him* who'd rejected me. And then there was Katie, relishing the chance to have me run around serving her again, like I used to when we were partners in bitchiness.

The crowd in front of the counter had finally begun to let up when the heavy front doors of the Mercury swung open and a small figure appeared, bedraggled and hunched over.

'Toby!' I said, coming out from behind the snack bar. 'What are you doing here?'

'I just wanted to hang out with you.' His voice had a pleading note to it. 'Can I stay?'

'Come and sit here, Tobes,' I said, clearing a space at the counter for the laptop. I was used to having Toby there when Mum needed a babysitter. I constructed a wall of junk food in front of him.

'This is a cinema, not some kind of free-food centre!' called

53

Noah from the ticket window. Noah's sleaze-to-boss ratio altered on date night.

Luckily my rate of ignoring him remained the same. 'I'll pay for whatever he eats,' I said, and didn't point out that at the inflated prices we charged, the cinema could afford to give a few snacks away.

Toby climbed slowly up onto the barstool. 'It's so crowded.'

'I can fix that,' I said.

Toby glanced at me dubiously. I reached to the control panel near the cash register and pressed the bell that made session chimes ring. 'Watch.'

The moment they heard the chimes, everyone made a dash for the cinema doors. There was no allocated seating at the Mercury.

Noah frowned and leapt over to the front of the mass. It was his job to tear the tickets and let people in. 'Bit early, isn't it?' he muttered as he swung past.

I didn't care. Five minutes later all the couples had gone and Toby was clacking away happily at the laptop. All was right with the world again. Even Noah cheered up once he'd done a till-reading and saw how much money we'd taken. It's amazing the amount of poor-quality confectionery that people will buy when they're on a date. Noah didn't even complain when I removed the Mercury CD and plugged in my iPod to play Luxe.

I began to restock the takeaway cups as 'Steeple Chaser' started playing, and when the foyer filled with the sound of Dallas's voice I got a sudden, unavoidable urge to dance. The feeling swung me up and away and promised to help me forget all about everything. Date night. Katie and Cameron. Dad. Weird websites that made my skin crawl and that I somehow couldn't quite forget, no matter how hard I tried.

To hell with it all. I closed my eyes as I started to dance. *You're not at the Mercury anymore,* I told myself. *You're at a Luxe gig.* Straight away I could picture it. The place was packed and there was no room for dancing, and somehow we were dancing anyway. Dancing and going crazy. But then I felt someone watching me. Dallas from Luxe.

When our eyes met he smiled and he stretched out his hand and suddenly I was being pulled up onto the stage. In my fantasy, Dallas paid no attention to anyone around him. Only to me.

'Olive,' called Noah suddenly. 'What are you doing?'

'I'm expressing the joy of life,' I called back, my eyes still closed. 'Through movement.'

'Maybe you could express your joy of having a job,' suggested Noah. 'Through serving that customer.'

My eyes opened. On the other side of the snack bar counter was Lachlan. He raised his hand, his eyes crinkling a little at each corner. 'Hey there.'

'Oh … Hi.'

Why wasn't there an emergency number to call when your face was so hot it was in danger of spontaneously igniting?

I turned down the music. Tugged my skirt back into place. The giant plastic ice-cream above the snack bar began a round of high-pitched whining while Lachlan waited patiently. He looked different out of school uniform. Less like everyone else. I found myself noticing things about him that I hadn't seen before. Tiny imperfections that made him, I don't know, more interesting somehow. Like the tiny C-shaped scar on his chin, from some childhood accident on a bike maybe. And the crease beneath his left eye that appeared when he smiled. The funny little tuft of hair that stuck out at the side of his head – the one that my hand itched to smooth down.

Then there were his clothes. I mean, he was wearing jeans and a hoodie like just about every other guy that night, but the hoodie had been patched at the elbow. *Both* elbows. A lot of people would've just chucked a hoodie when it wore out like that. But Lachlan hadn't. He'd got it fixed. Maybe he'd even fixed it himself.

It's his favourite, I realised. And that's when I started thinking that maybe Lachlan Ford wasn't a sky puzzle piece after all. Maybe he was a bit of the grass. Or the trunk of a tree. Something with texture.

'The movie's already started,' I said, suddenly aware that I'd been staring. 'Sorry.'

'I didn't come for the movie,' Lachlan replied.

'Well, what did you come for?' I said without thinking. 'Bowling?'

And straight away I knew what Ami would've said if she'd been there. *You putz. He came for you.* This was one of the reasons I needed her around. Without her I said stupid, stupid things.

Lachlan pulled at the cord of his hoodie so it was way too

short on one side. Then he pulled it back the other way. 'I – just dropped by for an ice-cream. They're supposed to be good here.'

'Better than the popcorn that's for sure,' I said, scrambling to regain some dignity. 'What flavour do you want?'

Toby looked up, puzzled. 'Is there another flavour now?' he said. 'I thought there was only vanilla.' Then he turned to Lachlan. 'Boringest flavour ever.'

Even the way I blush is weird. It's my neck, not my face, that turns red. 'I forgot,' I muttered. 'We only have vanilla.'

Then I tripped over, like someone had sneaked in and swapped my real feet for a larger pair.

Lachlan didn't react at all. Not to my neon neck, my tripping or anything. 'Vanilla's good.'

Amazingly, I was able to hand Lachlan the ice-cream without further humiliation. He shoved it into the pocket of his hoodie and I waited for him to turn and leave. But he didn't. He started to hum along to 'Steeple Chaser'.

I stared. 'You *know* this song?'

'I've heard it once or twice,' said Lachlan.

OK, so that was kind of sweet, this sporty guy trying to make out he'd heard a Luxe song. I mean, Luxe weren't on iTunes and they didn't have a distributor yet – the 'album' was a collection of tracks I'd downloaded from their website. There wasn't even any official album art, which is why I'd had to make my own with a picture I'd found of Dallas on MySpace. I couldn't bring myself to friend him, but I did look through his pictures and borrow one that I liked.

'Olive is obsessed with Luxe,' piped up my big-mouthed brother cheerily. 'She's always listening to them.' I pulled a *shut-up* face at Toby, which he didn't seem to see. 'Luxe, Luxe, Luxe. All the time.'

'Maybe they'll do a gig here one day,' said Lachlan. 'What's that local pub called?'

'The Rainbow,' I said.

'Right. Maybe they'll play there.'

I made my eyes big and wide. 'You're a genie, aren't you? And you're going to make my wish come true.'

Lachlan smiled, and with a shock I realised I was kind of flirting with him. 'It's at least possible, isn't it?' he said.

Well yeah. Most things are possible in theory. It's possible that there's life on other planets, or that Ralph could be taught to *stay*, or that one day my mother will learn to speak fluent Spanish. But a lot of things are also very unlikely. It was unlikely that I'd ever see Luxe play. Or that anything good would ever happen to me again.

The lightness I'd felt while dancing started to ooze out of me like toothpaste from a tube, and I thought I was about to lose my balance and crash to the floor. I steadied myself by leaning against the cash register and focusing on the small panel where the prices came up. The numbers glowed green.

Lachlan leant across the counter. 'Hey, what's wrong?'

Stuck to the wall just above the cash register was a small mirror, curved like an eyeball. The thief mirror, Noah called it. He – or possibly his dad – had put it there so that whoever was working the snack bar could make sure no-one was stealing stuff when they were busy at the till. The curve meant that you could see pretty much the entire cinema reflected in it – but in a distorted way. Looking in it now, I could see my own face looming like a monster's, my body stretched, and my nose sticking out like a toucan's beak.

Behind me in the mirror was Lachlan. He looked perfect. It felt wrong for us to even be in the same reflection together.

This is all just a joke to him, I reminded myself. *And I'm the punchline.*

There was no other explanation. No matter what Ami said. I was angry with myself for starting to think otherwise – even for a moment. People like me and Lachlan didn't belong together.

I turned back around, my folded arms a barrier across my body. 'I'd better get back to work.'

'Am I distracting you from your dancing?'

I didn't return the smile and Lachlan's soon faded. 'Oh. OK,' he said quietly. 'See ya.'

I stood there stiffly until he'd walked out the double doors and into the night.

I thought I'd feel lighter once he'd gone. I knew I'd done the right thing by sending him away. And even if by some miracle it *wasn't* a joke, people like Lachlan didn't fit into my world anyway. My new world.

But the heavy feeling didn't go. In fact, it grew stronger as the evening dragged on. By the time my shift ended, I felt heavier than I ever had since starting my meds.

On Monday morning Katie was sitting on her desk, her friends clustered around. I didn't need to listen in to know what they were discussing. You would have thought they were organising the Olympics from the amount of time they'd spent discussing the formal. The theme was Winter Beach Party, and they were agonising over whether it would be better to decorate the hall with fake sand dunes or fake icebergs, or with sand dunes that looked like icebergs, and whether the glitter around the welcome sign should be silvery-white or yellowy-gold. You know – the big issues.

'Look at their faces,' I said to Ami. 'They're genuinely worried about it.'

Ami gave me a look. 'Wasn't it *you* who came up with the theme, way back when?'

That was the problem with Ami. She never let me forget anything.

As we walked past Lachlan's row, he reached out and grabbed hold of my hand. 'Hang on,' he said, and I found myself stopping, even though after his visit to the Mercury, I'd vowed I was going to avoid him. It's hard to do that when someone's warm fingers are wrapped around yours, though.

Play it mucho relaxed, I told myself, hoping my hands weren't sweaty. *Don't show him how he affects you.* 'Let me guess,' I said. 'The ice-cream gave you food poisoning?'

'No, I just wanted to –'

But then Katie swooped, like a bird protecting its territory. 'Lachie,' she breathed. 'Thank god you're here. We really need a guy's perspective on something.'

I couldn't help smirking at Lachlan as Katie pulled him over to her desk. It was unsurprising, really, that someone with the physical dimensions of a stop sign was such an effective blocker. I told myself I was grateful, trying to ignore the lingering heat on my hand.

Miranda was already seated when I reached the back row, her hands folded on the desk, leaning forwards. My eyes were drawn to her wrist and for some reason I felt a surge of relief when I saw that the pink thread hadn't returned.

Miranda was looking pretty good. Her dermatitis seemed to have cleared up and her skin had an almost-healthy pinkish tinge to it. Her hair was shining, closer now to blonde than its previous mousy tone. Even her body looked more solid. It reminded me of how the eating-disorder girls at the clinic looked when they finally started eating again.

Ami noticed the change too. 'Looks like our shapeshifter is starting to take shape,' she murmured. I was pretty sure she was kidding, despite the wary look on her face.

Katie and the others were so deep in conversation that they didn't even notice when Miss Falippi hurried in late, her herbal tea sloshing onto the floor as usual. I'd inspected one of those tea spills once. It looked like dirt and bark, the kind of mixture little kids concoct in the sandpit.

Miss Falippi didn't seem to notice the mess she'd made. She

looked in a bad mood, and was frowning at the meeting taking place on Katie's desk. 'That's enough talking now, people,' she said. 'Plenty of time to discuss social events during lunch.'

Katie pouted and slithered down into her seat. Lachlan, looking grateful, returned to his. I felt his eyes turn towards me, but I concentrated on rearranging my pens. Miss Falippi began writing notes on the whiteboard and Katie turned back to whispering with Paige.

'I said that's enough, Katie,' said Miss Falippi, without looking around.

Katie was quiet for a moment, but gradually started up again. There was a loud click as Miss Falippi snapped the lid back on the marker.

'Sparks,' I muttered to Ami, 'are about to fly.'

'Or maybe whiteboard markers,' Ami whispered back as Miss Falippi turned around. 'She's holding that one like a spear.'

'Katie Clarke,' said Miss Falippi. 'This is *unacceptable* behaviour.'

'I didn't do anything,' said Katie, doing her doe-eyed thing.

When Miss Falippi cracked the shits, it was like a flash flood, pouring from nowhere, swift and brutal. 'That's *it!* I won't have this rudeness in my classroom. I'm taking you off the school-formal committee.'

Katie gaped. This was a new experience for her – getting told off – but somehow I knew exactly what she would do.

'What about Olive?' she said. 'She's *always* talking and you never punish her.'

'Just ignore them,' whispered Ami as every pair of eyes in the room turned to fix on me, including Lachlan's. But at least his were friendly.

He gestured towards Katie with his thumb. *Wonk,* he mouthed, shaking his head in this funny, dramatic way. I knew he was doing it to make me feel better. And it did work, at least a little bit. Then there was the sound of a chair scraping against the floor next to me, and suddenly the focus of the room shifted once more.

Now everyone was looking at Miranda, who was standing up. 'Katie wasn't talking,' she said, her voice clear and confident. 'I was.'

Miss Falippi looked off balance for a moment. Then her eyes narrowed. 'Oh, really? And who were you talking to?'

On one side of Miranda was an empty chair. On the other side was me – and we never spoke.

Miranda's eyes flicked towards me and she gave me this strange, sneaky smile, like I was somehow part of this game she was playing. 'I was talking to myself,' she said.

Miss Falippi's mouth was ruler straight. 'Are you sure about that?'

Miranda nodded. 'Yes.'

'Fine,' said Miss Falippi crisply. 'Then you are forbidden from attending the formal. You will also stay back for detention with me this afternoon and write an essay on the importance of silence. Tomorrow you will read it for the class. Understood?'

Miranda looked at Miss Falippi, steady and unafraid,

wearing the same superior look as when Katie had gone mental at her. Like all of this was beneath her. 'Understood.'

Miss Falippi glared around the room. 'Let me be clear,' she said. 'If one more person speaks out of turn today, I'll ban the whole class from attending the formal.'

The rest of the morning passed in total silence. No-one wanted to be the one to send Miss Falippi over the edge.

Just before the bell, I saw Katie quickly turn and nod at Miranda. A thank-you nod. Miranda nodded back.

SIX

Ralph bounded up to me as I unlocked the front door that afternoon, his tongue lolling out. A note had been tucked into his collar.

Your mum and Toby have gone to the shops. They'll be back around dinner time. Can you please take me for a walk? I am driving your mum crazy. Lots of love, Ralph.

'Your handwriting is really improving, Ralphy,' I said, scratching the itchy spot between his ears. 'I'll change, then we'll walk. But try to act your *dog* age OK? No running off.'

Before, I used to head to the beach for our walks so Ralph could work on his wave-biting skills and growl at the seaweed monsters. But the beach was out of the question now, of course. I could handle being near the swimming pool because it stayed pretty flat. But the ocean, with its swells and waves and hidden currents, made me clammy. Even Dr Richter had advised me to avoid it for the time being. *'We don't want to trigger a relapse,*' she said.

Besides, from the way Ralph was leaping about I figured he needed an exercise challenge. That meant heading through the forest behind the school and running up the hill.

Dad used to take me for walks in the forest all the time when I was in primary school. I never told him but I was always scared going there, mainly because of the stories we'd all heard from the older kids about the cannibal who lurked in the trees. *Never leave the path*, we used to warn each other. *That's how he gets you.* The forest was dark and damp and full of gnarled tree roots that could trip you up. In the fairytales Mum had read me as a kid, the woods were always places where witches lived or where uncaring parents abandoned their children. It was always our forest that I pictured as I listened.

That afternoon though, the sun was bright and warm, and I was actually looking forward to going in. It felt like I hadn't done any exercise in ages. As we crossed the highway into the forest, I unleashed Ralph and straight away he started tearing around chasing imaginary rabbits. I put on my headphones and warmed up for a run, pretending that I was in a tropical garden scented with fruit and flowers rather than a dank forest that stank of rot. I started to hum, jogging along at an easy pace behind Ralph.

We hadn't gone far when Ralph froze, his hackles rising.

'What's up, crazy dog?' I said, taking off my headphones and stopping beside him. 'Did those phantom bunnies get away again?'

But then I saw what had caught his attention. Up ahead

on the path was a figure silhouetted against the dwindling light. At first I was certain it was Miranda, but a moment later I wasn't. The figure was too far away and too hard to see. I had this uneasy feeling that whoever it was, they were watching me. Waiting. There was a sharp twinge in my head then, and I closed my eyes against the pain. By the time the throbbing had passed and I straightened up, the figure was gone.

Ralph was sniffing the air, muscles tensed.

'Ralphy,' I pleaded. 'Stay with me.'

But before I'd even finished the sentence he'd leapt off down the path, barking loudly. The light was disappearing rapidly and the cold night air was settling.

'Ralph?' I sounded whiny, childish. 'Come *here*.'

But Ralph ignored me, as usual, and there was nothing I could do but follow the path, praying he'd stick to it. The forest had become very silent. No birds. No insects. It was as if every living creature had disappeared.

And then, very faintly, I heard something. The crack-snap of twigs and branches breaking underfoot. 'Ralphy?' My breath snagged in my throat.

No, definitely not Ralph. This was a person and, from the sound of it, they were running through the forest's thick undergrowth. Towards me.

My chest constricted. *Breathe, Olive. Don't freak.* Lots of people ran in the forest all the time. Totally normal, non-scary people. But my throat refused to relax.

The noise grew louder. Closer. And then I could hear another noise too – a low gasping sound that seemed to echo all around. Panic scrambled through me.

A person stumbled into view, lurching unsteadily through a gap in the trees. Miss Falippi? I'd never seen her look like this before. Hair full of leaves, clothes covered with mud. She had this wild look in her eyes, and she kept twisting around to see someone or *something* behind her.

It's like a movie, I thought, feeling dazed. The scene where the panicked woman is chased through the forest. As she stumbled closer I was shocked by how unfocused her eyes were, and how red. I'd heard the druggy rumours about Miss Falippi, of course, but I'd never taken them seriously.

Miss Falippi stopped and leant on a tree a couple of metres from me, breathing raggedly. Did she even know I was there? She seemed so wired. I took a step forward and touched her lightly on the arm. 'Miss Falippi? Are you OK?'

Miss Falippi spun around, a look of complete terror on her face, like I was some kind of monster. 'Stop following me! I said you could leave, didn't I? Please … just go.' She started to whimper then. 'Oh, what have you done to me?'

My throat was tight with fear. Miss Falippi's eyes were so dilated they seemed completely black, and her forehead was beaded with sweat. She wasn't wearing her locket and for some reason this scared me most of all. She looked wrong without it. Unprotected.

'It's Olive, miss,' I said gently, finding my voice again. 'Olive Corbett.'

Miss Falippi's eyes scanned my face, frowning – finally seeming to recognise me. 'Olive? *You're* in on this?' she hissed. 'I would have *never*...'

'I'm just walking my dog,' I said, trying to sound reassuring and calm despite the burning in my chest. 'But we should leave now. It's getting dark.'

Miss Falippi suddenly flung up her hand like she did in class when she wanted silence. 'Shh!' Her eyes darted around fearfully. *'Is that...her?'*

I listened and although I heard nothing, I had that awful prickling feeling that comes when you sense someone is hidden nearby.

'Hello?' I said loudly. 'We need some help here. Is anyone there? *Please.'* I thought I saw something then – a pale flash between the trees – but seconds passed and no-one appeared. My fists clenched. 'There's no-one there,' I said, not very convincingly.

Miss Falippi swung round, her eyes even more crazed than before. 'I know your type,' she whispered hoarsely. 'You girls will stop at nothing.'

I tried again to get through to her. 'It's just Olive, Miss Falippi. I am not sure what's happened but maybe I can –'

Miss Falippi stepped away from me, her hands outstretched, her face purple with rage. 'Get away from me,' she shrieked. 'Leave me alone!'

She turned and stumbled off through the undergrowth, coughing and moaning. I didn't follow. She'd made it pretty clear she didn't want my help. I was taking some deep breaths when Ralph bounded out from behind a bush, looking pleased with himself. From the way he smelled it was clear he'd rolled in something disgusting.

'Oh, Ralph,' I said, nearly bursting into tears at the sight of his sweet, silly face. 'Look at you. Come on. Let's get out of here.'

o

When I got home Mum and Toby were still out, so I splashed water on my face and shoved down a round of meds. Had I taken any that day? Sometimes when I was tired I lost track.

I called Ami and when she turned up almost instantly, I nearly cried again – but then the anger came crashing in. 'Where the hell *were* you?'

I knew it was unfair, but I couldn't help it. I felt like she'd let me down. Ami took one look at my furious expression. 'What's happened?' It was a relief to let it spill out – the horrible noise of Miss Falippi's breathing, her paranoia, the madness in her face. My voice shook as I described the feeling I'd been unable to shake, that there was someone else in the forest.

Ami listened the way she always did – not interrupting, just hearing me out. 'You did the right thing,' she said when I'd finally finished. 'You tried to help and she wouldn't let you. What else could you do?'

I nodded slowly. It was the reassurance I'd wanted. But I still felt freaked. Ami squeezed my arm. 'Hey,' she said. 'Let's clean up Ralph before your mum sees him. I bet you by the time that's done, you'll have forgotten all about Miss Falippi.'

Usually I hated cleaning Ralph. His long fur tangled easily around gunk and burrs, and he had a habit of escaping from me while still wet and romping around, spraying water everywhere. But that evening I threw myself into the task with the sort of dedication I usually reserved for making Luxe posters.

Ami sat on the edge of the bath, pointing out the bits I'd missed and generally trying to take my mind off what had happened. And it worked. Pretty much. By the time Mum and Toby came home and Ralph was burr-free, I'd gotten close to convincing myself that what had happened in the forest was no big deal at all.

o

In the morning Mum had yet another rush of orders to deliver, so I got Tobes ready and took him to school.

I hadn't slept well. Every time I'd closed my eyes, Miss Falippi's manic face had appeared in my mind. *You girls will stop at nothing*, she kept saying over and over. Throughout the night, her expression morphed from fear to fury, then back to fear. I was relieved when morning came so I could plod through the things I needed to do. This task, then this task, then this one. They kept me distracted.

The bell had long since rung by the time I arrived at school. My footsteps echoed as I hurried across the deserted quad, making deals with fate as I went.

If Miss Falippi is all right, I'll hand in my work on time for two weeks, I decided. As I reached the main building where all our classrooms were, I ramped up the deal. *I'll pay attention for a month.* All the doors in the corridor were shut except one. Ours. It was obvious from the noise drifting out that there was no teacher in there. My hands were damp. *If Miss Falippi is OK, I'll be a perfect student for a year.*

I could feel Lachlan watching me as I walked in, but I focused on Ami instead. She smiled at me reassuringly as I took my seat beside her. 'She's probably just late,' she whispered, but there was an edge to her voice that gave her away. Ami was as worried as I was. I fixed my eyes on the doorway, willing Miss Falippi to appear, bracelets jangling, tea sloshing, locket dangling.

And then there was a familiar voice, just outside the door. 'People. Get out your books. We're going to learn about Cerberus today – the three-headed guard dog of Hades.'

The talking died away instantly. People slid reluctantly into their seats. Ami nudged me. 'See? Everything's fine.'

But I knew something was wrong. I could feel it, squeezing my heart.

'Anyone who doesn't have their books out when I walk in will not be going to the formal,' continued the voice. It was so clear and strong – the opposite of how Miss Falippi had sounded in the forest. 'Am I making myself clear?'

My heart was beating fast then. Why wasn't she coming into the classroom?

Then the moaning began. People were looking around at each other nervously now, but no-one moved.

'What have you done to me?' the voice whimpered. 'What have you done?'

I jumped to my feet, my chair clattering to the ground, just as someone sauntered through the doorway. Miranda. She saw me standing and smiled.

'Well it's good to see that *someone* was going to help poor old Trippy Falippi. I mean, if that had actually *been* her.' She rolled her eyes and flailed her arms around. 'Help me! I'm dying!'

It was the voice we'd all heard coming from outside the door. Miss Falippi's voice. But now it was coming from Miranda's mouth. The nausea rose up through me. She *must* have been there in the forest. But she hadn't come to help.

There was a moment's silence. Then Katie began to laugh. 'Oh my *god!* That was amazing. I seriously thought that was Miss Falippi out there.'

Cam guffawed. 'Awesome!'

'That's not cool,' said Lachlan, shaking his head, but he was drowned out by Paige and Justine's giggling.

'What a pathetic, sick joke,' I said, anger making me tremble.

Miranda's eyes were on me straight away. 'It's Miss Falippi who's the joke. How does a drug addict like her get to be in charge of a classroom anyway?'

I glared at her. 'What are you talking about?'

Miranda's teeth glittered. 'Haven't you heard? Miss Falippi was found wandering around the forest last night, completely wasted.'

'Miss Falippi was actually on drugs?' said someone.

'God yes,' smirked Miranda. 'I saw her slip stuff into her herbal tea when she thought no-one was watching.'

Katie shook her head, looking disgusted, and I heard a few other people starting to mutter too. I was suddenly aware that Miranda was watching me closely.

'Don't pretend you care,' she said. 'She's a stupid old freak, always blabbing on about nothing. She kept me here for an hour last night while she slurped away, thinking I didn't know what she was up to.' She smiled slyly. 'So I put a little something extra into her cup. Detention ended pretty quickly after that.'

There was a moment of silence, which Katie broke by laughing again. 'You are *too* funny, Miranda.'

I saw Lachlan out of the corner of my eye, sitting there stonily. Did he, like me, think that Miranda hadn't sounded like she was joking?

Katie patted the back of the seat beside her. 'Come and sit here, Miranda,' she said. 'Justine, move over.'

When Justine stayed where she was, Katie shook the chair impatiently. 'Move!'

Justine got up robotically and shuffled along to the spare seat right at the end of the row. She kept her head down but I could see that her cheeks were pink with humiliation. By the time Mrs Deane walked in, Miranda and Katie were sitting side by side, chatting like they'd been friends for years. Their hair, I realised with an uneasy lurch, was now almost exactly the same shade of blonde. The same length too.

'Where's Miss Falippi?' I asked Mrs Deane, somehow tearing

my eyes off the weird sight of Katie and Miranda gossiping.

Mrs Deane gave me one of those *I'll let your interruption pass this time because there's something more important I need to say* looks. 'Miss Falippi is unwell. I will be supervising the class until I've found a substitute.' She sat down, folded her hands. *End of conversation.*

But I couldn't let it go. Not that easily. 'What's wrong with her?' My mouth was dry.

When Mrs Deane spoke it was obvious we were hearing the official story. 'Miss Falippi has been under a great deal of stress recently. She's taking some time off.'

○

By halfway through recess, it seemed everyone knew about Miss Falippi and her supposed drug problem. There were even people claiming she'd acted high in class sometimes. And when some cops showed up as the bell rang and headed for Mrs Deane's office – well, that was all most people needed as proof.

Miranda spent the break with Katie. Justine and Paige were there too, but they may as well have been invisible for the attention they received. Katie fussed over Miranda, redoing her hair, adjusting her uniform so that she was wearing it in the *correct* way. Miranda was the new toy. At the end of the break, I saw Katie tie the pink thread from her wrist around Miranda's. A strange feeling came over me as I watched them get up and walk away together, arms linked. Part of me was surprised at Katie, taking someone under her wing – not that Miranda looked like she really needed caring for anymore. The other part of me was … not jealous, exactly, but I did feel an odd, anxious protectiveness towards Katie.

A little breeze picked up and started blowing the break-time rubbish around in circles. I looked down and watched a line of ants busily working on an apple core.

I turned to Ami. 'What should we do? About Miranda?'

Ami's response was instant. 'Nothing. We stay the hell out of her way.'

o

She's really come out of her shell. That's an expression I'd never liked. It seemed to me that most of the creatures living in shells were the sort you'd rather have stay in there. Snails. Crabs. Things with stingers. But over the next few weeks I heard people say these words about Miranda over and over again. And they said it like it was a good thing.

At first Ami and I kept away from Miranda as much as possible. But I'd be lying if I said I wasn't still fascinated by what was going on – and not just because focusing on her distracted me from daydreaming impossible things about Lachlan.

It was hard to believe that the thin, frail, practically mute creature who'd turned up in our classroom a couple of months ago was the same person who now seemed to be everywhere and part of everything. Miranda was filling out. Her once-baggy uniform was now shorter and fitted perfectly, always casually askew in some Katie-ish way. Her sudden healthfulness hadn't rubbed off on Katie, though – just the opposite. Katie had always been too skinny, at least to everyone except herself and her agent. 'If I can just lose this last kilo,' she was always telling me fretfully, 'my agent says the jobs will come flooding in.' It didn't matter how many times I told her it was crazy, she wouldn't give it up.

Katie's agent must have been thrilled with her now because the curves – such as they were – had started falling off.

It wasn't just weight Katie was shedding. Every time I saw Miranda, she had another one of Katie's possessions. At first it was just small things like hair clips and pens and magazines. But the things gradually became bigger and more valuable. Her purple earphones. Her favourite scarf. Her iPod. I half-expected her to rock up with Katie's personal diary – the one she kept locked with a small silver key. But the biggest shock was the day I spotted Miranda wearing Katie's earrings. Everyone knew about those earrings because Katie bragged about them constantly. They were 'twenty-four-carat white gold' with a 'two-carat diamond in each stud'. She only dared to wear them to school because they were insured. No-one could touch them, not even Paige and Justine. But at assembly one morning, there they were in Miranda's ears, sparkling and twinkling like stars when she swished her hair to one side. And that's where they stayed. Until the night of the formal, of course.

Miranda had become part of the school-formal committee, although whenever I saw them having a meeting it was mainly Katie and Miranda examining the streamer samples while they listened to music with one purple earphone each. Paige and Justine would sit a little way off, their faces grim, surrounded by uneaten packets of rice crackers and bags of grapes. There seemed to be a protective barrier forming around Katie and Miranda, and it was becoming harder for people – and snacks – to get through.

Still, I was surprised when the news went around that Justine and Paige were officially no longer friends with Katie. Maybe it was the suddenness. Or the way that no-one seemed to know – or care about – what had happened. Apparently they'd just failed to measure up in some way.

'They probably wore the wrong shade of nail polish,' said Ami. 'You know. Something unforgivable.'

When Justine was ejected from The Katie and Miranda Show, she just faded into the background. Maybe it was a relief. But it was different with Paige. I suppose I'd always thought that there wasn't any real friendship between her and Katie – that Paige was prepared to put up with being Katie's slave because of the associated benefit. Status. She'd stuck at it for a long time too, hovering on the edges for months as things soured between me and Katie, and pouncing when my position became vacant. I knew she was thrilled with her promotion, but I never considered for a minute that Paige might genuinely like and care about Katie.

Yet when Katie deleted her as a friend, Paige seemed devastated. She continued to trail along behind Katie, watching everything she did. Miranda put a stop to that quick smart. The story went around that there was some big fight and that Paige had refused to go away until Katie herself told her to. Which

Katie did – right to her face one lunchtime in front of everyone. I don't know what Paige looked like as she walked away – neither Ami or I were there – but I picture her as looking kind of dignified. I do know what she said as she went, though, because for the rest of the day everyone went around imitating it.

'I'm really worried about you, Katie. I think she's trying to *kill* you.'

The imitations were all pretty much the same – using the quavering, emotional voice of someone about to lose control. Some people gave her a speech impediment – saying the r's like w's. It was probably exactly how they imitated me when I was in the clinic.

When Paige finally left Katie and Miranda to it, I was relieved. I knew I didn't have a shred of evidence, but I couldn't shake the feeling that if she'd resisted, something would've happened to her. Like what had happened to Miss Falippi. Getting in Miranda's way was starting to seem like a health hazard.

Once Paige was gone, the invisible wall around Miranda and Katie closed up completely. The only other person who was allowed into their space was Cameron. The three of them walked around everywhere together – the untouchable trio – laughing and acting like they were the only three people in the entire world. The only three that mattered.

SEVEN

One Wednesday afternoon, I brought Toby home from football practice and we found Mum busy frying up what looked like a pan of large, brown erasers.

'Oh!' said Toby, glancing at me. 'Tofu schnitzels.'

I was just as concerned as he was. Mum seemed to think tofu schnitzels were a treat. She only cooked them when she was worried about us. More worried than usual. We needed to tread carefully.

'Yummm!' I said, breathing through my mouth. 'Can I help?'

'Just take these over to the table,' said Mum, sliding the sizzling brown things onto plates and tossing a salad. 'We've all been so busy I thought it'd be nice if we had a special dinner together.'

I took the plates and we all sat down. 'Thanks, Mum,' I said.

'Yeah, thanks!' said Toby. His smile was stretched so wide it made my facial muscles ache just looking at him.

I picked up my fork and attempted to spear the schnitzel with it. Looking over at Toby, I was surprised to see that one of his schnitzels had already vanished. Grinning, he pointed to his bulging pocket. Not such a bad idea. But difficult to do with Mum looking straight at me.

'So, Olive,' she said. 'How's school? Who are you hanging out with these days?'

I managed to hack off a cube of schnitzel and shove it into my mouth. 'It's fine,' I said, hoping only to answer the first question. I considered mentioning the cops who'd shown up in home room that morning to inform us that in the weeks to come, they'd be *interviewing each student with regards to some very serious allegations.* But as if Mum needed another reason to stress.

Her face went pink with relief. 'I'm so glad,' she said. 'So you're not still spending time with Ami?'

I hated the way Mum said Ami's name. Like it was in inverted commas or something. Like she still didn't understand that Ami was the only person in my life who really got me.

Things went quiet then. Toby, perhaps sensing the sudden drop in temperature, put a big piece of schnitzel into his mouth. In the silence I could hear it squeaking between his teeth as he valiantly attempted to chew it.

'Ami helps me,' I said.

Mum kept cutting her food into smaller and smaller pieces. 'Aren't there others you can talk to?' she said, not meeting my eyes. 'What about Katie? You girls used to be so close.'

'She's got a new best friend now.' I didn't add that the new friend was probably a parasitic shapeshifter who kept stealing her stuff. It seemed a bit dramatic for dinnertime.

'Oh. What about the others?' Mum persisted. 'You used to have so many friends.'

'And now I don't,' I said, kind of loudly. 'Now I just have Ami.'

I guess I could have told her about Lachlan, but what would I say exactly? *There's a guy at school that I sort of like, but I'm too fat and weird to go out with him and Katie's probably blabbed to him that I'm crazy, like she did to everyone else.* I don't think so.

Mum's cutlery clicked on the plate as she put them down. 'I don't like you relying on this *Ami*,' she said. 'Honey? I'm worried about you.'

I so didn't want to be having this conversation. I needed to get away, get some fresh air. Dr Richter was always telling me that exercise would help. My chair scraped across the floor. 'Thanks for dinner,' I said flatly, fighting to stop the frustration spilling into my voice. 'I'm going for a ride.'

o

It was already getting dark as I headed off, streaking along the road as fast as I could. The streetlights had come on and there was just the faintest light-blue glow over the horizon. I had a tailwind and it wasn't long before I'd left Jubilee Park far behind. When I arrived at the intersection near the edge of town, I stopped. The left-hand road soon curved around and would lead me back into town. The other road followed the coast. My hands began to sweat a little, thinking about the rise and fall of the ocean.

Just keep your eyes on the road, I told myself. *Forget that the water is out there.* The lights changed and I didn't move. Being so close to the ocean – especially alone – was über terrifying, but I knew I wasn't ready to go back home yet. The frustration was still burbling inside me. I put my head down and headed out along the coast road. I rode fast, not looking to the sides except for the occasional sideways glance for traffic, trying to funnel the surge of fear into my pedalling.

It was darker now but I didn't need light to know exactly where I was. In my mind I saw the darkened weekender houses and the closed-for-winter surf shops flash by. The deserted playgrounds with their stunted trees and scratchy, burr-filled grass. I hadn't consciously chosen a direction, but I knew where I was heading. To the lookout. The place Dad and I used to ride to all the time.

The lookout was really just a slight bulge in the road where cars could pull in to photograph the ocean, but it was a long enough ride from our house to make your muscles tingle. It had one of those signposts with pointers telling you how far it is to London and New York. Like it knew you'd rather be somewhere else. Dad and I would stop there and gaze at the horizon, and I'd ask him jokingly if that was the end of the world. He'd laugh and say, 'No, Pet. There's a lot more world beyond there.'

Riding along here was bringing stuff into my head. Things I usually managed to block out. About Dad. About how bad things had been just before he left. How I'd started sneaking out on weekends and lying about cutting school. How I was obsessed with looks and boys and manipulating the world – playing people off against each other to get what I wanted. Especially Mum and Dad. How angry I'd become if I was ever denied anything. I was the kind of girl who caused bad things to happen. The kind of girl who deserved bad things to happen to her in return.

I realised I was gripping the handlebars so tightly that my fingers were burning.

After Dad left, Mum started leaving pamphlets around the house for *kids from breaking homes*. I'd scoffed at them, but I did flick through one, just long enough to see the line about how *your parents will always love you and their separation is not your fault*. That was either bullshit, or the gods of family breakdown had made an exception for me.

The fact that he'd left because of me was indisputable. I was always the cause of Mum and Dad's arguments, and then their fights spilled over into money and shitty days at work. So after the Incident, and after I came out of the clinic, I decided to kill off the old Olive for good. I owed it to what was left of my family to shut up, swallow my meds and not cause any more trouble.

o

When I sensed that the lookout was near, I slowed and pulled in. It was too dark to see the ocean and at first I didn't notice the bike – a racer – leaning against the wall. And even when I did my first thought was, *That's weird. Someone's left a bike here.* But of course, a moment later I saw the bike's owner sitting cross-legged on the wall, staring out at the ocean.

Lachlan looked so peaceful. So smooth and untroubled. I felt a pang of envy. *Nothing bad could ever happen to someone like him.* Lachlan Ford was one of those people who would just cruise through life, steadily and easily.

I used to be like that too. Although I guess I was less of a cruiser and more a steamroller, flattening whatever was in my path. The old Olive did what she wanted, when she wanted.

I steadied my breathing. *Get going. Before he sees you.* Because if Lachlan had smiled at me right then I suspected that all the medication in the world wouldn't be able to stop me bursting into tears. Silently, I pointed the wheel of my bike towards home. Put my foot on the pedals. And rode straight over some broken glass. I heard the viper-hiss of air as my front tyre deflated.

Lachlan must have heard it too. Or maybe he'd known all along that I was there. As I busied myself with examining the flabby mess that was my front tyre, I heard him jump off the wall and walk over – in that unhurried, casual way of his. 'Got anything to fix it with?'

Just like that. No greeting. No mention of the fact that I'd been avoiding eye contact every day in home room and ignoring him in the halls these last few weeks. My heart leapt and once again I felt the annoying flicker of doubt. The one that made me wonder if maybe Lachlan's apparent interest was genuine and not just some kind of cruel gag. But I quickly squashed this. There was just no way it could be true. God knows what his weird pseudo flirting was about though. Maybe he did it with everyone.

'Of course I do,' I said. I kept a small puncture repair kit in a bag under my bike seat. It was something Dad had been big on – knowing how to mend stuff yourself. *You can't rely on anyone else to patch things up for you,* he'd say. *Better you learn for yourself.*

I upended my bike and released the wheel. Then I fished out the tool that helped remove the tyre from the rim. I could feel Lachlan close beside me, watching, warmth radiating from his body.

'Need a hand?'

'No thanks.' Then I added, a little tersely, 'You don't have to stick around. It's under control.' Did he think I wasn't capable of changing a tyre? That all girls had to wait around for *big, strong* guys like him to help them out?

'Actually, I do have to stick around.' Lachlan gestured to the racer. 'I've got a flat too,' he said, a little sheepishly. 'Can I borrow your repair kit?'

I stared at him curiously. 'How long have you been waiting?' He'd looked so calm sitting there on the wall, gazing out to sea. Not like someone who was stranded with a flat.

'Half an hour? Maybe longer.'

'You didn't call anyone?' I said. 'Or start walking back into town?'

Lachlan shrugged. 'No. I figured someone would come along eventually.' He grinned at me. 'And someone did.'

I dropped the bike pump. Picked it up again. 'Butter fingers,'

I muttered. I scooped up the stuff from the repair kit and held it out. 'Here.'

Lachlan looked at the kit doubtfully. 'Feel like giving me a hand?'

'Don't tell me you don't know how to patch a tyre!'

'Of course I do,' Lachlan said quickly. 'But not as well as you. You're like a tyre-fixing machine.'

How was it that he always managed to make me laugh?

'OK. I'll help you,' I said. 'Watch and learn.'

He smiled gratefully. 'Thanks,' he said. 'Next time I'll change yours.'

'Yeah, sure,' I said. As if there would be a next time.

So I helped Lachlan fix his tyre and pump it back up. Then somehow, without even discussing it, we started riding back into town together like it was the most natural thing in the world. *It doesn't mean anything*, I told myself sternly. *It's just the logical thing to do.*

We didn't speak much on the ride back, but it was a comfortable, easy silence. I didn't exactly forget the stuff that had been on my mind – Mum going off about Ami, my growing concerns about Miranda – but they kind of fell away a little. Even the ocean, falling and swelling only metres away on the other side of the road, didn't seem quite so scary right then.

We stopped at the intersection at the outskirts of town.

'Usually I go right here,' said Lachlan. 'But how about I ride home with you? It's pretty dark.'

'No thanks, Mr Lifesaver Guy.' I was aiming for cheery and

casual, but it came out sounding defensive and rude.

Lachlan studied my face for a moment. 'Is it just me you say no to?'

'Hey, don't get cocky,' I said, glad that he couldn't see the rising blush on my neck. 'I say no to heaps of things. Commercial radio. Leggings that look like jeans. Tofu schnitzels. At least, I'd say no to them if I could.'

'*Tofu schnitzels?*' winced Lachlan. 'I don't even know what those are and I'm saying no to them.'

I laughed. Despite myself. 'Good decision.'

A car drove up to the lights, filled with people and pumping with music. The passengers turned to stare when the car stopped, laughing about something. *Hey, everyone! What's wrong with this picture?* I imagined them snickering as they looked at me there next to Lachlan.

Lachlan didn't seem to have noticed the car. He was watching me. 'Are you still saying no to school formals too?'

'Yeah,' I said, making a close examination of my handlebars. 'I'm still saying no to those.'

The traffic lights changed and the car took off. For a moment Lachlan didn't move. I stayed there next to him, although I don't know why. I guess I was waiting for something.

Finally Lachlan raised his hand. 'Well, bye then, I guess. See you around.'

'Yeah,' I said. 'See you.'

As Lachlan took off down the street, I was suddenly aware of the wind blowing hard and cold across my neck. I hadn't noticed it before. It was like I'd been wearing a scarf and it had suddenly been removed.

EIGHT

'Well hello, beautiful,' said Noah from the ticket office as I rushed in on date night a few days later.

'Enough with the sarcasm, thanks,' I said as I slotted myself behind the snack bar counter.

'I wasn't being sarcastic,' insisted Noah. 'You look good, even with a red face and helmet hair. So, is this just a social visit?'

'OK, OK,' I said, ruffling up my hair with my hands. 'Watch me, I'm working.'

And I did work, solidly, for the next half an hour or so. Scooping popcorn, squirting soft drink into cups, passing back change. Ami sat on the end of the counter, swinging her legs and making quiet jokes about the customers' purchases, but I was too flat out to join in. I even forgot to keep an eye out for Lachlan. It wasn't that I wanted him to come in for another ice-cream. But I half-thought he might.

It was after the first surge had passed and I was at the cash register that I saw Cameron reflected in the thief mirror, coming in the front door. On his arm was someone skinny and hunched.

'My god,' said Ami. 'Look at Katie.'

'No.' I shoved the drawer of the cash register closed and turned around. 'It *can't* be.'

Shapeless. That was the word that came to my head as I looked at Katie that night. Standing next to Cameron – so buff and solid and high-school handsome – only highlighted the difference between them. No-one would've picked these two as a couple. They barely looked like they belonged to the same species.

I found myself staring, practically open-mouthed. What the hell had *happened* to her? Was she sick? It was only a month or so ago that Katie had torn the pink thread from Miranda's wrist and tried to humiliate her in front of the whole school. Since she'd strolled around the pool in her bathers, her supermodel glow radiating in waves.

Katie wasn't even a shadow of her former self. She was the whisper of a shadow.

The Mercury door swung open again and this time Miranda walked in, wearing one of Katie's dresses. It bothered me, even though Katie and I had swapped clothes all the time when we were the same size. Maybe it was that the dress would have been way too big for Katie now, and yet it fitted Miranda perfectly. In fact, it looked better than it had *ever* looked on Katie, especially across the chest. You could feel everyone in the foyer turning to look. Miranda had become the sort of girl that people openly gaped at. And once their eyes were fixed on her, it was hard to look away. Cameron, I noticed, didn't even bother to try.

Miranda waltzed up and pushed her way between Cameron and Katie, draping an arm around each of them. 'Hi, my honeys,' she said. Cameron's whole face glowed at her touch. 'Do we have tickets?'

'Not yet,' said Cameron, the eager puppy. 'I'll go and get them now.'

Cameron unhooked his arm from around Katie and walked towards the counter. Katie swayed for a moment, then leant against the wall, her hands pressed against her concave stomach. I saw her say something to Miranda. I couldn't hear it, but it was clear from her eyes what she was saying. *I'm hungry.*'

For a moment, Miranda crossed her arms and looked at Katie. But finally she sighed and walked briskly towards the snack bar where I was waiting, my hands pressed onto the smooth lino surface.

'I'll take a bottle of water.'

I got a bottle from the fridge and took a choc-top out of the freezer, placing them in front of Miranda. She stared at the ice-cream, like it was something I'd just coughed up.

'I didn't ask for that,' she said. 'Just the water.'

'It's not for you,' I said. 'It's for Katie. She always has one. This one's on the house.'

I was suddenly determined for Katie to get her ice-cream. It was her first date night in weeks, and that probably meant her first non-diet food in ages too. It felt like some fundamental law of nature would be upset if she didn't get a choc-top.

'You think I'm *stopping* her?' said Miranda icily.

I leant forward on the counter. 'I don't know. *Are* you?'

Miranda held my gaze for a few seconds before swivelling round. 'Hey, Katie? Honey? Do you want a choc-top?'

Katie was still leaning against the wall. But now her eyes were closed. A word formed on her lips. But the sound that came out didn't match the expression of longing on her face. 'No.'

Miranda turned back to me and smiled that victorious smile she'd recently perfected. She picked up the bottle of water and strolled off.

Fifteen minutes after Miranda had gone, I was still fuming, smarting from the humiliation of defeat. I just couldn't shake it. So, after a bit of angry restocking – slamming down coffee cups so hard they buckled – I went over to the freezer and fished out a fresh choc-top.

'What are you plotting?' asked Ami.

'Katie is going to get an ice-cream,' I said determinedly. 'I'm going to deliver it myself.'

Ami frowned. 'Aren't we steering clear of Miranda?'

'I'm not asking you to come with me,' I said, heading towards the closed cinema doors. But Ami slid off the bench and followed me. Just as I knew she would.

My plan was pretty basic. Sneak into the cinema, wait until my eyes adjusted to the dark, locate Katie, deposit the ice-cream in her lap, and sneak out again. More complicated was my motive for wanting to do it in the first place. Was it because

Katie looked like she needed help? Or was it about proving something to Miranda? I decided not to dwell on it.

The soundtrack was blaring loudly as Ami and I slipped into the cinema. As my eyes adjusted, heads and shoulders of varying heights and widths began to emerge.

Ami nudged me. 'Over there.'

Sure enough, up the back of the cinema, not far from where we were standing, were the outlines of a tall guy with a long-haired girl on either side of him. Katie had her head resting against Cam's shoulder and he had his arm draped around her neck. Miranda was slumped down in her seat. I smiled in the darkness. *Easy.* I could just lean over Katie's shoulder and hand her the ice-cream. But as I stepped forward Ami stopped me.

'Something's not right. It's all around the wrong way.'

I peered at the three shapes again and saw what she meant. The girl with her head on Cameron's shoulder – the one he was holding so close – wasn't Katie. It was Miranda. Katie was the one scrunched up in her seat. And when I edged a bit closer, I heard soft, snoring sounds coming from her. I hesitated. Should I shake Katie awake and tell her what was going on? I curled my hand around the choc-top and the plastic wrapper crinkled. It wasn't very loud, but it was enough to cause Miranda's head to turn.

My eyes had adjusted to the gloom enough for me to see her face quite clearly. She looked at me, and when she smirked, it was clear she knew exactly what I'd been planning to do. I froze, half-expecting her to speak, but she turned back again without saying a word. A moment later she gave a contented sigh and nuzzled her head deeper into Cameron's shoulder.

Ami and I looked at each other. The choc-top was softening in my hand. 'Just let her sleep,' Ami whispered. 'Maybe tell her another time.'

I nodded slowly. But I knew I probably wouldn't talk to Katie about it. It wasn't like she would listen.

By the time Ami and I were behind the snack bar again, the ice-cream had begun melting through the perforated plastic onto my hand. I dumped it into the rubbish and went to wash the sticky mess away. We didn't say much for the rest of the night, but I was pretty sure Ami had the same word going around in her head as I did. A word that kept coming back no matter how often I tried to evict it.

Shapeshifter.

NINE

'No way, Ami,' I said. 'I'm not going. *Forget it.*'

You think you know someone. And you think they know you too. You especially think they know the things that you are absolutely *not* prepared to do. Ever.

Ami had started talking about the formal. As in, suggesting that we go to it. At first I thought she was kidding. I mean, if there was one thing I'd been clear about since I came back from the clinic, it was that I wouldn't be doing crap like that any more. And I'd thought Ami was with me on that. It was one of the things we'd *bonded* over, for god's sake! But now she seemed to have changed her mind.

'It could be fun,' Ami said.

'It will be horrific,' I retorted. 'And cheesy. I used to be on the committee, don't forget.'

'Horrific, cheesy fun,' said Ami, shrugging. 'What's wrong with that?'

'It's not my thing,' I muttered.

Ami folded her arms. 'What *is* your *thing* these days, Olive? Hiding in your room doing nothing? Ignoring the hot guy who clearly has a thing for you?'

'Listening to Luxe isn't *nothing*,' I retorted. 'Anyway, aren't we supposed to be staying away from Miranda?'

We had been, too. Since that date night at the Mercury, I'd been trying extra hard to shut Miranda out of my mind – attempting not to notice that her personality and magnetism was growing stronger every day while Katie kept fading into the background. But all the same, that rubbishy shapeshifter website kept floating at the edges of my mind, especially whenever I noticed how limp Katie's hair was looking next to Miranda's luscious locks.

'I don't think it's Miranda you want to avoid,' said Ami flatly. 'I think it's Lachlan.'

'Couldn't we just hire a bunch of DVDs instead?' I pleaded. I was starting to feel clammy. 'Eat corn chips and salsa?'

'Look, I can't *make* you go,' said Ami.

'That's right,' I agreed quickly. 'You can't.'

'It's just that …' Ami stopped and bit her lip.

'What?' I said, like a total *dummkopf.* 'What is it?'

'It's just that I'd really, really love to go,' Ami sighed. 'And you know I can't go without you.'

Of course then I started thinking about all the things Ami had done for me. How she'd made school bearable. How she hung out with me at work, making me laugh and keeping the boredom at bay. The countless hours she'd spent talking to me about Dad and making me feel that maybe, one day, I'd feel OK again. I wondered yet again what I would do without her.

'All right, all right,' I said. 'I'll go. But only for a *micro-second*. Do you get me?'

Ami squealed and danced around.

'And I'm going to avoid Lachlan all night,' I said. 'So don't get any ideas about that.'

'You can hide under a table if you want,' said Ami. 'I'm just happy we're going.' And then, because she liked to torment me, she mused, 'I wonder what Lachlan will wear?'

o

Once I'd agreed to go, Ami and I spent quite a bit of time coming up with costume ideas for the winter beach-party theme – something a bit more interesting than the inevitable bikini tops and little fur-trimmed skirts for the girls, and tuxedos paired with board shorts for the blokes. My first idea was to cover myself in blue make-up and go as someone with hypothermia, but then Ami suggested going as a shark attack victim. Nothing to do with winter, but too good an idea to pass up.

This involved a number of visits to the local op shop, which of course I was happy about. When I first started going there it was because none of my old clothes fit – neither my body nor my personality – so I'd bundled pretty much everything I owned into a bag and chucked it away. But I had limited money for replacements, hence the op shopping. I never expected to find things I actually liked – but that's exactly what happened.

The hunt part became addictive. In normal shops you just walk in and see something that looks OK, then check for your size. It didn't work like that in op shops though. I had to be patient. Sometimes – often – I came home empty-handed. But there were times when I found something so lush that it made all the failed visits worthwhile. The best bit was that my purchases only ever cost a couple of dollars.

Sourcing my formal outfit was one of those sweet experiences. I found a dress right at the back of the shop, folded up with the 50-cent bed sheets, and even before I smoothed it out I knew it would be perfect. A bit mouldy with age and tight in the waist, but beautiful anyway – pale minty-green with little beads sewn on to the bodice. Something that a girl from the 1950s probably wore to *her* school formal. Except that she wouldn't have worn it the way I was planning to.

Later, as I held the scissors above my new purchase, I found myself hesitating. Poor dress. It had really come down in the world. But then I thought about how amazing it would look when I'd finished and I stopped feeling like I was destroying the dress and told myself that this was more like *re-creation*. I had to do it anyway. This would be my way of letting everyone at the formal know that I wasn't taking the event seriously.

o

On the night of the dance, I put the dress on and smeared the skin that was exposed by the 'shark bite' with fake blood.

I didn't even mind that my pudgy stomach was showing. Blood smears can be very flattering when they're applied vertically.

Ami directed me while I did my hair. Prissy on one side. Chaos on the other. When I'd finished, she nodded. 'Perfect.'

I had to go into Mum's room to see my reflection. My mirror was another thing I'd removed, post-clinic. The shark-attack side was only visible if I turned to the left. From the other angle I looked completely normal. It was this side that freaked me out the most.

'I look so …'

'Pretty,' smirked Ami, drawing out the word so it rang in my ears. 'Preeeeetty.'

I clasped my hands together. Fluttered my eyelids. Channelling the 1950s girl who'd once owned the dress.

'Maybe some dreamy guy will dance with me tonight,' I said in a sugary voice. 'That would be so *peachy.*'

I put on my shoes. Mint-green kitten heels – another op shop purchase and one I never thought I'd actually wear. They were perfect, especially with just a tiny splattering of blood.

'Well Cinderella, I wonder what *Lachlan* will think of your outfit?' said Ami.

'That's something we'll never know,' I said, ignoring the sudden lightness I felt. 'Seeing as I'm going to avoid him. And we'll only be there for half an hour. *Max.*'

All the same, it was an interesting question.

o

The formal was being held at the town hall, a lush old building down on the esplanade with all these crazy turrets. It was painted a pale creamy colour and because it was the tallest building on the street it loomed up against the evening sky like an oversized sandcastle. As Mum turned onto the esplanade, I started catching glimpses of people from school. Sadly I'd been right about the bikinis and little fur-trimmed skirts. Seriously. Some people are insane.

My feeling of dread had started to reach dangerous levels before Mum even stopped the car, and the moment I stepped out onto the footpath I knew this was a huge mistake. No matter how *rad* my costume was. But by then Mum had already pulled away, leaving me and Ami on the footpath. Music – *scheiss* music – blared from the town hall. Two girls arrived, dressed as mermaids, their skirts so narrow around their ankles they could hardly walk. They clutched each other to keep from falling. Each one was wearing a little icicle tiara that went nicely with their cold little smiles. They stopped on the steps, listening to the music.

'Oh my god,' screamed one mermaid.

'I *love* this song!' screamed the other, nearly tripping on her tail.

'I've changed my mind,' I announced, pivoting on my heel. 'I'm going home.' There was a bus stop nearby – I could be home in twenty minutes.

Ami threw herself in front of me. 'No! You promised me you'd stay for a bit. Just remind yourself that we're here to have fun. Or will that break some Princess of the Alternative rule?'

'No,' I said, laughing. 'We're allowed to have fun. We just don't like bad music.'

'Well, put on your headphones and listen to your own music,' said Ami, clearly exasperated. 'I bet you brought some. Let's go inside.'

'Everyone is staring,' I muttered as we walked up the steps and through the ornate wood and glass doors.

'That would be because of the gaping, bloodied hole in your dress,' Ami pointed out.

Oh yeah. I'd forgotten about that. I straightened up. The only thing worse than turning up in a bizarro costume is looking like you regret it.

Inside the hall, set to one side, was a table for refreshments. None of it looked very refreshing – just a bowl of flat orange punch and a few platters of chips. Clearly Miranda and Katie hadn't wasted much of the budget on food.

Nearby Cameron and his friends were standing together, all of them wearing tux jackets with ties shaped like tropical fish. Either they'd planned it or they'd all had the same dumb idea. Cameron looked edgy. He kept fiddling with the fish, his eyes continually flitting towards the door like he was waiting for someone to appear. Not Katie, obviously, because she was standing right near him, silent and grey as a shadow.

'It's a worry, isn't it?' As usual Ami said exactly what I was thinking. 'She looks like she's being drained of life.'

I nodded, my eyes still on Cameron. I was pretty sure I knew who he was looking for, and when his face suddenly began to sparkle I followed his gaze. Miranda had arrived. And it wasn't just Cameron who turned to look. We all did. Almost like we had no say in it.

'Hi, Miranda,' said Cameron, stepping forward and holding out his hand. Like he was a prince. 'You look …' He stopped. Because silence described how Miranda looked, better than any word could. In any language.

I found myself remembering how Miss Falippi had told us about the Sirens. How they sang songs that were irresistible to the sailors, who would wreck their ships and die because they were so desperate to get closer to the music. Although Miranda wasn't actually singing anything, I could sort of feel the pull myself – like an undertow.

Miss Falippi. I realised I hadn't thought about her for ages. I'd heard a rumour the cops were going after her for drug possession, but I didn't hear what happened. She'd resigned without ever coming back.

Somehow Lachlan walked up without me seeing him until he was right there, totally unavoidable. Ami – my supposed friend – not only failed to warn me, but had now completely disappeared.

'Hey.' Lachlan was smiling – and not in a 'so you came anyway' way or a 'what the hell are you wearing?' way. He just looked pleased. Pleased to see me there.

I'd thought about what to do, of course, if this situation arose. Make an excuse and get away from him as quickly as possible.

No chatting. No getting dazzled by his pretend flirting.

'Oh. Hi,' I said. 'I was just …'

But for some reason I forgot all my pre-planned excuses and felt this weird little quiver in my stomach – probably because I hadn't eaten much dinner. Groping around for something to say I noticed Lachlan's outfit - an old-fashioned suit, in pristine condition, and the funniest shirt I'd ever seen.

'Where did your shirt came from? It's so lush.'

Lachlan eyed me cautiously. 'Does *lush* mean "something a wonk would wear?"'

'No. I really like it,' I said. 'It's so … ruffly!'

'It was the ruffliest in the entire formal-hire shop,' he reported proudly.

'I like your jacket too,' I said.

Lachlan stroked one of the lapels. 'This belonged to my Grandpa.'

'So you decided to skip the whole beach theme huh?'

'No, I've got this.' Lachlan fished out something hanging around his neck – a large, hooked tooth, threaded onto a piece of leather. 'This was my Pa's too. He told me he'd pulled it from the mouth of a live shark.'

I laughed. 'How long did you believe that?'

'Way too long,' Lachlan admitted. 'Especially as it's got this on it.' He turned the shark's tooth over and pointed out the writing on the back. *Made in China*. 'By the time I realised it wasn't true it didn't matter.'

'He sounds interesting,' I heard myself say, even though I

was breaking my own rules. *It doesn't hurt to be nice to the new guy, Olive*, I imagined Ami saying.

'He was ... someone who didn't like to swim between the flags, I guess.' Lachlan squinted at me. 'You remind me of him, actually.'

My instinct was to crack a gag. *I remind you of an old man? Maybe I should use a better moisturiser.* But even I could see that he hadn't meant it that way. My mouth was dry. I imagined again what Ami would say. *Get it together, Olive.*

'The trouble with avoiding the flags is you end up like this,' I managed to croak, pointing to the shark bite in my dress. The way Lachlan's gaze brushed over me made my exposed skin turn to goose-pimples, despite the blazing heat of the hall.

'I guess that's why it's good to have your own personal lifesaver around,' he said. 'Watching out for you.'

A new song started playing. Lachlan tilted his head. 'Come and dance?' he said. Casually. Like it was possible I'd say yes.

'It's such a wonkish song,' I said weakly.

'I'm a wonkish dancer.' There was something very determined about him. 'Come on.'

So hopefully that explains how I ended up dancing at my school formal – or at least as much as it's possible to explain something so unexpected. But here's the really strange part. Once I'd calmed down a bit, I started to enjoy myself. Lachlan wasn't such a bad dancer after all. He lost himself in the music – moving about in this cute, happy way, his long limbs flopping around. And he didn't do that other thing that some people do, where they spend the whole time checking if there's someone better they should be dancing with. Lachlan looked at me. Only at me.

When the song finished he took hold of my hand and held it like it was something very precious. His eyes were soft. 'Stay for another song?' he said.

That's when I heard it. People nearby, snickering. I knew what it meant. I wrenched my hand away, angry with myself for being so stupid.

'Hey,' said Lachlan. 'What's wrong?'

I glared at him, my throat aching. 'Have you won your bet yet?' I said, my voice hard and fierce. 'The one you made about dancing with the ugliest girl at the formal?'

'What are you talking about?' he said, looking horrified. 'I –'

I cut him off. 'Isn't it embarrassing, being seen with me? Even as a joke.'

'Olive. *Stop.*' There was something in Lachlan's voice that made me pause, just for a moment. He looked so serious. 'Why would I be embarrassed about dancing with you? You're the most amazing, most beautiful, most ... *real* person in this whole school.'

I had to look away then. The ground was covered in gold glitter. I guess it was meant to look like sand. 'Sometimes I don't feel real,' I said, hating how pathetic it sounded.

'Well maybe you're *un*real then,' said Lachlan softly. 'Which is probably why I want to kiss you.'

Usually you can rely on your body to do the basic things on

its own. But right then my body totally forgot about respiration. I had to gulp at the air, trying to get the process started again. I don't know if someone was messing around with the heating, but suddenly it was even hotter than before in that hall. Hot, bright and way too full.

'I need to go outside,' I wheezed. Thank god my legs remembered what they were for. I ran.

o

It was the darkness as much as the cool breeze that helped me control the swirling, tumbling feeling in my chest. I slowed to a walk and a moment later I heard Lachlan running to catch up. He didn't speak, just fell into step beside me. Silently we moved away from the crowd out the front who were laughing and smoking furtively in the shadows.

I turned down the path that ran along the side of the town hall. The unpainted bricks were exposed and rough along here and I stopped, leaning my face against them, cold and solid on my cheek. Lachlan stopped too, just behind me. I watched a tiny spider – smaller than a raindrop – making a web in the gap between two bricks. It had probably taken it all night to create that web and I could've destroyed it with the tiniest movement of my finger. The spider too.

'I freaked you out, didn't I?' said Lachlan. 'With that kissing thing.'

'No,' I lied. 'I just wasn't expecting it. I don't really *know* you. I mean, I've had maybe three conversations with you in my life.'

'Well yeah.' Lachlan's smile was small, but so sweet. 'They've been three good conversations though, don't you reckon?'

I didn't answer. *Lachlan wants to kiss you.* I said it over and over in my head – like it was a foreign phrase that I couldn't quite translate.

Lachlan leant against the wall too, face turned towards mine. 'Why can't you believe me that I like you?' he said. 'That I want to hang out with you?'

My head began to throb. 'Lachlan,' I said. 'I can't. I just can't.'

'Can't what?' said Lachlan. 'Hang out or believe me?'

Noise from the town hall filtered down to us, louder and then softer as the wind changed direction. There was laughing and cheering. It sounded a lifetime away.

Lachlan turned his face up towards the sky. 'Sometimes you seem to like me,' he said, 'and then you jump away, like you're scared I'll bite. I don't get it. Is there something wrong?'

Yeah there's something freakin wrong, I thought. *Something wrong with me.* And I couldn't accept that Lachlan didn't know that, especially as he must have heard about my history by now. He should be running away as fast as he could before I wrecked his life just like I'd wrecked my family's.

But Lachlan didn't move. He just stood there beside me and I realised he was waiting for a response. I turned and looked at him. It was time to be honest. 'We don't match.'

Lachlan's forehead wrinkled with surprise. '*Match*? Who says we have to? We're not shoes.'

108

'But we're so different,' I said, trying to find a way of explaining it. 'You're a swimmer. You probably train all the time. And if you're not swimming you're probably off doing something else *active* and *sporty*. I bet you go nuts sitting inside for more than five minutes and you love nothing more than hanging out at the beach.' I knew I sounded blunt but maybe that wasn't such a bad thing, even though it was hard to look at him as I spoke. Now let's compare that with me, OK? I like hanging around on my own, listening to music no-one else has heard of and dreaming of the day I can get away from the ocean forever. Be honest, Lachlan. Do we *sound* like a good combination?'

Lachlan was quiet for a long time and I wondered if he was waiting for me to leave. But eventually he spoke. 'OK then. Who *do* I match?'

'Someone *cute*,' I said promptly. 'Someone sweet and pretty who'll mind your towel and cheer for you while you swim. Someone who says *ohmigod* all the time and who covers her mouth when she laughs in case she's got food in her teeth. Someone smooth and knot-free.'

Lachlan looked bemused. 'What's wrong with knots? They keep things together sometimes.'

I ignored this, not wanting to break the flow of my description. The words came easily because I was describing someone I knew. Someone I used to be. Pretended to be, at least. 'She's perky and chatty and involved in everything. She talks about you as *my beautiful swimming star* and constantly raves about your latest successes.'

Lachlan made a strange noise then. I stopped and stared. 'You're *laughing?*'

'Sorry,' said Lachlan, 'but this chick sounds kind of irritating. And ... fake.'

He was right, of course. The old Olive *was* fake. That was why I'd finally knocked her off. The new Olive was hard and broken, but at least she was real. But she wasn't the sort of person I thought Lachlan would want to kiss.

'What about you?' said Lachlan. 'What kind of *shoe* do you match?'

Truthfully? I suspected that there wasn't anyone out there for me, a bloated ex-mental-patient family-wrecker. And, as Ami had pointed out, most of the people I liked were about as unavailable as it is possible to be. As in dead. Or fictitious. But I wanted to give Lachlan an answer. One that didn't leave me looking quite so tragic.

'Dallas Kaye,' I blurted. 'He's the lead singer of Luxe.'

Lachlan gave me the strangest look then, like I'd just said something that really disappointed him. 'Yeah,' he muttered. 'I know who he is.'

Lachlan stepped away from the wall then, the gravel crunching beneath his shoes. Old-fashioned ones, I noticed, lovingly polished. Probably also his Grandpa's. Looking at them I had a sudden image of Lachlan cleaning those shoes earlier this evening and the thought of it made my insides crinkle up.

'I guess I see things differently,' he said. 'I don't think people are like some board game that you can only play one way. And

I'm kind of surprised that you do.'

My stomach crunched again as Lachlan shoved his hands deep in the pockets of his jacket and turned away.

'Hang on, Lachlan,' I said. 'Wait. Don't be dumb about this.' I knew it made no sense. All this time I'd spent trying to convince him to leave me alone and now that he was going I was holding him back.

Lachlan stopped. Turned to face me. His expression was so cool that I could hardly stand looking at him. 'The thing is, right now I *feel* like being dumb about it,' he said, swinging away from me again. A moment later he stalked off around the corner.

I stood where I was, longing for some kind of natural disaster to occur. An earthquake maybe. A hurricane. Anything to distract me from the way I was feeling. To break the icy silence that was closing in around me.

And then something did happen. Someone screamed.

TEN

For a moment I didn't move, unsure of where the scream had come from or even if it was for real. Then it came again, an angry scream, and I knew it wasn't a joke. It was coming from around the back of the hall. I got moving, running to the end of the path and into the little garden behind the hall.

A purple spotlight was trained on the fig tree there. It was probably meant to light up the area and make it look less scary but it had the opposite effect, washing the tree's bare branches and sinewy trunk with an alien glow. I stopped in the shadows, avoiding the purple light, deciding that it was better – safer – to remain unseen.

I spotted Katie right away. She was in front of the fig tree with her back to me. She was so still and pale, the rippling of the wind across her dress the only movement. I knew instantly that it was Katie who'd screamed – everything about her stance said fury. But what had she screamed at, exactly? It wasn't until

I stepped sideways that I saw Cameron and Miranda sitting on the wooden bench under the tree. They weren't touching, but there was something about the way they were sitting that made it clear they *had* been. Maybe it was the looseness of Cameron's fish tie. Or the slightly rumpled look of Miranda's hair. These days her hair never looked messy.

I can picture so clearly how their faces looked as they sat there, although when I think back now, logically it's not possible. The only light was trained up into the branches of the tree, not on the bench. Perhaps the moonlight was enough to illuminate them, though, because I can picture Cameron's face perfectly – knotted and twisted around with guilt and anxiety. His tension made Miranda seem all the more serene.

I shifted slightly and a twig cracked beneath my shoe. Neither Cam nor Katie reacted, but I thought I saw Miranda's eyes flick over to where I was standing in the shadows. It was just for a moment, but when she looked away again her mouth was twitching.

I knew I should go. *This has nothing to do with you.* But then Katie began talking and I found myself leaning forward, trying to pick out her words. Her voice was weak, like the screaming had drained her.

'I saw you. Don't try and deny it.'

Cameron stood, holding his hands towards Katie, palms upwards. 'Katie,' he said. 'Please.'

Katie's whole body was rigid and when she spoke her voice was the same. 'I *saw* you. What you were doing on the bench together. You're disgusting.'

'Katie,' said Cameron again, taking a micro-step towards her.

Katie staggered back. 'You're a cheater,' she hissed. 'And a liar. I hate you. I *hate* you.'

'Come on,' said Cameron. 'Calm down.'

Katie shook her head. 'You've been laughing at me, haven't you?' she said huskily. '*Stupid little Katie. Doesn't have a clue what's going on.* But I know now, don't I? My boyfriend and my best friend.'

Miranda laughed then – a laugh full of contempt, and I felt myself begin to simmer. How could she laugh?

Katie's hands clenched, her fists pitifully small. 'I was so *nice* to you, Miranda. I made you!' she said. 'And all you've done is steal from me!'

'I didn't *steal* anything,' sneered Miranda, rising from the bench and moving towards Katie. 'You gave me things. But you can have everything back if you want – starting with these.' Miranda lifted up the golden sweep of her hair and plucked Katie's earrings from her ears. She held them out, like they were a couple of dead beetles. 'They're not *real* diamonds, you know.'

Katie snatched up the earrings and flung them into the bushes. 'I'm not talking about those,' she said. The tendons in her neck were bulging.

'Do you mean Cam?' said Miranda, her voice full of scorn. 'You *loser*. I didn't steal him. He came looking for me. Can you guess why? Because you were boring him to death.'

Katie shook her head.

Miranda's smile glittered. 'Ask him yourself then.'

For as long as I'd known him, Cameron had been the Big and Popular Guy. But that's not how I would've described him right then. Right then he was the Shrunken and Nervous one. The one who looked like he was about to wet his pants. 'I – that's not –'

The wind picked up Cameron's stuttered words and flung them out to sea. Miranda turned her back on him and glided towards Katie. 'So is there anything else you want to accuse me of *stealing* from you?' she said. 'Go on. I'm dying to hear it.'

'I used to be popular,' whispered Katie, starting to sag. 'Beautiful.'

'So I stole those things, did I?' said Miranda. 'Get real, Katie. You think that if I could steal personalities I'd bother stealing *yours*? You just lifted yours straight out of a magazine anyway. There's nothing original about you. Nothing interesting either. That's why Olive dumped you, isn't it?'

I went cold. Katie gasped and bowed over as if winded.

'Miranda!' Cameron was probably trying to sound firm but instead he just sounded scared. 'This is getting out of control.'

Miranda paid no attention. She kept moving towards Katie, her dress swish-swishing with each step. 'So I suppose it's also *my* fault you don't eat anymore, is it?' she said. 'And that you've forgotten how to brush your hair? The hair that you also seem to have stopped washing?' Miranda's perfect little nose wrinkled with distaste. 'Can't you smell yourself? You *reek*.'

The awful thing was that Miranda was right – Katie *did*

smell. I'd noticed it myself the last few weeks. It was a musty, sour stench that clung to her, trailing behind in a cloud as she walked. The smell of neglect, I suppose. Or despair.

Miranda tapped her cheek thoughtfully. Then she smiled – like a brilliant idea had struck. 'You've always been so good at giving other people feedback on how they look,' she said. 'Maybe it's time I gave you some. You know. Just to check you're not turning into a road accident. There's no going back once that happens, remember.'

I'd be lying if I said I hadn't imagined this scenario – Katie being treated the way she'd treated others. The way she'd treated *me* since I'd told her we were no longer friends. I'd never imagined it happening like this though, when she was already so broken and so empty. Part of me wanted to intervene then, but Ami's warning rang in my ears. *'Stay the hell away from her.'*

Miranda had already begun walking around Katie, examining her from all angles. 'We may as well keep going with your hair,' she said. 'I can see your scalp. Not a good look, you'd have to agree. And your skin? Ew, Katie. So pasty white. You look like a corpse.'

Get angry at her, I willed Katie. *Push her away and leave.* But all Katie did was nod. Like Miranda was doing her a favour.

Miranda looked at Katie's dress and shook her head regretfully. 'Your clothes are so bland these days. I mean, what *is* that thing you're wearing? A sack? But I guess most things would look like a sack on you now.'

'I want to take the test,' said Katie and even though her voice was whisper-thin there was a certain determination to it. 'The one you said all the models in Europe have to take before a show.'

'No,' said Miranda sharply. 'You can't. Not here.'

Katie raised her arms and held them out to the side. 'You don't need a tape measure to get the numbers,' she pleaded. 'You can tell just by looking at me, can't you? Please. Just look at me.'

'Actually, you're right,' said Miranda suddenly. 'I *can* tell just by looking at you. Bad news again, Katie. Your numbers are way too low.'

In the distance, the waves crashed and rolled.

'Too *low*?' whispered Katie. 'I didn't know that could happen.'

'Of course it can. God, Katie. Have you looked in a mirror recently? You're just bones. It's disgusting.'

I couldn't control the yell that came from me then. *'Stop it!'* I couldn't just watch from the shadows any more. Not while someone was being mauled alive right in front of me. Even if they didn't want my help.

Katie and Miranda turned to look at me. Katie's expression was so vague I wasn't sure she even knew who I was. But it was clear from Miranda's expression that she did. With a chill I realised she had known I was there, all along.

'Are you standing up for Katie now?' she said. 'How very strange. Considering how you dumped her.'

I mustered up the fiercest expression I could, doing my best to ignore the pounding pain in my skull. What was it about Miranda that made my head ache? 'Just leave her alone,' I said.

Miranda snorted. 'With pleasure.'

Katie stood fixed in place for a moment, looking at Miranda. Then silently she fled into the darkness.

My heart began to race as I looked at Cameron, slumped on the bench, head in hands. 'Aren't you going after her?' I demanded.

'She doesn't want to see me,' he mumbled.

I couldn't even look at him. *I was right to mess with him*, I thought savagely. *That cowardly piece of shit.*

'I'll go then,' I spat. 'Alone.'

I guess it's pretty strange to go searching for someone you don't like very much, but there was no way I could let Katie run off on her own like that – so upset and so obviously sick. I'd let Miss Falippi go. I wasn't going to make the same mistake again.

I turned and stormed off, but before I could get very far, there was a hand on my arm – one full of warmth and reassurance. 'Wait up. I'll come too.'

How long had Lachlan been there? It didn't matter. He was there and I was glad. *Crazy* glad. He raised an eyebrow. 'But only if you want my help, of course.'

I didn't quite trust myself to speak, so I nodded.

ELEVEN

We started by searching around the perimeter of the hall, checking behind every bush and tree and dark space. I even looked into the fancy fountain with the carved dolphins out the front – and saw nothing but my own face bending and wobbling on the water's surface. Next we searched inside, pushing our way past the laughing girls on the dance floor, the cuddly couples and the guys getting secretly drunk behind the potted palms. I checked the toilets and the cloakroom. Katie wasn't there. Ami had also vanished.

Lachlan and I met on the front steps. Lachlan looked at me. 'Where to next?'

Katie could be anywhere. 'Let's look down the street,' I said.

It was good to get away from the hall and we walked along together, checking the doorways, the bus shelters and behind the bins lined up in the alley beside the Rainbow Hotel. Then we took the path that led down to the beach. As my heart began to thump, I told myself I wouldn't lose my grip. So what if this was the first time I'd been back since the Incident. I'd ridden alongside it not so long ago. Walking on the sand wasn't so different, was it?

You won't even be able to see the water. It's too dark. Just get on with it.

As we got nearer, I tried to remember everything Dr Richter had told me to do when I felt the panic coming. Control my breathing. Remind myself that *I was not my past*. I couldn't let Lachlan hear me breathing like a wonk, because then he'd ask what was wrong and I'd have to lie, or tell him what I'd done.

The wind was growing steadily stronger, making the jaggedy bits of dress around the shark bite flutter like tiny flags. As we stepped off the path onto the sand Lachlan stopped and looked at me. 'She's probably not here, you know,' he said. 'I bet she caught a taxi and went home.'

I knew he was probably right. And if the situation was reversed, Katie wouldn't be out searching for me. If I quit now I'd be home in half an hour, safe and warm in my fortune teller's tent, letting Luxe smooth everything away. But that was the soft option. The old Olive option.

I kicked off my shoes and dug my feet into the cold sand. 'You go if you want,' I said tightly. 'I'm going to look a bit longer.'

'I'll stay too then,' said Lachlan, beginning to remove his jacket. 'You take this.'

I shook my head. 'I'm not cold.'

Lachlan swung the jacket over his shoulder and we trudged

along, calling Katie's name and scanning the sand for people. A chant began circling in my head: *This is pointless, useless, hopeless.*

Lachlan stopped, head tilted, listening. 'I heard something,' he said.

A lot of trucks used the beach road, especially at night, avoiding the speed cameras and the traffic lights. I stood beside him, listening hard. At first, nothing. And then the faintest of noises. It could've been a seagull. Or a cat. But somehow it just wasn't either of those things. There was something in it — some tiny note of distress that caused Lachlan and me to sprint towards the high wall that divided the beach from the road. Lachlan reached it first and scrambled up. At the top he leant back, holding out his hand. I hesitated. I was pretty sure I could get up that wall myself. Then I imagined what Ami would say. *For god's sake Olive, just let him help you.*

So I reached up and Lachlan grabbed hold and hoisted me over. A moment later I was on the footpath beside him. The sound came again, much closer now. And clearer.

'Look,' said Lachlan, pointing to a crumpled pile in the middle of the road — too small to be a person. Too still. *It's a bag of rubbish. Someone's chucked it out of their car window.*

Then the shape moaned and in a flash Lachlan was there, crouching down. 'It's Katie,' he called.

I hesitated on the curb for a moment — trucks and cars had a habit of appearing from nowhere along this stretch of road — then I ran over to join them. Katie was curved into a C. I took one of her hands. It was icy. 'What happened?' I asked softly.

'Did you fall? Were you hit by a car?'

Katie shook her head slowly, the street lights revealing how streaked with dirt her face was.

Lachlan stared along the road and I could tell he was worried. 'Can you stand up?' he asked Katie. 'Can you walk?'

'No,' said Katie, her voice cracking. 'I can't.'

Lachlan looked at me. 'We have to get her off the road,' he muttered. 'There's something coming.' He put his arms around Katie, saying gently, 'I'm going to pick you up now, OK? Tell me if anything hurts.'

In one swift movement he'd scooped Katie off the road and carried her – cradling her like she was a child – over to the footpath. I'd only just made it off the road when a truck whooshed past, horn blaring.

Lachlan folded up his jacket and slipped it under Katie's head.

'Am I dying?' she whispered.

'Of course not,' said Lachlan. 'But I'm going to call an ambulance. Just so you don't have to walk back into town. OK?'

Katie nodded, and Lachlan pulled out his phone and walked off a little way. A moment later I heard him speaking to the emergency services, explaining where we were, what the situation was – like he'd done this a thousand times before. And I suddenly felt ashamed for sneering at him for being Mr Lifesaver Guy. He was amazing.

Katie smiled sleepily. 'It's funny. I was so cold just before but I feel toasty warm now.'

I looked at her drooping eyelids. Surely that wasn't a good sign. 'You have to stay awake,' I told her, rubbing her arm.

'Just a little sleep,' Katie said softly.

When Lachlan returned, he took one look at Katie and frowned. 'We need to keep her awake and warm,' he muttered to me. 'Let's lie down next to her. We'll try to warm her up that way.'

To be honest, my reserves of body heat were pretty low by then – the shark-bite costume wasn't such a good idea, all things considered – but I lay down beside Katie, my body pressed up against her side. I half-expected her to push my arm away angrily, but she didn't. Lachlan lay down on her other side, his back to the road, and stretched his arm over Katie's body so that it came to rest on my shoulder.

Katie's eyes were still closed and her breathing was beginning to slow and deepen. 'OK, Katie,' I said loudly. 'Let's imagine you're famous. Your agent has booked you for this fantastic acting job in Paris and I'm a journalist writing a piece on you.'

'And who am I?' asked Lachlan.

'You're the photographer,' I said.

One of Katie's eyes flickered open. 'Which magazine do you write for?'

'Uh … Yen. Now, I understand that you are 172 centimetres tall?' I said, in a poncy journalistic voice.

Katie's eyes sprang open and glared at me. 'Olive, I'm 175.'

When Lachlan laughed, his hand shook my shoulder.

'Sorry,' I said. 'Of course, 175. Now, Katie. I believe your first big break was winning a Sweetest Smile on the Beach competition run by your local paper. Can you tell us what you think is behind your huge public appeal?'

The three of us lay like that for ten minutes while we waited for the ambulance. Squished up tightly together, me asking Katie questions to keep her awake, all the while intensely aware of Lachlan's hand on my shoulder. Every time his fingers moved across my skin, I wondered whether he was doing it on purpose.

Finally there was the blare of the ambulance's siren, the flash of lights, coming closer and closer.

o

Lachlan and I rode in the ambulance with Katie. The ambos wrapped us all up in these shiny silver blankets that looked like something you'd find in a spaceship. At the hospital Katie was whisked away, leaving Lachlan and me to answer about a billion questions. They kept asking us what had happened, why Katie was so skinny, what medication she was on, and we answered everything the same way. That we didn't know.

This was followed by the drama of calling Mum. I'd been planning just to return home and not mention any of this, but the hospital insisted that we were picked up. Naturally Mum freaked when I called from the hospital, and it took many minutes of talking over the top of her to explain that this time I was there because of Katie, not because of anything I'd done.

Finally the moment came when everyone stopped asking questions and taking details, and it was just me and Lachlan alone in the waiting room. And I found myself wondering if

I should tell him everything, unprompted. About Dad, the Incident, my meds. The reason I looked so different to those six-month-old photos on the school blog.

I knew Katie would have blabbed already, but I thought maybe it'd be different hearing it from me. God knows how distorted and stretched the gossip had become in her hands.

I guess I felt like I owed it to Lachlan. The truth. Because once he'd heard the full story, he might understand that I hadn't turned him down because I didn't like him, but because I *did* like him. Because I knew he deserved better.

When I turned towards him, he was watching me with this expectant look on his face. Like he knew I had something big to say, something important.

A moment passed. And then another. *Go on, you wonk,* I ordered myself. *Speak.* But I couldn't. The words seemed to catch and be drawn back inside me.

The waiting room door was flung open and Mum rushed through, smothering me with her arms. 'Oh, sweetie,' she said, sobbing. She hauled me to my feet, oblivious to Lachlan sitting next to me. 'Let's get you home. You must be exhausted.'

I looked over at Lachlan, wishing there was some easy way I could explain, just from the look on my face, how messy and complicated my life was right then.

Lachlan nodded at me, and then looked away. 'Bye, Olive,' he said quietly.

o

All the way home in the car, I could still feel where Lachlan's hand had rested on my shoulder. I replayed his goodbye over and over in my head. Remembering the tone of it. It had seemed so sad. Disappointed. But the worst thing was how final it sounded. Like Lachlan had given up on me.

TWELVE

The local paper published an article about what had happened that night. *Young heroes save tragic teen beauty.* God knows how they heard about it. They'd sourced pictures from our school blog. One of me with my arm around Katie, both of us with big smiles. I looked at that photo for a long time. I wasn't the only one who'd changed. The Katie who Lachlan and I had found crumpled on the road was nothing like this girl with glossy blonde hair and a wide smile.

A close friend of the victim said that Miss Clarke's physical and mental state had declined dramatically recently. 'She was totally obsessed with the idea that she was overweight, even though the opposite was true,' the friend reported. 'She said she'd rather be dead than fat. And she just wouldn't accept help.'

'One guess who that *close friend* is,' I said to Ami. It's strange reading about something you were part of, written by someone who wasn't there. Things get twisted around. The article made it sound like Katie had lain down on the road, that the whole thing was a suicide attempt.

'No-one's going to believe that,' I scoffed.

'Don't bet on it,' said Ami grimly.

Soon after the article appeared the news went round at school that Katie was being treated for anorexia. And Ami was right. No-one seemed in any doubt that Katie had chosen to lie down on the road, wanting to die. I guess to them this seemed like the logical explanation. But they hadn't seen the confused expression that was on her face when we'd found her. The one that was so clearly saying, *how the hell did I get here?*

The next thing that happened was that a whole lot of rumours sprang up about the fight between Katie and Miranda at the formal. Who had said what. Again, nothing matched with what I'd witnessed.

Miranda was just talking to Cameron and Katie went crazy at her for no reason. I heard that over and over. *The jealousy was eating her up.* Everyone just bought the lies completely. I didn't hear a single person say they didn't believe it.

Meanwhile, Miranda drifted around looking all sad and noble, acting like she was *devastated* about it all. 'Poor Katie,' she'd say, shaking her head sorrowfully. 'It's so tragic that anorexia has messed up her head.'

Everyone nodded and said how brave Miranda was. What a great friend.

At first I fumed about how stupid everyone was not to realise that Miranda was manipulating the situation to suit herself.

But after a while, I wasn't so sure. That's the trouble when you're the only person who believes something. You start wondering if you're wrong. And it seems so much easier to let go and just be carried along by the current like everyone else.

My doubt grew like one of those weeds that you see in cracks in the footpath – the ones that can eventually push up concrete. Ami believed my version of the events, of course. But she hadn't been there. The person I found myself really wanting to talk to was Lachlan. To find out if he'd seen things the way I had. But Lachlan seemed to be staying out of my way. I hardly ever saw him – and when I did, he was always looking in the other direction.

I knew I had no right to feel upset. *It's what you wanted,* I kept reminding myself. *You should be relieved.* So why wasn't I?

I arrived at school one day to find Ami waiting for me by the lockers. She looked at me closely. 'You're starting to doubt yourself, aren't you?' she said. 'About what happened at the formal.'

'Maybe a little,' I admitted.

'Well you shouldn't,' said Ami firmly. 'You were there. You saw it all.'

'I guess,' I said, and then paused, trying to decide if I was actually going to say what I'd been thinking for a while now. 'Ami. The way Miranda destroyed Katie ...'

Ami nodded slowly. 'Everything lines up doesn't it? All that crazy shapeshifter stuff.'

My throat constricted. 'But it can't be true, can it?' I needed

Ami to tell me this was rubbish. 'This is the real world. There's no such thing as –'

'Isn't there?' said Ami, interrupting me as she leant in close. 'But it explains *everything.*'

I fell silent for a moment. It was usually Ami who pointed out why my crazy theories were pure wonkishness. Having her say something like this – it was unnerving.

'You don't really believe that, do you?' I whispered. 'That stupid website? It's – it's not *logical.*'

'It was a stupid website,' agreed Ami. 'But sometimes the illogical answer is the only one. She's *dangerous*, Olive. She admitted she slipped something into Miss Falippi's drink and then got everyone believing our hippy home-room teacher was some kind of addict. Now she's trying to kill Katie.'

Kill Katie. I shivered. Was it really as serious as that?

Ami's eyes were narrowed. 'And don't tell me you haven't noticed how she now looks exactly like Katie. Or at least, like Katie used to look. It's *just* like the website said. Miranda is draining her.'

'But we're the only ones who think there's something weird about Miranda,' I said desperately. 'So why would we be right?'

'Because we're special, Olive,' said Ami darkly. 'That's why we can see what's going on when everyone else is blind to it. You aren't affected by her the way everyone else is.'

What about Lachlan? He didn't seem affected by her either. Did he think there was something weird about her too? I wished I could just bowl up to him and ask, without caring how insane I sounded. I swallowed. 'I don't know, Ames. It seems so unbelievable.'

Ami was silent for a while. And then she said in a low voice, 'You know about parasitic wasps, don't you?'

'Well, yeah,' I said. 'I've only been sitting next to those insect posters for six months. Why?'

'Remember how the mother wasp doesn't lay her eggs in a nest or a hive? She lays them directly into the body of another insect – you know, like into a caterpillar.'

'Right, so the eggs hatch in a dead caterpillar,' I said, pulling a face. 'Gross.'

'Not dead,' corrected Ami. '*Alive*. The wasp larvae stay inside the living caterpillar as they grow, feeding on its blood and flesh until they're big and strong enough to bite their way through its skin.'

'That's disgusting.' My own skin was tingling, like there were things crawling over me.

'There's more,' said Ami. 'The baby wasps release this chemical that messes with the caterpillar's brain, so it doesn't realise what's going on. It'll even try to protect the infant wasps as they're eating their way out through its skin because it thinks they're part of its own body. Then once the baby wasps are gone, the caterpillar is left to die.'

'Ami!' I said, feeling nauseous. 'What has this got to do with Miranda?'

'Well, I just wonder if that's what shifters are like,' said Ami. 'Not like elves or goblins or whatever magical creatures people think of when they hear the word shifter. Freaky disturbing stuff happens in the natural world all the time. We just don't think of it as happening in the human world. But why shouldn't it?'

I felt unsteady. Ami was watching me very carefully. She nodded at me. 'You know it's the truth,' she said quietly. 'Katie is the juicy little protective caterpillar. But she's almost completely dried up.'

The corridor was full of people but somehow I could hear the rhythm of my heart, beating loudly.

'If we're wrong, Miranda's just a bitch,' Ami said, her voice soft but steady. 'But if we're right, Katie's in danger.'

I slammed my locker door, just as the second bell went. 'I'm going to see her,' I said. 'Right now.'

'You better hurry,' said Ami. 'In case Miranda gets there first.'

o

The clinic was one of those ugly boxy buildings – the sort that made your heart sink as you approached it. This I could say from personal experience, as it was the same clinic I'd spent time at myself after the Incident. Inside, someone had attempted to make it look a little friendlier. Paintings had been stuck up on the walls, mostly done by patients. One wall was covered with paper honeybees inscribed with positive messages. *Bee confident. Bee kind. Bee a friend.* Out the back was a garden.

The panic that had propelled me there had worn off a little by the time I arrived. I felt my confidence slip further as I pushed through the front door and smelled that familiar smell of overcooked vegetables. It was unlikely that Katie would be thrilled to see me – I'd probably just be a reminder of how far she'd fallen. But I was here now and it felt stupid just to turn around. I took a deep breath. *Bee brave,* I told myself. *All you have to do is go in and just warn her to stay away from Miranda.* That seemed reasonable, and do-able.

The woman at reception smiled as I approached. 'Hello,' she said. 'We haven't seen you for a while.'

'I'm here to visit Katie Clarke,' I said quickly.

The woman looked at the visitors list and shook her head. 'Sorry. It's relatives only at the moment.'

Patients at this clinic were able to indicate people they did and didn't want to see. You couldn't forbid the doctors or nurses from coming, of course, but just about anyone else could be on the 'no visits' list. When I was here, I'd made it clear that I didn't want to see anyone from school.

'She's my cousin,' I lied.

The nurse scrutinised my face. People used to say we looked alike. 'She's in Room 12,' she said finally. 'Don't stay too long. And keep things calm, please.'

o

My shoes made mouse-like noises on the polished corridor tiles. *Room 8, Room 9.* I tried to work out what to say to Katie that sounded halfway believable. *You know your supposed best friend Miranda? I think she's draining you of your personality and spirit.* It was going to be tricky.

I stopped outside Room 12. I could see my distorted reflection in the glass. Even stretched out long and thin like that, it looked anxious. *This could be such a mistake.*

But I went in anyway. It was air-conditioner quiet in there and for a minute I thought I'd got the wrong room. This one was unoccupied. Then there was a noise from the bed and I saw Katie lying there, asleep. She barely made a lump under the sheets.

I stood by the door, awkward and awful. This was all so wrong. If Katie had been in hospital just a couple of months ago, it would have been overflowing with flowers, teddies, giant cards. People would've camped in here around the clock, and Katie would've been propped up in bed, behaving like royalty. I could picture Justine and Paige fussing around, arranging all the flowers in vases, and Cameron lying on the bed next to Katie, joking that this hotel was so good he was going to stay too.

But apart from a few things probably brought in by her family – some magazines, a single bunch of flowers – the room was totally bare. It was just Katie. And me.

I started backing out. There was no point hanging around if Katie was asleep. Maybe I could call her, or email even. That would be better, probably.

As I was reaching for the door handle, there was another noise from the bed. Katie's eyes were open, watching me.

'What are you doing here?' Her voice gave no clue as to what she thought about finding me in her room. There was this strange *blankness* about it and I couldn't tell if she was cross or surprised. *Maybe she's pleased to see me,* I thought, although

I knew that was unlikely.

'Just dropping by to say howdy. I've never known anyone who's been rushed to hospital in an ambulance before. I was wondering what it was like.' My voice sounded high and fake, my words like they'd been scripted by someone else. A moron.

Katie grimaced. The bed covers rippled as she shifted her legs beneath it. 'I wouldn't recommend it,' she said.

'At least you get some time off school,' I said stupidly. That was a mistake. Being reminded of school was probably the last thing Katie wanted.

She twitched the corner of her sheet. 'How *is* school?'

My mouth was apparently out of control. 'You're the hot topic of conversation, of course. You even made it to the front page of the paper.' Another mistake. The article hadn't exactly been the sort you'd cut out and keep for your scrapbook.

Katie wasn't listening anyway. 'Everyone hates me,' she said. 'All my friends. Cam. Everyone.'

'No, they don't.' I went and sat on the chair beside her bed. 'They feel terrible about what happened. They...told me to send you their love.' It's OK to lie, isn't it, when the person you're lying to looks so sad and sick? It's not so much lying as making up a story.

Katie must have known it wasn't true, but I could see she desperately wanted to believe it all the same. She fell back on her pillows and let my fairytale wash over her. 'How sweet,' she murmured.

'How long are you going to be in here?'

Katie shook her head slowly. 'I don't know,' she said. 'They want me to "fill out" a bit.' She gave a hollow laugh. 'But there's no way that's going to happen if they keep serving me up plates of disgusting gunk.'

'What do you feel like eating?' I asked.

'A choc-top.' When Katie grinned I saw a flash of how she used to be – that spark in her eye.

'I'll bring you one,' I said. 'Next time I visit.'

'Do you remember when we tried to make our own?' said Katie suddenly. 'Back before –' her eyes flicked away for a moment. 'Well, back when we were friends?'

Funny. I'd forgotten about doing that. 'I still don't know how they get the chocolate to stick on properly,' I said. 'Ours just fell off in big globs everywhere. But they were still pretty awesome.'

Katie looked awake now – properly awake. 'Olive, do you think I've got an eating disorder?'

Her question took me by surprise. Katie *had* always worried about her weight. And there was no denying that she was scarily thin. I remembered what I'd come here to do.

'Yeah,' I said. 'I do.'

Katie's face fell. She squashed back down into the pillows.

'But I don't think you have anorexia or bulimia or anything,' I added quickly. 'Your disorder is that you're *being* eaten. From the inside out. And not just your body. Your mind too.'

From the corridor came the sound of someone pushing a trolley with squeaky wheels. I remembered that squeak from when I was here.

Katie's eyes were fixed on me. 'What do you mean?'

'That stuff you said to Miranda at the formal. You're right. She *is* stealing from you. She's trying to steal your whole life.'

Katie was trembling now and I knew that I had to choose my words carefully. If I suddenly launched into a description of shapeshifters, with a bit of wasp stuff thrown in, Katie would reach straight for the call button and have me ejected. I needed to say the things Katie probably already suspected.

'She wants to take everything from you,' I said.

For a moment Katie didn't respond. Then she nodded.

I leant forward. 'She makes herself stronger by making you weaker.'

'Yes.'

'You can't trust her, Katie. She's not your friend, no matter what she says.'

Katie's face screwed up. I'd gone too far. 'No, it's *you* who's not my friend. You *dumped* me, remember? Without ever telling me why. I came to the clinic to visit you. I was *worried*. But they said you didn't want to see me. Then when you came back to school you acted like you didn't even know who I –'

'Hang on a minute,' I said angrily. 'Don't put that all on me. It was as much your fault as it was mine.'

'What the hell are you talking about?' Katie's voice cracked.

'It's not like we could still be friends after what you did,' I said, my temper fizzing. 'You told everyone about my dad leaving. And about my ... *Incident*. So excuse me for not wanting to be friends anymore.'

Katie was speechless, and I felt a small surge of triumph. She'd obviously thought she could get away with betraying her *best friend* and that everything would be fine. And then she said something that floored me.

'Ollie,' she said, looking me right in the eye, 'I never told anyone *anything*. I mean, I wrote about it in my diary – I had to, to cope with everything – but you know that's completely locked and hidden. Anyway, we've been friends since primary school. How could you think I'd actually blab all that personal stuff?'

'But everyone acts like they know,' I said, finding my voice. 'Like I'm a leper who's going to –'

'I said you were away because you had glandular, you *idiot*. The only reason everyone avoids you now is because you act like a pain in the arse who's too good for us.' Katie crossed her thin arms, and I saw the blue veins beneath her papery skin. 'So why the hell should I trust you now, about Miranda, when you've obviously never trusted me?'

The hum of the air conditioner had triggered an echo in my brain. I could feel it, high and insistent like a mosquito. I massaged my temples with the heels of my hand, trying to get things straight. If Katie was telling the truth, and *nobody* at school knew about what had happened, then not even Lachlan knew. So his interest had been genuine. And maybe I'd completely screwed things up with the one guy at school who was decent and lovely. I felt a cold hand squeezing my heart, but I had to put all thoughts of him out my mind. I had to focus.

Of course, things with Katie weren't that straightforward.

Our friendship had been shattering in slow motion for a long time before Dad left, and before I did what I did. But what could I say to her now that wouldn't just make everything a whole lot worse? Did she really want to hear how I felt like I'd been forcing myself into a badly fitting friendship? How I'd started to despise all the things she was interested in, and only pretended to care so I wouldn't upset her? And how when Dad left, it just exploded inside me and I couldn't pretend anymore? I figured that these were things she didn't need to hear. Especially now.

'I'm sorry, Katie,' I said. 'Things were really … screwy for me then. I know I was a bad friend and I know you're pissed off. It's just …'

Katie watched as I struggled to think of an explanation. 'I guess I was jealous of you,' I said, and it was partly true. I'd been jealous of how easy her life was.

Katie's eyes opened wide with disbelief. 'You were jealous of *me?*' she said. 'That's crazy. You're the smart one. The funny one. The cool one. The one everyone liked. Even …' Katie pushed up her knees under the sheets and hugged them. 'I sometimes got the feeling that even Cam had a thing for you.' She laughed, embarrassed. 'I was always so scared he'd dump me and chase after you instead.'

I felt a pang of pity for Katie, and another feeling too. Regret.

Maybe I could have handled things better with her. Maybe I'd been too quick to give up on our friendship. There were things that Katie and I needed to talk about. But not now.

There was other stuff – life and death stuff – to deal with. I had to make her promise to cut Miranda off.

I reached over and squeezed her hand. 'I'm so sorry, Katie. About everything. I know it's hard but you have to trust me on this. Miranda is *really* dangerous and you're her number one target at the moment. You have to stay away from her. Please tell me she's on your "no visits" list.'

Katie's hand suddenly gripped onto mine, tense and surprisingly strong.

'What's wrong?'

Katie had frozen – even her breathing seemed to have halted. Her head was turned slightly to one side, listening. I listened too but at first all I picked up was the food trolley, squeaking its way around from room to room. Then I heard two people talking as they walked down the corridor, coming closer.

I recognised the nurse's voice straight away. When I was here, she was the one who always seemed to be in a foul mood. She'd walk into your room and sigh, like you were keeping her from what she'd rather be doing. She had one of those stern faces that seemed incapable of cracking a smile – even a fake one. But I could hear her laughing and chatting in an über-friendly way.

'She'll be so pleased to see you,' I heard her saying as she came closer. 'And you'll be helping so much too.'

'It's no problem,' the other person replied. 'I *want* to help – she's my best friend after all.'

I knew who it was. Someone who sounded exactly how Katie used to sound.

Katie knew too. Her bony fingers hooked into my arm. 'Don't let her in,' she whispered. 'Please. She can't see me like this.'

THIRTEEN

I pulled away from Katie's grip and stood up. 'Don't worry. I'll sort it out.' I walked towards the door like I had some sort of plan, when actually I had no idea what to do. Throw myself up against the door or fling it open and wrestle Miranda to the ground? And then what? Call the police? *Arrest this girl immediately. She's a personality thief. A shapeshifter.*

I reached for the door handle – maybe planning to walk out and confront Miranda in the corridor – but as I took hold, I felt it turn beneath my hand. Then the door pushed open, sweeping me to one side, and there was Miranda. I jumped in front of her, blocking the entrance, standing close enough to feel her breath against my skin – cold and with no scent. *Snow-breath*, I thought, shivering.

'Olive,' she said. 'How totally not surprising to see you. Move it. I'm here to see Katie.'

I stayed put. 'She doesn't want to see you.' My legs were

tensed and ready but I didn't really know what for. I'd never confronted someone like Miranda. A shifter.

'Don't be stupid,' snapped Miranda, pushing past me with surprising strength. Her thick hair flicked into my face. 'Katie is my friend. My *best* friend. Of course she wants to see me.'

Katie's hands fluttered up to cover her face. 'I'm sorry, Miranda. I look so terrible.'

'Katie!' I knew it was bad to yell at someone who was so weak, but this was beyond frustrating. 'Don't apologise. It's her freakin fault you're in this state.'

Katie's crying grew louder. She pushed back the covers and scuttled into the bathroom, clicking the lock behind her.

Miranda didn't try to stop her. Didn't even glance her way. She was watching me instead – her mouth smiling but her eyes still and cold. 'It's *my* fault, is it?' she said.

I jumped as someone came up behind me and put their hand on my arm. It was Ami. She gave me a reassuring squeeze. 'Don't let her psych you out,' she murmured. I hadn't seen her arrive but I was so glad she was there.

Having Ami there made me feel a thousand times better. 'I know what you're doing to Katie,' I told Miranda, pleased by how strong I sounded. 'All those wonks at school might be blind to your crap, but I'm not. I watched what you did – pulling her apart bit by bit while you pretended to be her friend.'

Miranda flicked her hand dismissively. 'You know what your mistake is? You've been listening to Katie and taking her seriously. Her brain has been starved. She's completely paranoid.

143

Delusional. You *of all people* should know something about that.'

My head had begun to pound.

'Don't listen to her,' whispered Ami. 'We are right about this. We need to tell Katie what we know.'

The door opened and a nurse appeared. The cranky one. 'What's going on?' she said, glowering at the empty bed. 'Where's Katie?'

'She's locked in the bathroom because *she* upset her.' Miranda pointed at me. 'She should leave.'

'*Me*? I'm not the one Katie's terrified of,' I shot back. I was shaking – from anger – but I knew it made me look scared. '*You're* the one who should go.'

'Don't be ridiculous,' said the nurse crisply. 'Miranda is part of the recovery team. She has volunteered to sit with Katie during all her meals and encourage her to eat. She's Katie's healthy-weight role model.'

That left me unable to speak. How could anyone mistake Miranda for a role model?

The nurse checked the clock. 'It's Katie's meal time now. You'll have to go.'

'No. I won't,' I said. The nurse brought the stubborn child out in me. Ami gave me the thumbs up.

'No-one is considering how Katie feels,' said Miranda, 'Let's ask her what *she* wants.' She walked over to the bathroom door and knocked on it firmly. 'Hon?' Miranda's voice was gentle. Soft enough to stroke. 'Come on. Open up.'

There was a long pause, then finally the sound of the lock

being turned. A moment later Katie stood in the doorway – a greyish silhouette against the ultra-bright light of the bathroom.

Miranda reached over and lightly touched Katie's arm, making all the tiny hairs instantly rise. 'Do you want me to leave?' she said. 'Because if you do, just say and I'll go,' she snapped her fingers, 'like that.' It was somehow threatening.

Katie's eyes – already bloodshot from crying – began filling with tears again. 'Please don't leave me. I want you to stay.'

Miranda's face swung back to mine, gleaming with triumph.

'You've got to explain to Katie how much danger she's in,' urged Ami quietly. 'Make her understand.'

'Katie,' I said. 'Think of everything she's done to you. All the things she's taken. Tell her to leave.'

But Katie shook her head. 'I want her to stay.'

The nurse went over and took hold of Katie's arm, leading her back to bed. 'Enough of this nonsense.'

When Katie was tucked back in Miranda sat beside the bed, where I'd been sitting moments earlier.

'I'm going to check on the food trolley,' said the nurse. She glanced in my direction as she left the room. 'When I come back I want you gone.'

Miranda smiled. *I win*, the smile said. *You lose.*

It felt like everyone – Miranda, Katie, Ami – was looking at me then. Waiting for me to do something.

Rage blew across Ami's face. 'She can't get away with this! Olive, you have to do something.'

I've thought so many times about that moment. What I *could* have done. Maybe I could've grabbed Katie and bolted for the door. She looked so light I could've carried her. But where would we go? Maybe I should've run after the nurse and explained that Miranda was the last person to be left in charge of Katie. But what was the point? Katie didn't want to be saved.

Ami was beside me, whispering and pushing me. 'Tell her. Tell Katie what Miranda is. You have to do this, Olive. It's the only way.'

Miranda was speaking to Katie in a creepy, sing-song voice. She was stroking her hair. 'You'll look so funny when you're fat. None of your clothes will fit. You'll have to give them all away.'

I took a step towards Miranda, not wanting my words to be dampened by the hum of air conditioner. 'I know what you are.'

Ami nodded.

Miranda looked up at me. 'Do you?' she said, the lullaby tone replaced by something hard and cold. 'What am I?'

'You're a parasite. A *shapeshifter.*' Once I'd got those words out everything else started to flow. 'You crawl in under people's skin and leach them of what makes them who they are. You drain them until there's nothing left.'

Something flashed across Miranda's face then. Shock, maybe. Or fear. Before I could decode it, it was gone, submerged by Miranda's loud, angry laughter. 'Do you know how insane you sound?' Then the anger faded and I saw something gleam in her eyes, sharp and bright. 'But of course you don't.'

I frowned. 'What does *that* mean?'

'Olive,' said Ami, suddenly seeming agitated. She pulled at

my arm. 'Let's forget about this. We've made a mistake. A big one. Let's go.'

'I'm not going anywhere,' I muttered, shaking her off. I fixed my eyes on Miranda. 'Tell me what you mean,' I ordered.

Miranda's top lip curled back. 'You had a breakdown, didn't you? Tried to kill yourself and ended up here, in the clinic.'

Once when I was a little kid I held my hand inside our deep freezer for five minutes, just to see what it felt like. My fingers went white at the tips and it was an hour before they felt normal again. That coldness was nothing compared to what I was feeling now.

'I'm better now,' I said thickly. And I was, wasn't I? I'd been doing my baby steps. Taking my meds – most of the time.

Ami started crying then. Strange – I'd never heard her cry before. Not even when she was telling me about her dad leaving and how hard it had been. 'Please, Olive,' she said. 'Please let's just go.'

I didn't look at her. That's the thing I regret the most. I didn't turn around and look at Ami one last time. But by then my head had begun to swirl and I couldn't tear my eyes away from Miranda and that nasty little smile of hers.

'You really think you're better?' Miranda sneered. 'Having an imaginary friend at your age is *normal*, is it?'

The wall clock ticked. In one minute, the door to Katie's room would swing open and the food trolley would be pushed in by a woman in a baggy blue uniform and soft-soled shoes. The smell of fatty lamb and watery vegetables would flood the room. Behind the trolley would be the nurse, coming to check that I had left. She would arrive just in time to see my eyes lose focus, my body begin to sway. It would be her who rushed over to catch me as I fell. She would check my pulse and call for assistance. Orderlies would arrive with a stretcher and take me away.

But none of this had happened yet. The door to Room 12 was still closed. Miranda was looking around with this look of amused curiosity. 'Is Ami here right now?' she asked. 'I bet she is! I can always tell because you do that funny muttering. Can you point to her for me, Olive? I'd love to know exactly where you think she is.'

I didn't look around. The spell was broken. I knew that if I turned around Ami – my best friend, my *only* friend – would have vanished. For good. The clock kept ticking. My eyes began to blur and my legs turned to liquid.

FOURTEEN

'OK, Olive. Let's do our *breathing*.' Dr Richter was doing her encouraging smile. 'In ... and out. That's the way. Keep that space in your chest broad and those airways nice and open.'

While I *breathed* I looked out the window at the garden. The people who tended it were obviously told to keep everything smooth and calm. Nothing ugly. Nothing upsetting. Flowers were removed before they had a chance to wither or curl. There was nothing jagged or spiky. Everything was soft and gentle and perfect here in Crazy Land.

The most solid-looking thing in the garden was the hedge. I guess that was because the hedge wasn't just there to be admired, it had a job to do. It had to protect the patients from the outside world, and it had to protect the world from us.

Once I'd *breathed* enough, Dr Richter nodded and smoothed away an invisible wrinkle on her skirt. I sometimes tried to imagine Dr Richter doing something that wasn't neat and elegant. You know. Like swearing after stubbing her toe. Or picking a booger from her nose. But it was impossible.

'Your mum will be here soon,' said Dr Richter. 'Are you ready to leave?'

'Yeah,' I said. 'All packed.' It wasn't like I'd brought all that much with me anyway. A couple of changes of clothes. PJs. Toothbrush. iPod. The shredded remains of my dignity.

When Dr Richter laughed it sounded like raindrops falling delicately on flower petals. Don't get me wrong – Dr Richter was OK. She'd helped me in the past, teaching me *strategies* and stuff. But I wondered whether she could really understand what it was like being me.

'I meant, are you ready to get back into life? To continue your journey towards sound mental health as an outpatient.'

Dr Richter made this conversation feel casual, or at least her version of casual. But it wasn't, of course. Last time I was here, as in, after I'd tried to kill myself, I'd said some dumb, flippant thing just as I was about to be discharged and ended up staying for another two weeks. So instead of spitting out the words I was thinking – *what life?* – I produced what I hoped was a dazzling smile. 'Yes, I am.'

Dr Richter clicked her pen, something she did a lot. If she hadn't been a doctor, I would've called it a nervous habit. 'And what about Ami?' she said. 'How are you feeling about her?'

'I miss her.' *Oops.* 'I mean, like I said, I guess I always knew she wasn't real,' I added hastily. 'She was just ...' I forced down the lump in my throat. Dr Richter probably wouldn't approve of crying over the loss of someone who'd never existed. 'She was just helpful sometimes.'

When I was a kid, I'd invented imaginary friends all the time. A boy called Bim-Bim, who was usually to blame when something was broken. And a girl called Spanner. I can't remember where the name came from but I know she was some sort of superhero who would whoosh in if I needed rescuing. No-one thought having imaginary friends was a big deal back then. Mum even encouraged it – asking how they were and sometimes laying places for them at the dinner table. I was an only child for a long time so it made sense to create my own perfect friends who loved everything about me and were happy to play my games endlessly.

I guess it's common for kids to do that sort of thing. When you're older it's considered weird. But I created Ami for the exact same reasons I'd invented Bim-Bim and Spanner. Because I needed her. I'd come out of the clinic heavier, blurrier, than when I went in, and no-one understood how I was feeling. Not Mum. Not Katie. Ami was someone I could trust.

Dr Richter was still eyeing me, a look of practised understanding on her smooth face. 'Don't forget,' she said, 'that what you referred to as "Ami" was actually the process by which you monitored your thoughts and feelings.'

A *process*. Is that all Ami was? I made myself nod. 'Ami was really just me,' I regurgitated dutifully. But I allowed myself a little private joke. *Me but with way better hair.*

Click click. 'What do you think it will be like back at school?'

I picked at the seam of my jeans pocket. I was tired of these constant questions and the way I was forced to recall, over and over, the very things I was trying to forget. Like school. I knew exactly what it would be like. I might have been wrong about Katie telling everyone what happened last time, but Miranda was different. As if she'd resist spreading such juicy gossip.

I bet they'd all had a big old belly laugh about it. *Freakazoid Olive and her imaginary friend. And wait till you hear what she thought Miranda was!* Would Lachlan laugh along too? At least Dr Richter couldn't torture me with questions about him – I hadn't mentioned him to her once. I couldn't even let myself think about him. Every time he crept into my brain I pushed him away. That was way more than I could deal with.

'Actually, I'm thinking about not going back,' I said. 'I want to change schools.'

Dr Richter scratched her chin with her pen. 'What are you so afraid of, Olive? Is it to do with the girl you accused of being a witch? This Miranda?'

I sighed. 'Shapeshifter.' Outside I could hear a gardener pruning the hedge, making it perfect, cutting away all the messy shoots. 'I called her a shapeshifter, not a witch.'

Dr Richter crossed her legs. Removed another invisible crease. 'You understand that it wasn't true, don't you?' she said quietly. 'There's no such thing as shapeshifters. Those headaches you reported getting when Miranda was around were to do with your medication, combined with stress. And the girl's very pale irises – well, that could be caused by a lack of sunlight, or a vitamin deficiency. From what I hear Miranda had not been properly cared for in the past.'

I gripped the arms of my chair. *They weren't just pale,* I wanted to yell. *They were mirrored. What kind of a vitamin deficiency does that?* But of course I couldn't say that. I nodded.

'I want you to put yourself in Miranda's position,' said Dr Richter, crossing then re-crossing her legs. 'Imagine what it must have been like, hearing you say those things about her while her best friend was in hospital.'

I remembered Miranda's sneering face. The pleasure she got from destroying Ami right in front of me.

'It must've been awful for her,' I deadpanned.

Dr Richter scrutinised my face, checking for sarcasm. I kept my expression smooth and impenetrable – another useful skill I'd picked up from Dr Richter.

'You can't escape from Miranda, you know,' she said suddenly.

My heart tumbled. 'What?'

'I mean that if you run away to a new school you won't deal properly with this episode. You need to face what's happened.'

The sight of Dr Richter's hovering pen made me silent. I was familiar with that pen's power. Just a few marks from it scrawled on a form could have me staying here for months.

'She's a particularly hard person to like,' I mumbled unconvincingly.

Dr Richter lowered her pen and folded both hands around it. 'Olive. You have to face the fact that you made some false and very cruel accusations. I believe it's best for you to stay at the same school until you've dealt with this and made peace with Miranda. I've already advised your mother not to move you.'

'You can't do that!' I said, fighting the rising tears as hard as I could. Make peace with Miranda? That was impossible. And how could I go back to school, where *everyone knows* how crazy I am? Last time I'd invented Ami to help me cope. But this time I would be on my own.

'Believe me, this is the best and quickest way for you to heal,' said Dr Richter. 'Once you've come around to the idea, you'll see I'm right.' She reached over and patted my arm. I guess it was meant to be soothing. 'Don't look so worried, Olive. You have nothing to be ashamed of. Clinical depression and anxiety, and even temporary conscious psychosis, are not uncommon in adolescence. I'm sure a number of your school friends have had their own troubles. It will be fine. Better than fine. Your new – what does your mum call your medication?'

I let myself slide back down in my seat. 'Vitamins,' I muttered.

Dr Richter nodded. 'Yes. Your new *vitamins* will help. Less paranoia and … fewer delusions. The headaches should stop too. Once that's sorted we'll focus on moving on. I know you're upset, but you might be surprised by what happens once you get over these irrational feelings you have about Miranda. You might even end up being friends.'

I didn't snort. It took monumental effort, but I didn't snort. I couldn't resist a tiny bit of sarcasm, though. 'Maybe,' I said, shrugging. 'Maybe Miranda and me and Katie will become *besties*.'

Outside there was the sudden growl of a lawnmower. I'd been staying in a different part of the clinic these last few weeks, but I hadn't caught so much as a glimpse of Katie, let alone her *healthy-weight role model*. I figured she'd beefed up enough to go home.

The noise of lawnmower seemed to make Dr Richter jumpy. For the first time since I'd met her, she seemed a little flustered. A genuine wrinkle appeared on her skirt and she didn't even notice.

'Let's just focus on Miranda,' she said quickly, not meeting my eye.

o

Mum leant against the doorframe and smiled. While I'd been waiting for her to turn up, I'd planned exactly what I would say to convince her that sending me back to school was a stupid idea. But she looked so tired standing there that I decided to let it pass for now.

'Ready?' she said.

I nodded. 'Bring it on.'

Outside in the corridor I heard tinny, electronic noises. 'Toby,' said Mum. 'Put that wretched game away and come in.'

There was a scuffling sound and Toby shuffled in, his eyes glued to some bleeping game thing.

'Hi, Tobes,' I said.

'Hi,' he said, not even looking up.

Mum grimaced. 'That stupid toy. I hate it already.'

She insisted on taking my bag out to the car and finalising the paperwork while I *rested*. 'Toby will keep you company,' she said as she hurried out.

Toby sat cross-legged on the floor, the game chirruping away.

'Come and sit here,' I said, patting the space on the bed beside me. 'I've got something for you.'

Toby didn't move. 'I just want to get through this level.'

So I slid down beside him, watched him play for a while. 'Where'd you get that from anyway?' I asked. It wasn't the sort of thing Mum usually forked out money for.

'From Dad,' said Toby.

'Wow, cool,' I said, managing to sound calm, like there was nothing astonishing about that. 'Did he ... *Dad* ... send it?'

The game trumpeted a tinny little fanfare. Toby's thumbs pressed buttons furiously. 'No. I stayed with him a couple of times last week while Mum was here with you. He came and picked me up and took me to his place in town. He's got a new car that doesn't even have a back seat so I got to sit in the front next to him.'

Mum had told me Toby was staying with friends. There was another fanfare. Toby still hadn't even looked at me. It was time to produce my secret weapon. 'Look,' I said, rustling the wrapper of the chocolate bar I'd bought from the vending machine in the corridor.

Toby's eyes lifted, just a little. 'Is it *real* chocolate?' he asked suspiciously. 'Or carob soy?'

'Oh this is real, my friend,' I said, removing the bar from

its wrapper and breaking it in half. 'Double-dipped.' Caramel oozed over my fingers. 'Here,' I said, holding out half.

Toby put the game down and took the chocolate. I saw him glance at the door.

'Don't worry,' I said. 'I have an orange for afterwards.'

We ate in silence, like we always did when we shared banned food. When the chocolate was gone, I peeled the orange.

Toby took a segment and played with it between two fingers. 'Will Ami come back?' he asked suddenly. 'When you're home?'

'Oh, mate,' I said, wrapping my arm around him. 'Ami has gone. For good.'

On the ground, the game continued bleeping and Toby pushed at it with his foot. 'I'll miss her,' he mumbled. 'Miss *hearing about* her, I mean. Mum said I'm not supposed to say that but it's true.'

'I'll miss her too,' I said, my throat aching. 'Heaps. But you know, she was just me, really. And I'm still around.'

Toby looked up at me and I was relieved to see a small but cheeky grin on his face. 'Ami was *way* funnier than you,' he said. 'And smarter.'

I gave him a playful push. 'Ha!'

Toby's smile faded. 'Why did you do that stuff, Olive?'

'What stuff?'

'Mum said you were picking on a girl at school, calling her names and spreading nasty stories about her. She said that you only did it because you were taking the wrong vitamins. Is that true?'

I shoved a piece of orange in my mouth, sucking the juice out until I felt I could trust my voice enough to speak again. 'I wasn't picking on Miranda, Tobes. I … I made a mistake. I got it in my head that she was a shapeshifter. Which is … kind of a thief, I guess, but they don't just steal people's stuff, they steal their personalities and looks too. If you let them. I thought she was trying to kill Katie.'

Toby looked at me, surprised. 'Why?'

I sighed. 'I looked up some dumb website. But it wasn't true.'

Toby frowned. 'Well, what is she then?' he asked, his voice serious. 'If she's not a shapeshifter, what is she?'

'She's just an ordinary person,' I said.

Maybe if I said it enough times I would start to believe it.

o

It's strange how different a place can look, even when you've only been away a week. I mean, there are the things that actually *have* changed – like the grass has grown or someone has replaced the old, curling 'no junk mail' sticker on the letterbox with a new one. But then there's the other stuff. The things that just don't match with the picture you've carried of them in your mind.

When we pulled up in the driveway of our house that afternoon, I noticed for the first time that there was moss growing on the roof. Heaps of it. Then as we walked inside I saw how worn out the carpet was in the hallway. The floorboards creaked too – had they always done that? Even Ralphie looked different. Shaggier. Greyer.

I took my stuff to my bedroom, feeling the familiar relief as I got closer to shutting myself inside. But like the rest of the house, my fortune-teller tent bedroom was looking very shabby. The red velvet curtains were covered in dust and had come unfastened from the wall in places.

I picked up the Magic 8 Ball and gave it a shake. 'Should I redo my room?'

The words slowly floated up in the green plastic answer window. *Maybe later.* I smiled. Sensible object, that 8 Ball. I put it back and floomped onto my bed, put on some music. Last time I came back from the clinic, there'd been one song, 'Celladora', that I listened to over and over. This time I chose a different track. Number three, 'Steeple Chaser'. I lay back on the bed and closed my eyes.

'Knock knock.' Mum stuck her head between the curtains. 'Can I come in?'

I sat up. 'Sure.'

Mum sat down and pulled one of the cushions into her lap. She seemed kind of nervous or something, fidgeting with the cushion's zip in this annoying way. Weird how I'd begun noticing all these funny little habits in the people around me since the clinic.

'Noah called,' she said. 'He's wondering if you could work on Saturday. If you're over your, ah, flu.'

I lay back down again. 'Actually, I thought I might take a few weeks off.'

Mum unzipped the cushion, then zipped it up again. 'Dr

Richter thinks it's a good idea for you to get back into things as soon as possible.'

Of course Dr Richter would think that. Dr Richter has never experienced date night at the Mercury. Especially when you no longer have your best friend there to help you get through.

'I'll see how I'm feeling,' I said.

Mum nodded. I kind of hoped she'd go then, so I could get on with lying on my bed listening to music. But she stayed there, zipping and unzipping. 'I called the school too,' she said after a moment. 'I spoke with Mrs Deane to let her know you'll be back next week.'

'I bet she was thrilled to hear it,' I said. 'Did she update you on all the *goss?*' That was a joke, obviously. Because if there had been any goss it would've all been about me.

'Actually there was something,' said Mum. 'It's about Katie Clarke.'

'Let me guess,' I said. 'Katie is threatening to leave school if I'm allowed back in.'

Zip. Unzip. Zip.

I was on the point of pulling that freakin cushion out of Mum's hands when she added quietly, 'Olive, I have some very bad news.' She cleared her throat. 'Katie is dead.'

FIFTEEN

Katie Clarke had died of heart failure. That was the official story, at any rate. Apparently her rapid weight loss put strain on her heart and it suddenly just gave up. It had happened in the early evening, during the dinner period. By the time the doctors got to her, it was too late. Only Miranda had been there to witness her passing.

At least she wasn't alone – that's what everyone kept saying.

The memorial service was at school the following Monday. At first I was going, then I wasn't, then I finally decided that I would. I arrived deliberately late – after everyone else had already gone into the hall – and hung at the back. The entire school was crammed in there and it was stuffy as hell. A few faces turned around as I walked in but I kept my eyes straight ahead – just in case one of the faces was Lachlan's. By now he must have found out, like everyone, about my *temporary conscious psychosis*. I wasn't ready for the look on his face when he realised I was back.

Now that he knew he'd been chatting up the school nutcase.

Katie's family were sitting up the front. Katie's mum was flagpole-straight but her dad was sagging in his seat, like he'd been deflated. Between them was Katie's little sister, Hannah. She kept turning in her seat to sneak glances at all of us. She'd grown heaps since I'd last seen her. She looked like Katie did when we'd first become friends.

Directly behind them was Miranda, her head slightly bowed. What was different about her? Her hair looked a little lank and unwashed. *But that's not surprising, is it?* I imagined Dr Richter saying. *For someone who has just lost her best friend?* It wasn't just her hair – even the way she sat seemed different, as did the small movements she made in her seat. She seemed … sad.

A thought appeared in my mind. One Dr Richter would not have approved of. *She's just pretending.* I shoved the thought away. Stuff like that was not going to help me get away from this place.

Miranda is not dangerous. This had to be my mantra from now on. *She's just a normal girl. Bitchy, but normal.*

We sang a hymn – awkwardly because no-one knew the words – and sat there in silence while *Goodbye England's Rose* was played over the PA system, even though Katie was neither English nor particularly rose-like. Then Mrs Deane stood on the stage and spoke about Katie. She abandoned her usual clipped, precise talking style for once and went on and on about how Katie had been an *integral part of the school.* How she'd shown an *avid interest* in everything that was going on around her. She talked about how many people had admired Katie. How we'd all looked up to her. 'Katie was a role model for so many students,' she said.

It was like listening to a fairytale – one that began *long, long ago* ...

I zoned out, unable to stand it. But the moment Mrs Deane's voice faded to a background buzz I found my own Katie memories rising. The sleepovers in primary school where we'd spend the entire night planning for high school and agonising over how terrible it would be if we didn't end up in the same class. Our first solo trip to the Mercury together – when Katie had laughed so hard that popcorn had flown from her mouth and landed in the hair of the guy in front of us. All the school events we'd organised together and how I'd teased her about her obsession with details.

It was strange thinking over those things. Stuff I hadn't thought about for ages. It reminded me how for a long time, it had felt really good being friends with Katie. And then, when things started to go bad – when the person I was inside no longer matched the way I looked – I'd hidden it from her for as long as I could.

Despite myself, I believed what she'd said in the hospital, about not telling everyone that I'd tried to kill myself. Katie Courtney Clarke could be shallow and self-centred, but she wasn't a liar. The old Olive was the one who was manipulative, deceitful and mean, and I'd projected all of that onto Katie.

When I tuned back in again, Mrs Deane was speaking directly to Katie's family. Katie's mother had started making little noises, horribly private sounds that it felt wrong to be hearing.

'I'm sure I'm not the only one here who feels that our school will be a much darker place without your daughter's sunny smile,' said Mrs Deane. 'We are glad we had the chance to be warmed by it.' Mrs Deane's eyes moved away from the Clarkes and swept the hall. 'For those who were close to Katie, the upcoming months will be particularly hard,' she said. 'We will support you as much as we can.'

Miranda's head stayed bowed, her hair falling down over her face.

There was another hymn and that was it. Katie Clarke was gone. The double doors were opened wide and everyone filed out – clearly relieved to escape from the stifling room. I stood at the back, watching them all leave, wondering if I should go and say something to Katie's family. But what would I say exactly? That I was sorry? It sounded so stupid. It would be better just to slip off with everyone else.

As I stood there dithering, I found myself looking right into Miranda's eyes. From across the room they looked kind of cloudy. And then, her face began to fold up. *She's going to cry*, I thought. *Maybe she really did care about Katie.*

But Miranda didn't cry. Instead, her mouth widened into a yawn – big and luxurious. When she'd finished, she gave me a little smile. I looked away, my heart pounding.

SIXTEEN

I squashed myself back into my old routine as best I could. In class I perfected my *paying attention* face. I did just enough homework to avoid being hassled by our new substitute teacher in home room. I stacked cups and scooped popcorn at the Mercury. My meds were ingested at regular intervals. I made it through each day like this, being measured and controlled. I tried not to think, and the only time I allowed myself to feel anything was when I burrowed into bed at night and put myself to sleep by listening to Luxe. Luxe was the one good thing in my day.

At school I slunk from class to class with my headphones on, although strangely no-one seemed to be gossiping as much as I'd thought they would. I'd steeled myself for the whispering and rapid changes of conversation when I entered a room, but for some reason it didn't happen. It was almost like they didn't know about Ami, and what I'd said to Miranda – even though that had to be impossible.

The hardest thing was coping without Lachlan. It's horrible to want to see someone so much it makes your whole body ache, while simultaneously living in fear of running into them. During my first couple of weeks back at school, I had the feeling he was trying to get my attention, but I refused to meet his eyes. I knew I was being a total coward, but I couldn't bear him telling me he was sorry to hear about my illness, and – even worse – seeing the pity in his face. Seeing that, I knew, would reduce me to a blubbering mess. When the teacher rearranged our seating and moved me to the front, I was relieved. It meant I didn't have to stare at Lachlan's back anymore.

o

The only person I did find myself watching was Miranda. That was a hard habit to break. I'd figured that she would fill the Katie-shaped space at school and take over all her duties. But it quickly became clear that she had no intention of doing this. She completely cold-shouldered Cameron, who, after a couple of weeks of following her around with a desperate look in his eye, gave up and slid away, looking wounded and confused. Miranda made no attempt to recruit new friends and went back to her old habit of sitting alone on her bench, hands folded together, eyes closed. At first people would sidle up to her – still suspecting that she was in charge and that this sitting-around business was all part of it. But Miranda completely ignored them and eventually they retreated for good.

As I was watching her do this one day, something from the

shapeshifter website popped into my head – the bit that described how shifters 'faded into the background' when they'd returned to their search phase. And even though I made myself repeat a hundred times *there's no such thing as shifters,* I still found myself waiting for her eyes to spring open and for her to *look* at someone the way she'd looked at Katie.

Obviously I didn't tell Dr Richter about this. She'd just alter my medication again and go on about the dangers of letting my imagination run away with me. That's also why I didn't tell her about what happened one afternoon about three weeks after I'd left the clinic.

I was unlocking my bike after school when a bug landed on me and disappeared down the back of my dress. I yelped and did one of those funny-looking dances that you do when you're trying to shake an insect out of your clothes while holding a bike. When the bug fell out, I shuddered. It was shiny black and nasty-looking, with a massive stinger. As it scuttled off, I noticed Miranda standing a few metres away, watching me, and even when it was obvious I'd seen her, she didn't break her stare.

I glared back at her, like it was one of those games you play as a kid to see who can go the longest without blinking. *This is stupid,* I thought after a moment, and was about to walk off when something made my fingers tingle. Had Miranda's eyes just *gleamed?*

Get a grip, Olive. Dr Richter had warned me that I might have a few low-level hallucinations – *visual tics,* she'd called them – while I adjusted to the new medication. And sure enough,

I realised what I'd seen was just the flash of sunlight on Miranda's face. *No such thing as shifters,* I breathed. *Just a normal girl.*

All the same, I found I was a bit shaky as I climbed on my bike. Sweaty too. Usually riding helps calm me down, but that afternoon it didn't. The whole way home I couldn't shake the feeling that someone was behind me, gradually coming closer until I could almost feel their breath on the back of my neck. But every time I turned around no-one was there.

o

Near our classroom was a large noticeboard. Only school-related events were supposed to be pinned to it – swimming stuff, auditions for the school play, band practice times – but people sneaked other things on there too. Once upon a time, the information on that board had shaped my life. Now I mostly ignored it. But one morning, not long after the bug incident, something caught my eye. In between flyers for a second-hand book sale and a school-fete reminder was a face – the lushest of all faces – printed on a rectangle of shiny sky-blue paper. I read the words over and over.

Luxe gig in Jubilee Park. Not in New York. Not in London. Not even in Sydney. The flyer said that Luxe would be playing at the Rainbow Hotel. That evening.

For one beautiful moment I was floating – almost laughing out loud with the idea that I would finally get to see Luxe play. That very night. Then I crashed back down to reality. *Don't be a wonk, Olive. That's never going to happen.* The Rainbow was super strict about not letting in underage people – there was always a bouncer on the door and he could spot a fake ID at a hundred metres. Plus there was no way Mum would let me see a gig that started at 10 p.m. on a Tuesday night. It just wasn't going to happen.

I leant my forehead against the noticeboard and felt all the joy slip away. *Just accept it. Stuff like that doesn't happen to you.* I lifted my head and stepped back. Straight into someone standing behind me.

Miranda.

The heavy exhaustion I'd felt a moment ago vanished. Now I was tingling with alarm. 'What the hell are you doing standing behind me like that?' I snapped.

Miranda didn't move. 'I was looking at that gig poster,' she said. 'Same as you.'

'Big fan of Luxe are you?' I muttered, turning away before she saw the way my hands were shaking.

Miranda didn't answer. She began to hum a familiar tune. 'Steeple Chaser'. I stared at her.

'There's another song I know too,' said Miranda. 'It goes, *Will I break it or make it with your half-hearted heart?*'

It was so strange hearing these words from Miranda. Maybe that's why I spoke. '"The Great Divided".'

'You're surprised,' she said. 'That I know Luxe.'

Yeah, just a bit, I thought. They had always felt like something private – something that belonged only to me. 'Where did you hear them?'

'Same place you did,' said Miranda. 'The internet.' Her mouth curved up. 'The lead singer is kind of hot, isn't he?'

'Dallas. Yeah. He's pretty lush.' *And the sun is quite warm.*

'I haven't told anyone, you know,' said Miranda suddenly. 'About Ami, I mean.'

My neck burned. 'Oh,' I said. 'Right.' Ami was the last thing I wanted to talk about. Especially with Miranda.

'You don't need to be frightened of me,' she said, leaning in closer.

'I'm not.' I tried to match her tone, cool and confidential.

'No? Well, prove it,' said Miranda. 'Come to the gig with me tonight.'

I tapped the flyer. 'It's over-18s,' I said, rolling my eyes. 'They won't let us in.'

'I'll get us in,' said Miranda. A statement. 'So there's nothing stopping you.'

I swallowed. *You have to face your fear, Olive.* 'Not possible,' I said. 'I've tried to get in there, like, ten times before.'

'Try eleven times,' said Miranda. 'This time it'll be different. I guarantee it.'

The bell rang. Down the corridor I could see our substitute teacher heading towards our classroom. She looked kind of anxious. It must be crap to be a substitute teacher. Always filling in for other people. Never staying anywhere long enough to belong. But maybe that was why they did it.

'Sorry,' I said tightly. 'I have plans already.'

Lucky for me, Miranda didn't push it. She just shrugged.

'No problem. But if you change your mind I'll be out the front of the Rainbow. Quarter to ten.'

o

Mum had a big rush order to get done that afternoon, so I helped Tobes with his homework. For dinner I made my specialty, known in our house as Something From Nothing. Tonight that meant scrambled eggs on toasted muffins with some carrot sticks artfully arranged on the side.

It kept me busy, but it wasn't enough to completely distract me from thinking about Dallas and the gig. I felt jingly, restless, and I kept wondering where Dallas was at that exact moment. Was he already in town? Every time I heard a car on the street, I wanted to run to the window. If it was Dallas driving past, I figured I'd just somehow *know*. I wished I could conjure Ami up again and get excited with her. I never really believed I'd get so close to meeting him, and only Ami could understand. But Ami was gone.

After I'd cleaned up the dinner stuff and convinced Toby that dentures were not as cool as he thought and that he should brush his teeth, I went to my room to attempt to do some homework. It was always a struggle, but that night it was impossible. In the end I put on some music and lay on my bed.

Around nine, Mum looked in. Everything about her was worn out. 'Your slippers have been chewed on,' I said.

'Not by me,' said Mum. 'I think Ralph's worried they're trying to eat my feet.'

I laughed. 'And everyone said he'd never make a guard dog.'

Mum smiled. 'Thanks for doing dinner, Liv,' she said. 'What would I do without you?'

Have an easier life, I thought. *Still be married. Worry less.*

Mum yawned. 'I'm going to bed,' she said. 'I'll be reading for a while if you want me. See you in the morning.'

There was the rattly whirr of our near-death bathroom fan and a few minutes later the click of Mum's bedside light.

I thought about climbing into bed myself, but I was wide awake. The band would definitely be at the Rainbow by now. They'd probably done a sound check and were finalising their playlist. Maybe the others were keyed up but Dallas was laughing and putting them all at ease. It was frustrating to know that he was so close by – but remained totally unaware of my existence.

The tree in our backyard creaked back and forth as the wind blew in from the bay. Nuts and leaves pinged like rain against the roof. I sat up. *Maybe I should go after all.* Why not? Sneaking out to a gig with Miranda would definitely be one way of proving I could *face my past.* I wasn't stupid enough to think I'd actually get into the Rainbow. But maybe I'd catch a glimpse of Dallas through a window. That wasn't completely impossible, was it?

I got up and crept out into the hallway, heart thumping. The house was quiet. I moved down to Mum's room and peeped in. The bedside light was still on but Mum's eyes were closed, an open book rising and falling on her chest.

At the front door I hesitated. This was pretty crazy. But the reasons to go kept appearing in my head. I'd be back in an hour – probably sooner. Mum wouldn't even know I'd gone. And this might be my only chance to see my music idol, the one guy in the whole world that I knew instinctively would understand me.

I grabbed some money, pulled on my sneakers. There was no time to change – and anyway, if I went back to my room I might lose my nerve. It wasn't until I was already on my bike, riding towards the Rainbow, that I realised I'd forgotten to take my meds. *Oh well*. I could take them when I got home.

o

The wind belted behind me, pushing my bike along at top speed. I barely had to pedal. The streets were deserted and it wasn't until I rounded the corner into the esplanade that I saw any signs of life. And there, shimmering with light up ahead, was the Rainbow Hotel.

I slowed down, weaving between the people standing around on the road out the front, smoking and chatting. Standing in the Rainbow's doorway was the bouncer – a boulder of a guy, his jaws working a piece of gum. I chained my bike to a pole and took a few deep breaths.

Don't worry. Miranda probably won't even show up, I told myself. But when I turned again there she was, standing near the chalkboard listing the upcoming events.

She smiled and came over to me straight away. 'Hey! You made it!'

I was surprised by how warm she sounded. Like she was

genuinely pleased to see me.

'Now, here's what we need to do,' she said, and there was an air of excitement in her voice that made my insides leap. I suddenly felt like this might actually work. Or it might not, but it'd be fun trying. 'Don't make eye contact with anyone, but don't look down either. Just look straight ahead and walk. Not too fast but not too slow either. Got that?'

My mind turned to Ami again. She wouldn't have wanted me to do this, especially with Miranda. *But Ami doesn't exist,* I reminded myself. And anyway, I had to prove that I wasn't afraid. I nodded. 'Sure.'

Miranda tucked a tendril of hair back into the loose bun she was wearing. It made her look older, that hairstyle. 'The main thing is that you act like you've got every right to be here,' she said. 'That's what they pick up on.' Miranda had obviously done this before. She walked briskly towards the Rainbow's entrance. 'Come on. Let's do it.'

I trailed along behind her, legs wobbling, my confidence leaking away. Nobody would ever believe that I – a girl with no make-up on and wearing scruffy runners – was an adult. I already felt the bouncer's eyes graze against me and I gritted my teeth, waiting for the inevitable, *Try again in a couple of years, sweetheart.*

But the bouncer didn't speak, even when Miranda and I were right there in front of him. When I braved a peek at him, he had this dazed look on his face – as if he was in a play and had forgotten not only his lines but how he even got on the stage.

He silently swung open the door for us and I held my breath as I walked in. I kept waiting for a hand to reach out and a voice to say, *Not so fast, young lady.* But there was no hand, nothing holding me back and then there I was – in the Rainbow. In the same building where Dallas, at that very moment, was preparing to come on stage.

I started laughing in a slightly manic way. 'I can't believe we got in.'

'I don't know why you're so surprised,' said Miranda, laughing too. 'I promised, didn't I?'

If I'd ever thought about what Miranda might look like standing in a dump like the Rainbow, I would've pictured her looking completely out of place and awkward. But she didn't look like that at all. She seemed comfortable and relaxed – like she belonged there. I remembered an early rumour from before she'd arrived that she had once dated the lead guitarist from The Heads. Looking at her then, I could see how that might be possible. My jeans suddenly felt dirtier and more worn-out than before.

'Come on,' said Miranda. 'Let's squeeze to the front.'

She reached out a hand towards me and instinctively I recoiled from it. Miranda's hand fell back heavily to her side. It was hard to read the expression on her face in the dim lighting, but her tone made it clear she was upset.

'I know you don't like me,' she said. 'I – I know you blame me for Katie's death. But I wish you could understand what it's been like for me. I wish you'd let me explain.'

'Go ahead,' I said, folding my arms. This would be interesting.

Miranda was quiet for a moment. 'I haven't exactly had the best *role models* in my life,' she said eventually. 'I've moved around a lot and I had to figure out how to fit in wherever I ended up. I made some stupid friendships because of that. Ones that didn't really suit me.'

Miranda stopped and turned her head for a moment. When she looked back I saw tears in her eyes. 'But despite what you think, I *loved* Katie. I still love her. I thought you might understand that, because you did once too.'

I felt a lump in my throat. Not because of what Miranda was saying, which was probably rubbish, but because Katie being gone really only sank in right then.

'You probably don't want to talk about it,' continued Miranda, 'but I guess she was kind of my Ami. We got each other, you know?' I was shocked to see the tears were streaming down her face but she didn't seem to care. 'A lot of crap things have happened to me. I've lost people. *Important* people. I don't know if you know what that's like.'

'I do, actually,' I said, with a little flicker of anger. *Ami for one. I lost Ami because of you.*

'Your dad,' said Miranda softly. 'He left, didn't he? Sometimes parents can't handle it when their kids have *issues*, can they? That must be hard to deal with. The guilt of pulling your family apart, I mean.'

It was a shock – hearing her say my private, inner thoughts out loud like that. Instead of my anger increasing, it was extinguished and all I could do was nod, near tears but determined to keep it together. Because how could I cry about my dad in front of someone whose parents were both dead?

'It's been pretty tough,' I managed to say.

'I'd offer to hug you,' said Miranda awkwardly. 'But I get the feeling that wouldn't go down so well.'

I laughed then. Kind of snottily. But at least I wasn't crying.

'I'm so glad,' said Miranda. 'You know – that you came here tonight. Even though you think I'm a … what's that word you use? Wonk. You came even though you think I'm a wonk.'

'I don't think you're a wonk,' I said, and without realising it, I'd put my hand on her arm.

Instantly Miranda put her hand on top of mine. 'Tell me about them,' she said suddenly. 'The band.'

'What do you want to know?'

'Everything you know.'

'Ah … that could take a while.'

'OK then,' said Miranda. 'Give me five words or less for each of them.'

That seemed do-able. 'OK, let's start with the bass player – Vincent. Über-talented musician. Painfully shy.'

'Got it,' said Miranda. 'What about the drummer?'

'Pearl,' I replied, starting to enjoy myself. It had been so long since I'd had a conversation with someone just for fun. 'Dodgy rhythm. Unique style.'

Miranda raised an eyebrow. 'And what about the singer? What do you think about him?'

'Dallas,' I sighed, 'is lush, lush, lush.'

'You're blushing,' Miranda said, smiling slyly. 'Even your ears.'

'Yeah, he has that effect.'

The stage lights bloomed into orange and the crowd began hooting and whistling. *Luxe was coming out.*

'Have you ever imagined this moment?' said Miranda, close to my ear. 'What it would be like when you saw Dallas for the first time?'

'Oh, just once or twice.'

'Right then,' said Miranda. 'You need to meet Dallas. After the gig.'

'Sure!' I chuckled. 'You set it up for me, OK?'

I've always been the sort of person who leaves the best thing to last. The tastiest thing on my plate. The biggest Christmas present. My dad teased me for ages about the time I'd saved my caramel-filled Easter egg for six months. By the time I unwrapped it the chocolate had turned white.

So when the music finally started, I stared at everyone else *but* Dallas. First I examined Pearl, with her thick straight fringe and her deep red lipstick. Then I concentrated on Vincent for a while, long and gangly and curled like a comma over his guitar. He had the super-pale skin of someone who spent way too much time inside. Exactly the sort of guy I'd be matched up with if I were doing some stupido magazine quiz. But the quiz would be wrong.

Next I looked out at the crowd, surprised at how many people were there. Clearly I wasn't the only one in Jubilee

Park who'd heard of Luxe after all. There were some Pearl wannabes, mimicking her urban cowgirl look. Then there were the bass-player dudes, there to see Vincent. He was young but he already had a big following online. Pity he seemed like the sort of guy who'd hate that. The bass-player dudes stood on their own, their heads nodding to the bass rhythm, their fingers marking out guitar chords against their legs. And finally there were the girls who were obviously there to see Dallas. Without even looking at the stage I could tell exactly where he was by watching the movement of their faces.

They're like a bunch of puppies, I thought in disgust, *watching a chop being waved around.*

It was only when the second song started that I forced my eyes over to Dallas. My whole body was buzzing. I'd listened to this person sing every single day for about six months. His songs had been my morning caffeine shot and my evening sleeping tablet. How would I feel when I actually laid eyes on him in the flesh? My head might explode. I braced myself for the wave of emotion that I knew would sweep me up and carry me away, and allowed myself to look at him.

Nothing. Nothing at all.

I nearly fell over backwards. I felt like I'd tried to lift something that looked very heavy, but had turned out to be weightless. Dallas was just as beautiful in person as in the photos I'd seen. More so, even. And his voice still made me shiver. But my crush had totally vanished.

Miranda nudged me, her eyes sparkling. 'Isn't he amazing?'

I nodded, but didn't reply. I found myself looking around for something to focus on. Something that would give me a chance to regain my balance. And then I spotted someone familiar in the crowd. Someone tall with dark, tousled hair, wearing a hoodie that had been patched at both elbows. Someone with a beautiful broad back. It was a back I knew well because, up until recently, I'd spent a lot of time sitting behind it at school.

SEVENTEEN

My mind began spinning. *He knows you're a Luxe fan. He came here hoping you'd turn up.* I clenched my hands with irritation. *Olive, you wonk. Stop it!* There was no way Lachlan would still be interested in me.

Except. Except maybe he *didn't* know about Ami, about the clinic, about the whole shapeshifter *scheiss.* Maybe Miranda had been telling the truth when she said she hadn't told anyone. I'd made that mistake with Katie, hadn't I? I'd been too stubborn to believe that sometimes people are better than you give them credit for.

My mind kept playing this annoying game of ping-pong for the rest of the set, driving me crazy and completely distracting me from the music. During the break I positioned myself with my back to the wall so at least Lachlan couldn't appear behind me. But during the second set I lost sight of where he was and my agitation built until I could hardly stand it. More than once

I looked over at the door, wondering if I could sneak out before Lachlan saw me. But the room was too full by then and anyway, I couldn't just leave Miranda without explaining what was up.

o

When the crowd called for an encore I actually groaned – something I never, ever thought I'd do at a Luxe gig. When the lights finally went up I was a nervous wreck. 'I've got to get going,' I said hastily to Miranda. 'Thanks for getting me in.'

'You can't go!' protested Miranda. 'Not yet.'

'It's late,' I said. 'There's school tomorrow.'

'*There's school tomorrow*,' Miranda repeated, her voice a higher, whinier version of mine. Then she smiled. Took hold of my arm. 'You *can't* go. I won't let you. You're going to meet Dallas, remember?'

'That was just a joke.' My eyes were darting around the room. The crowd had begun to thin but I couldn't see Lachlan anywhere. *Maybe he's gone*, I thought hopefully.

'No, it wasn't,' said Miranda, tightening her grip. 'Come on. It's time to meet *the guy of your dreams*.'

'No,' I said, pulling my arm free. 'I'm not going to hang around the door like some loser groupie.'

Miranda gave me a disdainful look. 'Who said anything about hanging around the door? He'll come out and find us.'

I snorted. 'Somehow, I don't think that's going to happen.'

'Let's just wait and see,' said Miranda. She marched over to the battered couch near the back of the venue and plonked herself down. Feeling silly – and dangerously exposed – standing there on my own, I went and sat beside her. Miranda nodded approvingly. 'For a minute there I thought you might be gutless.'

It was only a couple of minutes later that the door beside the stage opened and Dallas sauntered out, followed by Pearl and Vincent. All the girls in the room – the same ones who'd been busily pretending they weren't waiting for this moment – simultaneously tousled their hair and it looked like a breeze blowing through a field of wheat. Dallas didn't seem to notice. His eyes were sweeping the room.

'He's looking for you,' whispered Miranda. 'Quick. Start talking to me. He'll come over in a minute.'

But five minutes later, when Dallas hadn't appeared, Miranda glanced around and saw something that made her face screw up. 'Why would Dallas want to waste time talking to him?' she muttered.

I turned to see Dallas across the other side of the room, deep in conversation. With *Lachlan*. They were laughing.

Miranda stood up, smoothed her clothes. 'Let's walk past them. Dallas will blow him off once he sees us. It's you he wants to talk to, not that moron.'

'I'm not going over there,' I said, feeling a little leap of panic. 'It'd look so ... pathetic.'

Miranda gave me a pitying look. 'No,' she said. 'It's only pathetic when *ugly* people do it. Come on.'

I suppose I could have told her about my revelation – that I no longer felt about Dallas the way I had before the gig.

But I didn't. Maybe because I knew how stupid it would sound. How fickle and girly. But that wasn't the only reason. I'd decided – without even realising I'd decided – that I should keep my feelings for Lachlan to myself. And if I wasn't prepared to tell Miranda about it, then I had no choice but to do what she said.

So when Miranda strode off confidently towards Dallas, I followed along behind.

o

I was expecting Miranda to slow down as we came close to Dallas. But she didn't. Instead she just said *great gig* – barely even looking at him – and continued walking. Dallas was mid-sentence but he stopped when he heard her voice and looked around. Lachlan glanced around too and caught my eye. He didn't seem surprised to see me. But he didn't look exactly pleased either. It was a guarded kind of expression.

There was nothing guarded about Dallas though. His face broke into a huge grin and it was clear Miranda had been right. Dallas *had* been waiting for us. Well, for Miranda.

His finger tickled the air. 'Hey. Don't walk away. Come and talk to us.'

Miranda paused. 'Do we have time?' she asked me, like there was something way more important we should be doing.

'I guess,' I mumbled, feeling stupid. As we joined them, I could feel hate beams emanating from every other female in the room.

'I saw you in the audience,' said Dallas to Miranda. 'You liked the gig?'

'It was lush,' she replied, playing with an escaped frond of hair.

Pearl was standing nearby with Vincent. She snorted. 'It's the same after every show,' she said loudly. 'Some hair-twirling girl comes scampering over to flutter her fake eyelashes at Dallas.' She looked us up and down. 'How old are you two anyway?'

Humiliation dripped from every pore of my body.

'We're old enough to know when someone can't hold a rhythm,' Miranda flung back.

Vincent snickered, very quietly. Pearl seemed to grow – her annoyance making her both taller and broader. 'What would *you* know about rhythm? What would you know about anything?'

'I know one of your shirt buttons just fell off,' said Miranda. 'And that your eyeliner is crooked.'

This time Dallas laughed, and even I choked down a snicker.

Pearl's jaw clenched. 'These girls are under-age,' she said through gritted teeth. 'I want them chucked out.'

'Calm down, Pearl,' said Dallas. 'If you do that Vincent might also get turfed. And my brother.' He reached out and put a hand on Lachlan's shoulder. I stared at the hand and then at Lachlan's face. His eyes darted away, looking uncomfortable.

Pearl slammed down her glass and stalked off. 'I'm packing up my kit,' she called over her shoulder. 'The rest of you can keep playing at the crèche if you want. But if you want a lift, I'm leaving in twenty sharp.'

Dallas didn't even glance at her. I got the feeling that a meteorite could've crashed through the ceiling right then and he still would've kept gazing at Miranda.

'Who *are* you?' he said. 'I'm sure I know you from somewhere.'

She laughed. 'I'm just Miranda.' Her arm slipped around my waist. 'And this is my friend Olive.'

I tensed up. *Friend?* Since when?

'Well, I'm Dallas,' said Dallas. As if we wouldn't know that. 'And I'm really pleased to meet you.' His voice was so soft and intimate as he gazed at Miranda that I felt wrong standing near them.

Next Dallas gave Vincent a slap on the back that almost sent him sprawling. 'This is Vinnie. Our *wunderkind* and band mascot.' Then he swung his other arm around Lachlan's neck and mussed his hair. 'And this good-looking guy is my baby brother, Lachie,' he said. 'He's the reason we're here tonight. The clever little monkey set it all up. Even did the posters.' He chuckled. 'I thought there must be some little indie girl he was trying to impress. But then he turns up on his own.'

'Dal,' muttered Lachlan, unpeeling Dallas's arm. 'We know each other. We're at the same school.'

Dallas looked delighted. 'Is that right?' he said, shaking his head and looking at us. 'Have you noticed how hard it is to get information out of this guy? I bet you didn't know he wrote some of our songs.'

'No,' I said slowly. 'I didn't know that.'

Dallas whisked Miranda away to one side, leaving me

and Lachlan standing together. Uncomfortable? Yeah, just a bit. Vincent stood nearby, looking like he might die from the awkwardness of this situation – and he didn't even know what was going on. Lachlan wedged his hands into his back pockets and shifted his weight from one leg to the other. I suddenly couldn't stand it any longer.

'Why didn't you *tell* me?'

'Tell you what?' said Lachlan.

'Oh, I don't know,' I said. I think my voice might have jumped up an octave. 'Maybe just a little bit about who you *really* are.'

The bar girl came past, stacking glasses.

'You already seemed pretty sure of that,' Lachlan said. 'I'm the sporty lifesaver guy.'

'You could've corrected me!' I exploded.

The bar girl stopped, gathering up the empties on the table near us. The glasses clinked as they joined the stack.

'Would you have listened?' asked Lachlan quietly.

'Of course!'

Vincent coughed nervously. 'OK, it's time for me to go.'

'Tell you what,' said Lachlan, as Vincent disappeared. 'Ask me something now. Whatever you like.'

I examined his face. Was he teasing me? 'All right then,' I said, folding my arms. 'If Dallas is your brother, why do you have different last names?'

'He's my half-brother,' said Lachlan. 'Same dad, different mums. He uses his mum's last name.'

'You seem pretty close. For half-brothers.'

Lachlan nodded. 'Our dad did a lot of stuff with both of us when we were growing up. Took us on camping trips, hikes, that sort of thing. I thought Dal was just the best thing ever when I was a kid. We catch up when we can. It's been tricky since Mum and I moved out here.' He looked at me, smiling just a little. 'How am I going so far?'

'Not bad,' I said, trying not to let on how much I was enjoying just *talking* to him. I'd missed it. 'Next question. Do you really write songs for Luxe?'

'Dallas was exaggerating,' Lachlan said, embarrassed. 'There's only one thing I've written for them that they actually perform.'

'What's that?' I think I was holding my breath, waiting to hear what he'd say.

'"Steeple Chaser".'

I found myself watching the bar girl working her way around the room. Her glass stack was so tall now that it swayed like a reed over her shoulder.

'Did you arrange this gig?' I asked.

'If by "arranged" you mean "went in and asked" then yeah, I guess so. Maybe I should ask for a cut of the takings.' He grinned and took a swig of his drink. 'Anything else?'

Yeah, I thought. *Did you organise the gig to impress some girl, like Dallas said?* And if so, *which* girl? But I couldn't quite convince the words to come out.

Miranda's laughter – bright and high – made us both turn. She was leaning against the wall, her head tilted back and her long white throat exposed. Dallas's hand was resting just beside her on the wall.

'That must be ... bothering you,' said Lachlan uncomfortably.

'It's not,' I said quickly. 'Not one bit.'

'Really?' said Lachlan, and for a moment his face had this look – all shiny and hopeful. And for a moment it seemed possible that I could reach out and take his hand. Say to him, 'I've been so dumb.' And that he might nod and smile and say, 'Yeah, but I still like you.' And that everything might be OK. Better than OK. Everything might be little-twinkling-stars *sublime*.

But instead I blurted something stupid. 'Why didn't you tell me Dallas was your brother?'

Lachlan's face crunched in. 'So I could introduce you to him? Sorry, Olive. I guess I'm just not that self-sacrificing.'

'I didn't mean it like that,' I said. *You wonk, Olive. Wonk, wonk, wonk.*

'Don't worry,' said Lachlan, his voice all dry and horrible. 'Believe me, I'm used to it – Dallas has always been the big hot star. It's never been an issue because generally the girls who fall for him aren't –' He stopped.

'What?' I said.

Lachlan rubbed his hand slowly down his face. When he'd finished the anger was wiped away. Now he just looked sad. 'They've never been *you* before.'

I was suddenly only capable of starting sentences, not finishing them. 'But I – what I really –'

'It's OK,' said Lachlan grimly. 'I haven't forgotten what you said at the formal. You were right, we *don't* match. So don't worry. I'm not going to hassle you.'

Someone had opened a window and a waft of sea air blew through the room, heavy with salt. Lachlan breathed in deeply and his unhappy look faded a little. 'Feel like going for a swim?' he said suddenly.

'Who? Me?' I said, dizzy with how quickly the conversation had changed direction. 'Now?'

'Yeah,' said Lachlan. 'Why not?'

'Because it's night-time,' I said quickly. 'And freezing. And we don't have towels or bathers.'

Lachlan tilted his head, looking at me intently. 'When did you start hating the ocean so much?'

'Let's just say the sea and I had a falling out,' I said eventually, trying to sound jokey while fighting to keep my breathing under control. It was still so hard to believe that Lachlan didn't know what I'd done. What I'd *attempted* to do. But if he really didn't, there was no way I was about to fill him in here, standing in the Rainbow.

Lachlan kept watching me with those steady brown eyes. 'You don't have to tell me,' he said. He didn't sound angry. Maybe just a little disappointed.

Vincent reappeared, eyeing us warily. 'Lachlan, if you want a lift back with Pearl you have to come now,' he said. 'She's parked in a loading zone and she's not paying for another ...' he coughed, '... *effing* ticket.'

Lachlan put down his glass. Zipped up his jacket. Even from

where I was standing I could still smell him – a salty, warm-bread smell. 'Want a lift somewhere?'

'Um, no,' I said, when really I meant yes. 'I'm fine.'

Lachlan nodded. Like he was expecting that response. 'See you around then,' he said.

'Sure.'

Stop, I found myself willing him. *Turn around*. And just near the door, he did stop and turn. 'Hey,' he said. 'If you ever want to start over again, let me know.'

I gulped.

'With the ocean, I mean,' he said. 'Maybe I can help you patch things up.'

'Oh,' I squeaked. 'Yeah. I'll let you know.'

I waited, a goofy smile frozen on my face until he had disappeared, and then I fled outside and cooled my face against the flaky wall of the Rainbow. Maybe if I pressed hard enough I could sink into the bricks and disappear completely.

The door swung open and Miranda came out, her cheeks flushed. 'Hey, I'm sorry,' she said, coming over to me.

'Huh?'

'That you got stuck with Dallas's brother,' she said, shaking her head sympathetically. 'But I've been raving to Dallas about you. He's really interested, I can tell.'

I gave a short laugh. 'Somehow I don't think it's *me* he's interested in.' Tiredness was making me slump. 'Hey look. I'm going home,' I said.

'Oh *no*,' pouted Miranda. 'Not yet. Dallas will be devastated.'

'I think he'll cope.'

Miranda flung her arms around me, hugging me tightly. I don't know what I thought it would feel like to be hugged by her. Spiky maybe. Or cold. But the hug felt good – warm and friendly. When she pulled back, her eyes were sparkling mischievously.

'Sorry,' she said. 'I know that probably spun you out. But I'm just so glad you came tonight. It ... well, it means a lot to me.' She looked at me almost shyly then. 'See you at school tomorrow?'

I nodded, surprised at how natural this felt. 'Yeah. See you then.'

o

Later, when I was home in bed, I put my earphones in and played 'Steeple Chaser' on repeat. It sounded different now. Maybe because for the first time it wasn't Dallas's face I pictured as I drifted off to sleep.

EIGHTEEN

By the time Miranda appeared at school the next morning I'd almost given up on her coming at all. And the strangest thing was that I'd felt disappointed.

She grabbed my hands, her eyes bright. 'I *have* to talk with you,' she said. 'Now.'

'Sure,' I said. 'Go ahead.'

Miranda looked around with distaste. 'Not here. Let's ditch today.'

I hesitated. 'Well ...'

'Oh come on,' pleaded Miranda. 'Just for an hour. Seriously, I will bust if I don't talk to you.'

'Just one hour then,' I said. That wasn't breaking a promise exactly. Just bending it a bit. It didn't matter if I missed PE anyway – it wasn't like I'd be joining in.

When I used to drop school in the old days I would wait until no-one was around and then slink out as quickly as I could.

But Miranda just strode along like she had every right to be heading in the complete opposite direction to our home room. I trotted along beside her, fully expecting someone to jump out at any minute and ask what the hell we were up to. No-one did. We walked straight out of the front gate – past Mrs Deane's office – and down the street.

Around the corner from school Miranda stopped. 'I have something to tell you,' she said, chewing her lip. 'Something really bad. And I can't go any further until I get it off my chest.'

'What is it?' Crazy things had begun jumping into my mind. Things that would've set Dr Richter's pen clicking. *She's going to tell you she is a shifter. And that you're her next victim.*

'It's about Dallas,' said Miranda. 'Last night after you went, he asked me out.' She clenched her hands and pushed them together, her forehead creased. 'You hate me now, don't you? You'd just started *not* hating me and now you hate me all over again.' She sighed. 'I don't blame you. It must feel awful to have the guy you like ask someone else out. Especially when it's a guy like Dallas.'

I laughed with relief. 'It's not your fault that Dallas likes you,' I said. 'It'd be pretty pathetic if I got upset about that.'

The look on Miranda's face was hard to decode. She looked surprised, but there was something else in there. It almost looked like she was annoyed. 'Yes,' she said slowly. 'That *would* be pretty tragic, I guess.'

'So,' I said. 'How do you feel about him?'

Miranda closed her eyes and wrapped her arms around

herself, swaying from side to side. 'Dallas,' she sang. 'Dallas, Dallas, Dallas, Dallas.'

'You like him *that* much already?' I teased.

'You know that feeling when you really *connect* with a guy?' said Miranda. 'When he just completely *gets* you, even though you've barely said a word to each other?'

I thought of Lachlan. How surprising it was that he seemed to see and understand so much about me. How easy it was just to talk with him. 'Totally,' I said.

'Well that's how it feels with Dallas,' said Miranda. 'I mean, I only met him last night and it already feels like we've known each other all our lives.'

'So when are you going out?' I asked.

Miranda sparkled. 'Tonight!'

'Wow!' I said. 'So soon.'

I don't know why I was surprised. That was how it worked – for people like Miranda and Dallas. They met, they liked each other, they arranged to go out. Simple. I, on the other hand, had managed to convince the guy I was crushing on that I didn't care for him at all. Nice one, me.

Miranda eyed me warily. 'So you're not pissed off?'

'No.' I said. 'I'm happy for you.'

Miranda grabbed my hands and danced me around. 'That's *so* great! Hey, let's go shopping. I want to find something new to wear for tonight.'

'You won't find anything around here,' I said. 'Unless you want to wear a nice new tracksuit.'

Miranda flicked her hand. 'I don't want to look around here,' she said. 'Let's go into town.'

'Now?'

'Of *course* now.'

The idea of some mindless shopping in town was weirdly appealing. Maybe because it was something I hadn't done in ages, not since I was friends with Katie.

Miranda must have seen me hesitating. 'It's just one morning,' she urged. 'We'll be back this afternoon.'

'All right,' I said. One morning wasn't so bad. 'Train or bus?'

Miranda released her hair from its ponytail. It looked darker, like the colour she'd been using while she was friends with Katie had begun to fade and now her natural colour was returning. It was funny though. I couldn't quite remember what her natural colour had been.

'Neither,' she said. 'Let's drive.'

I laughed. 'Do you have a chauffeur, then?'

'I can drive,' said Miranda, without a trace of a smile. Then she gestured to the cars lining the street. 'Pick one,' she said. 'I can get it open in about fifteen seconds.'

'But the city is so crap for parking,' I said. *Just play along. Don't look like a wonk.* 'Let's get the train today.'

Miranda shrugged. 'Sure.'

o

Usually the train ride into town was pretty dull – travelling through endless bland suburbs and industrial estates. But that morning I enjoyed it. We talked a bit about the Luxe gig – Miranda loved their music as much as I did – and then we talked about bands in general. Miranda had been to heaps of festivals while she was living in Europe, the same ones that I could only read about online and daydream about attending. I was almost disappointed when we arrived in town.

'Where do you want to go?' I asked as we got off at Central. The last few suits were marching off the train and heading into coffee shops on their way to work.

Miranda looked around, her eyes kind of misty. 'It's weird to be here without Katie,' she said. 'Last time we were –' She stopped, cleared her throat. 'You know what? Let's follow someone.'

'What do you mean?'

'That's the way *I* find stuff,' said Miranda. 'I just look around for someone interesting and then I follow them.'

'Well ... OK then.' It seemed like a pretty weird way to shop, but this was Miranda's expedition.

We hung around the train station waiting for someone *interesting* to come by. For a while it felt like no-one would measure up. We'd been there for almost an hour, drinking hot chocolates and people-watching, when a woman with dark hair intricately twirled up on her head came past. She was wearing large sunglasses and her high-heeled boots clacked loudly on the concrete steps.

'Her,' said Miranda decisively. And we were off.

We followed the woman for several blocks, loitering outside a café when she stopped to pick up a coffee and pretending to examine the window display of a chemist when she went to the bank. Frankly, I thought Miranda had made a bad choice. The woman seemed kind of dull. But then she turned off the main street and into an alley, making a series of quick left and right turns until we found ourselves in a crowded laneway. Cameras flashed. At the end of the street was a building covered with thousands of silver balloons. The woman strode through the crowd and showed something to the security guard out the front of the building. Some sort of pass. The guard nodded and held open the door for her. The door handle was in the shape of a bird, swooping upwards.

'Interesting,' said Miranda. 'They must be opening a branch of Silver here today.'

I looked around. 'How do you know what it's called?' I couldn't see a shop name anywhere.

Miranda grinned. 'I just know,' she said. 'Let's go in. They have good stuff. You'll like it. And their opening parties are a-*mazing*.'

I hung back. 'We haven't been invited,' I said. 'And we're in school uniform.'

'Just relax,' said Miranda, tucking her arm through mine. 'It'll be fine. Or do you want to go back to school? You could be back in time for chem if you hurry.'

I laughed. 'No thanks.' I was a bit nervous about crashing this fancy-looking party but I didn't want to leave either. I was having fun. *Real* fun. For the first time in ages.

As we approached the door the security guard clicked his

finger at Miranda and grinned. 'Don't tell me. You *must* be Isabel's sister,' he said. 'Right?'

Miranda smiled, and shook her hair. 'We do look kind of the same, don't we?' she said sweetly. 'Is she around? She forgot to give me our passes.'

The guard almost tripped over himself in his hurry to open the door for us. 'Just go in,' he said. 'Say hi to her from me, OK?' Miranda stepped through, taking a firm hold of my hand like she thought I might make a break for it. 'Will do!' she chirruped.

Once upon a time, the building was probably a warehouse or a factory – cold and dank – but now it was a very fancy shop, all exposed bricks and a polished concrete floor. In each corner was an enormous vase of long-stemmed flowers and in the centre was a huge aviary rising up almost as high as the ceiling and filled with grey doves, each with a large silver bow around its neck. The clothes themselves were arranged on polished metal tables or strung on silver lines from the ceiling. There were no price tags on any of them.

Waiters in silver bodysuits glided around offering food and champagne to the guests even though it was only mid-morning. A DJ was hunched over his turntables. Everyone, including the waiters, was ridiculously perfect-looking. The guests were all laughing and talking – easy and comfortable and totally relaxed. *Of course they are,* I thought. *This is where they belong.* I felt awkward and completely out of place. I glanced at Miranda. If she was feeling like me, it didn't show. She swayed slightly to the music as she began looking at the clothes arranged in artistically crumpled piles on a table nearby.

A waiter swished over and offered us champagne. He didn't seem to notice that we were in school uniform. Miranda took two glasses and held one out to me.

'Come on now, *Pepita*,' she said. She was speaking in this strange voice – much deeper than usual and with some kind of foreign accent. 'You know Leon said we should have one before the parade.'

I smiled and took the glass, catching on straight away. 'Well all right then, *Ilsa*,' I said, with a theatrical sigh. 'But if I topple off the catwalk it's *your* fault.'

Miranda turned back to the waiter. 'What time are the models required backstage for the show?' she asked.

'In about an hour,' replied the waiter.

Miranda nodded. 'See, Pepita?' she said. 'Plenty of time.'

After the waiter had gone I started laughing. '*Pepita*? Where did that come from?'

Miranda giggled like a naughty kid. 'It was the first thing I thought of. I think he actually believed you were a model! I do know a Pepita in real life, though. Well, I *did*,' she corrected. 'It's ironic really. Poor Pepita hardly ever ate anything, then she choked to death on a carrot stick.'

I froze. 'Miranda. That's horrible.'

Miranda rolled her eyes. 'You moron,' she said, gulping her drink. 'I just made it up.'

'Oh,' I said, feeling stupid. 'Right.'

Alcohol didn't mix well with my meds, so the champagne

was growing warm in my hands, untouched. But Miranda downed hers and accepted another. Two pink spots had appeared on her cheeks. 'All right. I'm ready to try stuff on now,' she said, scooping up a couple of items, soft and light as clouds.

I looked around, waiting for someone to rush over and go nuts at her. 'Are you allowed?'

'It's a *shop*,' said Miranda. 'Of course I'm allowed. Come on. You're trying something on too.'

The change rooms were down the back and had been made to look like soup cans, each with a different label. Miranda handed me a black dress and pushed me into the tomato soup can. 'Don't come out until you've got it on. I'm going to try on the same one!'

The dress had looked pretty nothingy when Miranda had handed it to me. But once it was filled with a body – my body – it took on a form that was surprisingly beautiful. The material draped easily around my curvy silhouette, holding me together, looping my waist, feeling softer than anything I'd ever worn before. It also felt about a thousand times more expensive.

After a few moments there was a knock on my can. 'No hiding in there!' called Miranda. 'I want to compare.'

I came out self-consciously and joined Miranda in front of the large, ornate mirror. Miranda was wearing the same shimmery black dress, cinched at the waist and scooped at the back. She swished it around.

It was impossible not to compare our bodies. Miranda was so light and delicate, moving around as lithely as a dancer, openly admiring herself as she twisted to look at the back of the dress. My own weight had begun to drop – as Dr Richter had predicted – now I was on the new meds, but it was happening slowly. Next to Miranda I looked frumpy and awful, the dress bulging in all the wrong places. I couldn't believe that a moment ago I'd actually thought it looked good.

I saw Miranda looking at my reflection doubtfully. 'Ew, that dress is not right, is it?' she said. 'If you were a bit … Well, never mind. It was fun trying it on anyway, wasn't it? So, be honest. What do you think of it on me?'

'It makes you look amazing,' I said, edging back towards the soup can. I couldn't wait to get back into my uniform.

Miranda stopped twirling. 'No. I make *it* look amazing. Without me it'd just be a shapeless piece of material.' She twirled. 'Do you think Dallas will like it?'

I knew what my Magic 8 Ball would've said. 'Nothing is surer.'

'Right then. I'll take it,' said Miranda.

'You're kidding right? It'll cost a fortune.'

'I've got money,' said Miranda. 'Oona's always leaving her purse lying around.'

I looked at her carefully. Another joke? I couldn't tell.

'I'll get one for you too,' she added. 'It might motivate you to get into shape.'

'No thanks,' I said quickly. 'I'd never wear it.'

But Miranda had already started dancing back into her changing can by then. I wasn't sure if she'd even heard me. I got back inside my own can.

Once I'd changed I wandered out into the shop, doing my best to rearrange the dress properly on the hanger. Then I looked around. Miranda was standing with her back to me, watching the birds in the aviary. She was back in her uniform and there was no sign of the black dress. Some of the birds were on the floor of the cage, pecking at seeds, but most of them were huddled together on a branch, feathers fluffed up miserably. Several of them were tugging with their beaks or claws at the ribbons around their necks.

'It must suck being stuck in there with a big stupid bow around your neck,' said Miranda as I came up beside her. She sounded sad. 'Would *you* want to be in there?' she said. 'For a bunch of people to gawp at?'

I shook my head. 'Nope.'

'Me neither,' said Miranda. She glanced around the room with a look that I was beginning to recognise. The one that meant she was up to something. 'When I say *run*,' she murmured, 'Run. OK?'

'Run where?' I said.

But Miranda's hand was already on the handle of the aviary door, twisting it sharply. The next thing I knew, the cage door had swung open and the air around us whirled with grey and silver streaks and the sound of beating wings. It was so loud that it completely drowned out everything else – the sudden surprise and alarm of the other guests, the DJ's beats. Somehow, though, Miranda's voice managed to penetrate the chaos.

'Run!'

We took off out the door and pushed our way through the crowd in the street until we were around the corner. I was pretty sure no-one had followed us, but Miranda kept running and so I ran too. I felt strong suddenly, like I could run forever. We raced along the streets, dodging pedestrians, ignoring red lights, weaving between the cars.

'Stop!' I finally gasped, leaning against a wall.

Miranda wasn't even puffed. She started laughing. 'That was so freakin great!'

I laughed too – almost uncontrollably. I was stuffed but I felt elated too. *Do something that scares you. Because it scares you.* I'd thought that was the biggest cliché ever when Dr Richter had said that. But I was starting to understand what she meant.

'Imagine what it looks like in the shop right now,' said Miranda. 'Imagine that guard stomping around, trying to catch doves. All those beautiful people trying to avoid being shat on.'

I giggled. Then Miranda giggled. And that was it. We were gone again – laughing like we'd never stop.

o

We spent the rest of the day exploring, trying to go to as many places as we could before heading home. It might sound weird to explore a place you already know, but the city suddenly felt foreign to me. Not in a bad way though. I felt light and sort of fizzy as we wandered around, pointing things out to each other, chatting. The only time we stopped talking was when we were laughing – which we did a lot. All it took was Miranda waddling after some birds to get us both cracking up, almost doubled over, clutching our stomachs.

'Where's somewhere you've always wanted to go to around here?' Miranda suddenly asked me.

At first I couldn't think of anywhere – all the places I wanted to visit were overseas. But as we walked around I started thinking of buildings I'd only seen from the outside. Ones I'd passed by and wondered what they looked like inside.

I suggested the old ballroom in the dome of Central Station. I picked it because I was sure Miranda couldn't get us in. The ballroom had been closed to the public for years because of safety issues. But I'd underestimated Miranda. She convinced the stationmaster to let us in the dome by telling him we were doing a history assignment for school. She pulled out some crazy facts about the station that I assumed were made up, until I saw the stationmaster nodding his head. *Yes, that's right.* By the end of their chat I think he would've cut her a set of keys to the ballroom if she'd asked.

After that, we wandered around again until we found ourselves in another alley filled with tiny art galleries – the sort I'd never normally go into for fear of crashing into some million-dollar vase or something. Miranda stopped in front of one and looked through the window. It was empty except for a tall guy with dark, curly hair sitting at a desk, reading a book. From what I could see the paintings on display were all almost identical: a young woman whose face was framed by short red hair, her eyes looking directly at you. There must have been a hundred of them – some very small, some huge – taking up every centimetre of wall space.

'Let's go in,' said Miranda, pushing open the door. 'It's probably rubbish but we'll look anyway.'

It was unnerving standing in the gallery, surrounded by all those faces.

'If I was that girl I'd be keeping away from the painter,' I whispered to Miranda. 'Seems a bit obsessed.' I looked around. 'Do you think that's the artist over there?' He looked cute, but kind of intense.

'Yes,' said Miranda. 'That's him.'

The guy looked up from his book when Miranda spoke, and an expression of utter amazement appeared on his face.

'He obviously hasn't had many visitors so far,' I joked.

Then the guy rose from his chair and ran over to us, wild-eyed and talking to Miranda rapidly in what sounded like Spanish.

Miranda stood there for a moment. Then she shook her head. 'I'm sorry,' she said firmly. 'I don't understand you.'

The guy grabbed her hand, holding it to his chest and talking. Miranda pulled her hand away. 'I don't understand,' she repeated. 'You've mixed me up with someone else.'

The guy crumpled then, his face confused.

Miranda glanced at me sideways. 'Let's go,' she said. Outside, she exhaled loudly. 'You would not *believe* how often things like that happen to me.'

'He looked so crazy,' I said, unable to hide my fascination.

'I wonder what he was saying.'

'He was saying that all the paintings were of me,' said Miranda. 'Every one of them was a "tribute to my beauty".' She laughed. 'Pity they were *de mierda*.'

'You *understood* him?' I exclaimed, trying and failing to hide how impressed I was.

'Of course,' said Miranda. 'I lived in Spain with an uncle.'

The town hall clock chimed two. 'We should head home,' I said. There was no way we were going to make it to any afternoon classes of course, but I needed to get back before Mum got suspicious.

Miranda held up a finger. 'One more place,' she said.

She led me to this high-end hotel perched at the top of the city. It was a place I remember going past as a kid, desperately wishing I could go in. It had looked like a palace to me, with its carved stonework and gleaming bronze door handles.

The doorman nodded politely and held open the door for us. We stepped into a corridor lined with framed photos. To the right was a room filled with tables and chairs made of dark wood with brass claws on the end of each leg. A fire blazed. Except for an old man asleep in the corner, the place was deserted.

The waiter came over as we sat down. 'I'll have hot chocolate,' I said, but Miranda frowned.

'Don't be dumb, Samantha,' she said. 'We always have coffee.'

'Sorry, Penelope,' I said with a straight face. 'I forgot.'

'Put it on my father's tab,' Miranda instructed. 'Mr Kramer-Berkell.'

The waiter nodded. I managed to keep it together until after he'd disappeared.

'Did you also once know a man called Mr Kramer-Berkell? Let me guess. He died from the malaria he contracted while on safari.'

'No, I don't know any Kramer-Berkells,' grinned Miranda. 'The name just sounded right.'

When the coffees arrived I took a sip, not wanting to look stupid in front of Miranda. It was bitter and milky and hot. I remembered something. 'You didn't get a date outfit.'

Miranda sipped her coffee like an expert. 'Yes I did.'

I saw something poking out of the corner of Miranda's school bag then. Something black and shiny. 'You bought the dress?'

Miranda lifted a hand and wiggled the fingers like a spider. 'Nah, I used the old five-finger discount instead.'

'You *stole* it?'

Miranda sighed and dumped the dress on the table. Like I'd just ruined something. 'Don't freak out, you big square,' she said. 'It's fine. The head designer at Silver – Leon – is a friend of mine. I modelled for him for free when the label was just starting out. He told me I could have whatever I liked as payment.'

I'd only had a tiny sip of coffee, but my head was already buzzing. Maybe Miranda *had* worked as a model. Maybe she *did* know the head designer at Silver. It didn't seem totally impossible. 'Why didn't you tell me you knew the designer while we were in the shop?'

Miranda pushed her coffee away. 'Oh I don't know,' she

said crossly. 'Because it was more fun not to, I suppose. You do know about *fun*, don't you, Olive? It's that thing everyone else is having. Everyone except you.'

That stung, and the pain stayed with me even as Miranda's face softened. I had been having a good time with her – really. For several whole hours I'd been able to forget about Ami and Katie and Lachlan and the mess that was my life.

Miranda shoved the dress back in her bag then did up the zip, pulling it so quickly that it snared the fabric.

'Careful!' I said. 'You'll tear it.'

'Doesn't matter,' said Miranda. 'I've changed my mind about wearing it anyway.' She dumped the bag on the floor.

I fiddled with my spoon. The anaesthetic from the day's fun was wearing off now and I found myself missing Ami. Maybe it was because I hadn't thought of her for a few hours but the ache felt more intense than it had been for some weeks. I longed to be at home, curled up in my tent, listening to music.

Then Miranda sat up, her sulky expression gone. 'I know,' she said excitedly. 'I can borrow something of yours.'

'You're not serious, are you?' I said, surprised. 'All my stuff comes from the op shop.'

'You big wonk, that's called *vintage* now,' said Miranda. 'And you've got a great eye for it. Your look – well, it's unique. I like that.'

I could see Miranda's face in the handle of my spoon, her expression eager. 'I mean, I understand if you feel funny about me borrowing anything ...'

'It's no problem,' I said. To be honest I felt flattered that Miranda actually wanted to wear my things. Honoured, even. 'Do you want to come back to my place?'

Miranda did baby-claps. 'That would be *so* great!' she said. 'Now, are you ready to run again? They've probably figured out by now that the Kramer-Berkell tab doesn't exist ...'

NINETEEN

Miranda's *up* mood continued all the way home. She kept me entertained by doing imitations of the people sitting around us – the woman who kept sniffing and dabbing her nose with a disgusting hankie, the old man muttering to himself, the guy whose head was falling forward as he nodded off to sleep – until I ached from the effort of holding in my laughter. I was so distracted by her kidding around that it wasn't until we were on my street that my nerves kicked in. How would Toby react to Miranda? And what would Miranda think of my kooky mum? It could be a huge disaster.

'Our place is pretty messy and disorganised,' I said.

Miranda snorted. 'Wait till you see Oona's place.'

'Also, my little brother gets a bit shy around people he doesn't know,' I said. 'Don't take it personally. Oh and whatever you do, don't swear in front of my mum. She hates it. Even "bitch" sends her over the edge.'

Miranda draped her arm across my shoulder. 'Don't worry,' she said. 'I'm not going to sneer at your house or tease your brother. And I'm definitely not going to call anyone a bitch, OK? We'll get along fine. Just wait and see.'

Mum was doing a yoga stretch at the kitchen bench when we came in. If she was surprised to see Miranda Vaile – the girl I'd been *bullying* – she didn't show it. She just straightened up and said hi in this very casual way, like me bringing friends home was a regular occurrence. Then Miranda did an equally impressive job of admiring our ramshackle, disorganised house and Mum's collection of *world ornaments* – the sort of things that people buy when holidaying in exotic places, except that Mum hadn't actually been anywhere. She just bought things online.

'I'm sure you lived in some really amazing places when you were in Europe,' said Mum. 'Can you speak any other languages?' This was one of my mum's biggest dreams and she had a whole shelf devoted to language CDs, dictionaries and teach-yourself books. Not that she ever found time to use them. I looked at them way more than she did.

'Yes,' said Miranda. 'What would you like to hear?'

'Oh, just say whatever you like,' said Mum, flapping her hands. 'I won't understand it anyway.'

'No,' said Miranda patiently. 'I meant what *language* would you like to hear?'

Mum pressed her fingers together. 'Which is your favourite? You choose,' she said in this hushed voice.

'It depends,' said Miranda. 'I like explaining things in

German but I always daydream in French.'

Mum's eyes went all soft. 'Who wouldn't daydream in French,' she said, 'if they could?' The oven timer buzzed and Mum grabbed a wooden spoon. 'Are you joining us for dinner, Miranda? It's pumpkin and fava-bean stew.'

Miranda shook her head politely. 'Thanks,' she said, 'but I'm going out tonight.'

'Oh, what a shame,' said Mum. 'I had so many more things to ask you. How do you like the school?'

Miranda glanced at me and smiled. 'Well, it's way better now that I'm friends with Olive.'

I saw Mum's expression shift. It was only a small change – one that most people wouldn't have even noticed. But I knew what it meant. Miranda couldn't have said anything to make Mum happier.

The kitchen door swung back and Toby rushed in with Ralph galloping along behind. 'Olive!' said Toby breathlessly. 'Guess what I've taught Ralph to –' He stopped short when he spotted Miranda.

'Toby,' I said. 'This is Miranda. From school.'

Without saying a word, Toby turned and dashed back out again, Ralph following.

'Whoa,' said Miranda. 'He *is* shy.'

'Sorry about that,' I said. 'Hang on. I'll go and sort it out.'

I found Toby in our watermelon-slaughter corner, hunched up, head on his knees. Ralphy was snuffling around, chewing on old rinds.

Toby looked up at me as I came close, his eyes wide with alarm. 'Why is *she* here?' he whispered. 'She's the shapeshifter!'

I sat down beside him, between the dried remains of watermelons gone by. 'Tobes, there's no such thing as a shapeshifter. It was just a dumb thing I believed when my medication wasn't right.'

'Are you *friends* with her now or something?' said Toby, accusingly. 'It looks like you are.'

I thought about this. Were we friends? I still wasn't sure I trusted Miranda, but I'd had a great day with her. The best in a long time. I suddenly felt annoyed with Toby, like he was trying to take something from me. 'Miranda's just come over to borrow some clothes,' I said, straightening up. 'It's no big deal, Tobes.'

'You're not supposed to give her your things!' he said anxiously. 'That's how she'll *get* you. That's what you said!'

I brushed off some watermelon pips from my jeans, deeply regretting that I'd ever told him anything about shifters. 'She's not going to *get* me,' I said. 'You have to forget all that. Now come in and be nice. Or I'll never play kill-the-watermelon again.'

I held out my hand. For a moment Toby just sat there, not moving, but then he stood up. He refused to hold my hand but he followed me back inside.

When we came back into the kitchen, Mum was showing Miranda her *Cooking with Root Vegetables* cookbook. Somehow Miranda had managed to stay awake and keep smiling.

'Toby's got something to say,' I said.

'Hello,' mumbled Toby, trying to drill his shoe into the kitchen tiles. '*Verynicetomeetyou.*'

Miranda came over and squatted down next to Ralph. 'Who's this?' she asked, holding her hand out towards our dog, who sniffed at it gingerly, his tail and ears down.

Toby gave me an agonised look. *Go on*, I urged him with my eyes.

'Ralph,' muttered Toby.

'He looks smart,' said Miranda. It was obviously a lie and I could tell that Toby hadn't fallen for it, but he nodded tightly. I decided it was time to let him off the hook.

I turned to Miranda. 'Ready to look for clothes?'

o

When we first got to my room, Miranda spent ages just walking around – examining every ornament, every detail.

'I haven't seen one of these for ages!' she said, picking up my Magic 8 Ball and shaking it. 'Will Olive and I be friends forever?' she intoned dramatically.

There was that word again. *Friends.* It sounded less weird every time I heard it but there was something about it that niggled at me. Maybe it made me feel guilty – that I was somehow betraying Ami.

Miranda smiled as she watched the answer appear. 'All signs point to yes.'

'How about asking it what you should borrow for your date?' I said.

Miranda dropped the 8 Ball on my bed and went over to the wardrobe. 'I don't need a toy to tell me that,' she said, flinging the doors open. She went through my stuff methodically – taking an item out, examining it with an expert eye and then returning it to the wardrobe.

Eventually she held up the skirt that I'd worn on the first night of the Retro Horror Film-Fest. 'Now *this* is lush,' she pronounced.

'Really?' I said. 'I thought I was the only person in the world who would like that skirt.'

'The wonks around here wouldn't have a clue. Take it from me, this is a classic piece.' Miranda examined the label. 'You'd get a heap for it on eBay.'

'I knew it!' I said.

'Uh-oh,' said Miranda, hand covering her mouth. 'I shouldn't have said that. You won't lend it to me now, will you?'

'Sure I will. So long as you don't sell it,' I said, grinning. 'But it's going to be too big for you.'

'I can pin it,' said Miranda. 'It's perfect.'

She found a couple of other things she liked – a stretchy top to go with the skirt, and a necklace I'd made myself out of a couple of broken bracelets. I put on some music and stretched out on the cushions on the floor while she rifled, feeling something I hadn't felt in ages. Happy. I mean, I'd often felt happy when I hung out with Ami, but this was different. Ami *had* to like me, after all. Miranda didn't. If anything, she had lots of reasons *not* to like me – after what I accused her of. Yet here we were, getting along better and better. And it all felt so normal.

'What's this?' asked Miranda, holding up a bundle wrapped in a scarf.

I stared, breath catching in my throat. My Proof. How had she found it? I thought I'd hidden so carefully. 'Put that down!'

The sharpness of my voice made Miranda jump and the bundle came apart in her hands. The contents tumbled to the floor – things I hadn't looked at in months. Photos of my family having a picnic on the beach last summer. The dog-eared card with the picture of the little girl holding a basket of flowers. *You're Five Today!* A charm bracelet that had fallen free of the crumpled pink T-shirt I'd wrapped it in.

Miranda bent down and began picking up the things one by one, turning them over in her hands. 'What *is* this stuff?'

'Nothing,' I snapped. I wanted to snatch everything away from her and hold it all to my chest. The old feelings surged upwards, threatening to spill over.

Miranda opened the card and I felt that I could hear the words in my head as she read them silently. *Happy birthday, Pet. I love you more than you'll ever know.*

She picked up the bracelet next. It twinkled as she turned it around in the light. 'This is so pretty. You should wear it.'

I shook my head. 'No. I can't.' It's not a good idea to wear things that make you cry.

Miranda's eyes turned to mine. 'It's from your dad, isn't it?'

'He *did* love me you know,' I said fiercely. 'Once. These things prove it.'

Miranda laid the bracelet down. 'Of course he did.' Her voice was soft and soothing. 'Was he …' she hesitated. 'Was it because he left that you – you know – made that suicide attempt?'

My *attempt*. That was how the doctors always described it. It hadn't felt to me like I'd been attempting anything. It felt like the opposite. I fiddled with my sleeve.

I'd done a great job of hiding the anger and depression. I worked hard at making it look like my life was the same happy, shiny thing that everyone had always admired. Beautiful, popular, clever little Olive. But inside, I didn't feel like that. And the more time that passed, the more I felt like I was a fraud. Playing the part of someone I wasn't. It was terrifying – if I wasn't the person everyone thought I was, then who was I?

At school I managed – *just* – to keep the illusion going that nothing had changed. But at home it was impossible. The black, angry feelings would swell up inside me as I walked through the front door and some evenings I could barely speak. Mum just kept pushing vitamins into me and pretending it was all fine. But not Dad. I could tell that I was letting him down. By the time he left, he wouldn't even look me in the eye.

'It happened not long after Dad left,' I heard myself say to Miranda. 'He went without saying goodbye and I knew it was because of me. I felt like – such a failure.'

Miranda nodded sympathetically and suddenly it was all blurting out of me – everything that had happened that morning on the beach. I told her about how the old Olive used to head to the beach most mornings with Ralph for a run and, if it was warm enough, a swim. That morning had started the way it always did – or at least that's how it would've looked to anyone else. Trackpants and T-shirt on. The run down to the beach. My towel – stretched out neatly on the sand like I had every intention of coming back to it. Then I scratched Ralphie's ears, told him he was the best dog ever and strode into the water. When it was deep enough, I let the water pick me up and carry me off.

It was all so gentle – that's what I explained to Miranda. No fighting the current. Just going with it. My plan was to let the ocean draw me out further and further. I figured that either my water-logged clothes or the exhaustion would pull me down. I didn't think it would take very long. I felt like I was half-drowned already.

But the ocean rejected me. Instead of pulling me under, it kept pushing me back towards the shore. And on the beach Ralph went nuts, barking and barking. Even though it was probably the seaweed monsters and not me he was barking at, he still managed to alert a group of surfers. I suppose they thought they were *saving* me when they dragged me out.

I was admitted to the clinic straight away, put on twenty-four-hour surveillance because I was *a danger to myself* and forced to go to therapy session after therapy session to talk about my feelings. I was there for weeks. Dad never once came to visit me, even though I'm sure Mum would have told him what I'd done. That's what hurt the most – that he couldn't even bring himself to come and see me after I'd done the worst thing you could do.

After I'd finished explaining all this, Miranda and I sat there on my floor for ages. She didn't try to say any of the things people usually said – about what a tragedy it would've been if I'd succeeded and how I had so much to live for. She just sat there, silently absorbing it. Eventually she picked up one of the photos – me, Toby and Mum at the beach, arms around each other, smiling. Even Ralph's big hairy head had squeezed in there.

'Your dad's not in this one,' she said.

I pointed to a blurry shape in the bottom left corner of the photo. 'That's his thumb,' I said. 'He took the shot.' And I started laughing because I suddenly realised how ridiculous it was to keep a photo of someone's thumb. Miranda smiled but she didn't laugh. She continued to stare at the photo for a long time. 'You're lucky to have all this,' she said. 'I don't have anything to remember my parents. Everything was lost when I started being shunted around from relative to relative.'

I picked up a cushion and hugged it to my chest, feeling suddenly guilty. I shouldn't have snapped at Miranda before. I wasn't the only person who'd had bad stuff happen. 'How many people have you lived with?'

'God knows,' said Miranda bitterly. 'I stopped counting. I'd just get settled with a new lot when suddenly I'd be told to start packing again.'

'But why?' I said.

Miranda exhaled slowly. 'I guess I was a handful. Hard to control. I played tricks to try and get people's attention and they always took it the wrong way – like I was *evil* or something.

Passing me on was the easiest option.'

'I was a handful too, as a kid,' I said. 'According to Mum. I think that's why there's such a huge age gap between me and Toby.'

'The difference is your mum *loved* you,' said Miranda. At some point while I'd been talking she'd moved without me noticing, so that now she was positioned right in front of me on the rug. 'Unlike the people who got lumped with me. I tried really hard at first. To make them like me, I mean. Finally I realised what a waste of time it was. So I gave up.' Miranda was untangling the tassels of the rug with her fingers as she spoke, straightening them out strand by strand. As she did, I glimpsed a row of dark red scars along her forearm.

'Oh, Miranda,' I said, my breath catching in my throat. I remembered that day outside the Mercury with the heavy rain and the make-up on her arm. 'That must have sucked.'

Miranda's face had darkened. 'Do you know what it's like as a six-year-old to realise that your supposed guardians are *afraid* of you?' she spat. 'It makes you *despise* them. It makes you want to hurt them, and the things they love.'

Down the hallway in the kitchen I could hear Mum and Toby getting things ready for dinner. The clink of bowls, the metallic ting of cutlery. 'Why were they afraid?'

Miranda's eyes, when they met mine, were stones. 'Because I killed my parents,' she said.

My heart leapt. *Miranda Vaile the parent-murderer.* That old rumour, from so long ago.

'But weren't you just a little kid?' I said, trying to sound calm. 'Didn't they die in a car accident?'

She's kidding, I thought, willing Miranda's face to break into a sudden grin. For her to tease me for falling for another joke. Because if that was true – if she had murdered her parents after all – what else might be?

Miranda's expression didn't change. 'I remember the accident,' she said. 'Even though I was only two. We'd just driven past a playground with a slide shaped like an elephant. I was desperate to play on it but my parents wouldn't stop. I screamed and screamed. I felt so angry, strapped in my car seat like that – and I wanted to hurt them. I remember willing the car to stop, willing it with all my might. And then it did stop … by crashing into a tree.' Miranda's face was grey. 'They both died instantly.'

I reached out my hand. 'Miranda, that wasn't your fault.'

'Wasn't it?' she said savagely. 'My relatives all think it was. One uncle used to love telling me that my tantrum had distracted my dad and that's why he drove off the road. They were always so thrilled to get rid of me – passing me around like a virus until Oona finally agreed to take me in. But who knows how long I'll survive at her place.'

'It must be pretty interesting living with Oona,' I said, picturing her strange, fortress-like house perched up on the hill. This was my attempt to change the conversation. To move on to less painful stuff.

Miranda snorted. 'Interesting? It's like trying to breathe with a pillow held over your face.'

'Well, you're welcome over here any time,' I said, and instantly felt stupid. It had sounded a bit wonkish. But Miranda raised her head and I was surprised by how thrilled she looked.

'Really?' she said. 'You really mean that?'

'Of course,' I found myself saying. 'Come over any time you want.'

Miranda wiped the tears away and smiled. When I've been teary it takes ages for my face to return to normal. But a second later you couldn't tell Miranda had been crying at all.

'Thanks,' she said. 'You've got no idea how much that means to me.'

Mum's voice wafted down the hall, along with the smell of overcooked pumpkin. 'Dinner!'

'I better go,' I said, standing up. 'That stew is worse when it's cold. Anyway, you should get ready for your date. Can't wait to hear about it tomorrow.'

Miranda nodded. 'Let me just get myself together. And my things.' She put the clothes she was borrowing in her bag, and then wrapped up all my bits of Proof in the scarf and handed them back. 'Thanks, Olive,' she said, giving me a goodbye hug.

Near the door she hesitated. 'I know this will probably sound weird,' she said, 'but I feel like we've got some kind of *connection*. Because of the stuff we've both been through. It's like I can talk to you, tell you stuff, that I wouldn't trust anyone else with.' She chewed on her thumbnail and gave an embarrassed little smile. 'It's like we *get* each other or something.'

And the weird thing was, I felt exactly the same way.

TWENTY

Miranda turned up at school the next morning, dressed not in her uniform but in my skirt and top. *Something's happened*, I thought. There was something spacey about her, like she wasn't all there.

'Olive!' she said, nearly knocking me over with her hug. People walked past, staring. But Miranda didn't seem to notice. 'I just have to tell you about my lush date! You would've seriously loved it.' She looked so happy that it made me smile too.

'Where did you go?'

'We went into town and saw a gig,' said Miranda. She patted her cheek. 'What was he called? Elliott Furphy? Have you heard of him?'

'You saw *Elliot Furphy* play?' I said. 'At the Vault? That's been sold out for months.'

Miranda shrugged. 'Dallas is friends with Elli. We got in for free.'

'Oh,' I said, feeling a stab of jealousy. 'Right.' Of *course* Dallas would be friends with Elliot Furphy. Of *course* Miranda would see his band play for free. 'Was it good?'

'I didn't pay much attention,' giggled Miranda. 'I was a bit distracted by Dallas. He's so *incredible*, Olive. Look at my hands. They won't stop trembling.' She held her hands out. They looked pretty steady to me, although I did notice Miranda seemed to have picked up a bad habit of mine – chewing her fingernails.

'Sounds like it was a great date,' I said.

'It's *still* a great date! We've been up all night and we're going to hang out today.' She smirked at me. 'Jealous much?'

'That's why you're not in your uniform,' I said. 'I'm not sure how you're going to get away with skipping two days of school in a row though. What do you want me to tell Mrs Deane if she asks?'

Miranda was frowning at me. 'I asked you a *question*. Are you jealous of me?'

I laughed. 'Of course I am! Who wouldn't be?'

Miranda smiled, satisfied. 'I've gotta go. Dallas is waiting.' She turned to go, but then stopped. 'Hey, are you free tonight?'

I wasn't. Once a month Mum drove interstate to pick up supplies. She usually left one evening and came back late the following night. 'I have to look after Toby.'

Miranda wrinkled her nose. 'What a shame,' she said. 'We're going to see Elliot again tonight. It's the last gig – I thought you'd like to come.'

'Really?' I said. 'You think Dallas could get me in?'

'We already have your ticket,' said Miranda.

I sighed deeply. 'I wish I could.'

Miranda nodded sympathetically. 'Well, at least you'll earn some money, I guess,' she said.

'I don't get paid for babysitting Toby,' I said, laughing.

Miranda's eyebrows shot up. 'Wow,' she said. 'No offence, but it sounds like your mum is taking advantage of you.'

'It's no big deal,' I said. But Miranda had a point. I was doing Mum a pretty huge favour. And I did mind Toby a lot.

Miranda shrugged. 'Look, it'd be cool if you came. If you change your mind – or if your mum realises that she's asking too much – Dallas is picking me up at Oona's around nine.'

o

I felt grouchy and restless for the rest of the day, unable even to pretend that I was concentrating on school. The grouchiness only increased when I got home. Dinner was spinach and quinoa lasagne. *It'd be nice if we got some meat occasionally*, I thought grumpily, pushing my food around. *Just because she's vegetarian, why should we have to be?*

Mum gave me a concerned look. 'You don't seem a hundred per cent,' she said, that familiar look of worry on her face. 'Maybe I should cancel the trip.'

'Don't be crazy,' I said in a monotone. I wasn't in the mood to mollycoddle her tonight. 'You go.'

I thought that after she'd left, I'd accept that I'd missed out on the gig. But the irritation just grew. I bustled Toby off to bed way earlier than usual and then stomped off to my room, planning to do some homework and drown my sorrows by listening to music.

But my mind refused to think about French grammar and the music just made me more stir-crazy than ever.

Then a thought appeared from nowhere. *Why not just go to the gig? Toby's asleep. He'll be fine.* Once the idea had wormed its way into my head I couldn't seem to lose it. It grew stronger. *Why should you always miss out? You deserve some fun.*

I crept to Toby's room and peeked in. He looked so totally out of it that I felt sure he wouldn't stir until morning. I checked the time on my phone. Ten to nine. I'd have to hurry if I was going to make it to Miranda's place on time.

○

Maybe it was the excitement that made me ride up the hill so fast that night. Or maybe it was guilt. Whatever the reason, I was pressing the buzzer outside Oona's front gate just a few minutes after nine. Nothing happened. The massive security gates didn't budge and the front door didn't open.

The disappointment sat like a rock in my stomach. *They've gone already.*

Olive the Loser, missing out yet again. I was turning to head home when the front door swung open and the security lights flicked on, flooding the yard with an almost blinding light. Someone came trotting across the front yard towards me. Not Miranda, though. Oona. I froze, unsure what to do.

At the gate she stopped and peered at me – eyes shiny and dark as a bird's. 'Are you the new one?' she said. 'Miranda's latest friend?'

'Hello, Miss Delaunay,' I said, a little taken aback. 'It's Olive Corbett.'

Oona showed no sign of recognising me – either from the time I'd given her my umbrella or the countless occasions when I'd stood at her gates while Mum handed her vitamin pills through the bars. I wished I'd called Miranda's phone instead of ringing the buzzer. It didn't look like Oona was planning to let me in.

'Is – is Miranda around?'

Oona's eyes darted around. 'Luckily she's still inside,' she said, her voice dropping to a whisper. 'I must talk to you. Quickly.'

'Is it about your vitamin order?' I said. 'Mum's picking up some new supplies tomorrow. If you call her –'

'It's not about vitamins,' Oona snapped at me. 'It's about Miranda. I'm very concerned. She's in danger of – '

'Miranda's OK, Miss Delaunay,' I interrupted, trying to sound reassuring. 'You don't need to be so … protective of her.' *Like trying to breathe with a pillow over your face.* That's how Miranda had described life with Oona.

'You've misunderstood me,' said Oona tersely. 'Miranda is in danger of hurting *others*. I'm trying to protect people *from* her. You in particular.'

I stopped short and Oona smiled thinly.

'You're paying attention at last. I can see that you're strong, which is good. But you are certainly still at risk.' Her fingers gripped the bars of the gate and her voice dropped until it was almost impossible to hear at all. 'I should've taken her on earlier of course,' she muttered. Was she talking to me or herself? 'Things might have been easier if I had. She's so damaged now, and so stubborn. She ignores all my advice. Won't wear gloves. Continues to befriend people even though I forbade it.'

When Oona looked to me again her eyes were clear and she suddenly didn't look mad at all. 'Go home, Olive,' she commanded. 'Do you understand me? You must go immediately. Stay away from her. Keep everything you love away from her too. If you knew – if you saw what she did at that last place.' Oona looked stricken then, like she was remembering something awful. 'That poor, poor boy,' she whispered.

I gaped at her, not quite knowing what to do.

Oona was watching me. 'You don't believe me, do you?' she sighed. 'Of course not. I know what you all call me. I might be *loony* but I'm not deaf.'

There was a mechanical click then, and the gate began to swing open. A figure emerged through the glare of the security lights, storming towards us. 'Oona,' snarled Miranda. 'What are you doing?'

Oona's scrawny arm reached through the bars as the gate began to push her back. Her fingers clawed at me. 'Don't let her cut you off from your friends and family,' she whispered. 'It's *very* important.'

Miranda loomed up behind Oona. 'Let go of her.'

231

Oona's fingers dropped from my arm. Then she fled back into the house. I stood still as Miranda stepped through the gap in the gate, seething. 'She's got no right to interfere,' she stormed. 'What does she know? *Nothing.*'

'Don't worry,' I said, laughing nervously. 'I didn't take it seriously. It was funny.' I was trying to calm Miranda down of course, but I also didn't want to admit to myself just how unnerved Oona had left me.

There was a sudden rumble of an engine and a car pulled into the driveway, stopping right where we were standing. The anger lifted from Miranda's face immediately. 'Dallas!'

I felt hugely relieved too when I saw his friendly face through the windscreen.

Dallas rolled down the driver's seat window and poked his head through. 'Hi!' he said cheerfully. 'Climb aboard. I've got some killer tunes to play along the way. And I've got a surprise for you too.'

Miranda skipped around to sit in front with Dallas. I opened the back door and almost climbed into someone's lap. Lachlan's.

Miranda took one look at him and glared at Dallas. 'Why is he here?'

'Surprise!' said Dallas, oblivious to Miranda's anger. 'I invited him, although I think he only came to keep an eye on me. It's that lifesaver instinct coming out.'

Lachlan laughed. 'I'm off-duty tonight,' he said. 'You can look after yourself, Dal.'

He shuffled over then, giving me room to get in. The car

had a dry, sweetish smell, like hay, and the cracked vinyl seats snagged on my clothes as I slid into the car. I groped around for the seatbelt.

'No seatbelt, sorry,' said Lachlan. 'Better hang on. Dallas drives like a fiend.'

Sure enough, as we swung around a bend I found myself sliding across the seat until I was pressed against Lachlan. 'Sorry,' I said, moving back to my side as fast as I could.

'No problem,' said Lachlan softly.

'Hey, little Ol,' called Dallas from the front. 'Do you know this band?'

'The Ben-Day Dots,' I said, listening. 'First album.'

Dallas chuckled. 'How does a kid like you know about The Ben-Day Dots?'

'Well, because of Magenta Men,' I said. 'I read this interview where they mentioned –'

'Hey, Dal,' said Miranda suddenly. 'Did I tell you that story about the secret Boxers gig I saw in Paris?'

'You saw the *Boxers?*' said Dallas, turning back to her.

Instantly I was forgotten. And with no other distractions – except to hang on as we screeched around corners – I found myself wondering over and over what Lachlan Ford was doing there. I tried to feed myself the obvious answers. *He's here to spend time with his brother. It's nothing to do with you.* But my mind kept shooting off in sideways directions, imagining what would happen if I let my fingers slip out of the door handle so that I'd slide over and crash into him again. And if instead of apologising and moving away, I stayed where I was. Would he put his arm around me? Would he pull me closer?

By the time we pulled up outside the Vault, my nerves were jangling like wind chimes. I stumbled getting out of the car and almost landed in the gutter.

Miranda pulled me up, laughing. 'What's wrong with you, wonk-brain?' she said.

'Car sick,' I mumbled, and began walking over to join the end of the queue outside the Vault.

'What are you doing?' asked Miranda. 'We're guests of the band.' As the bouncer waved us through, she whispered in my ear, 'You'll be treated like a nobody if you act like one.'

The Vault was already pretty full and people were crowding into the main bar. 'Let's go in,' said Dallas. 'Wrangle our way up the front.'

'We're going to the toilets first,' said Miranda, grabbing my hand.

'Don't be long,' called Dallas.

In the brightly lit bathroom, I noticed something different about Miranda. 'You've had a haircut.'

Miranda ran her fingers lightly across her fringe. 'I did it myself. It's a bit zig-zaggy, like yours. Do you like it?'

I nodded, and then saw the top she was wearing. 'Hang on, isn't that *mine*?'

'Well yeah,' laughed Miranda. 'You lent it to me.'

'I didn't lend you that one,' I said.

Miranda inspected herself in the mirror. 'Does it matter?

We're friends, right?' Then she sighed. 'God. I look like such a wreck. I've had no sleep at all.'

'You look amazing, Miranda,' I said. And it was true. I would never be able to wear that top again now I'd seen how good it looked on her.

'That's because I'm in love,' said Miranda, stretching her arms up above her head. *'Love, love, love.'* The dreamy look on her face worried me.

'Um … Miranda?' I said. 'You do know that Dallas won't be staying in Jubilee Park forever, don't you? Maybe you should – you know – try not to get in too deep too quickly.'

Miranda threw me a pitying look. 'You're *so* jealous.'

'It's not that,' I said, feeling annoyed. 'I just think you should be careful. Protect yourself. Otherwise your heart will be broken when he goes.'

Miranda shook her head. 'He's not going anywhere,' she said. 'I'm going to make him stay.' She opened her bag and took out a lipstick.

'You're joking, right?' I said. 'He can't stay here.'

'Why not?' said Miranda, her mouth the shape of a kiss as she leant forward to colour it in. 'There's a studio near us he can hire out by the hour. Dallas has a bunch of new songs he can record there. I know some industry people. Once they hear the new songs, they'll be fighting over who gets to sign Luxe up.'

Miranda seemed so confident. Like she *could* actually make these things happen. She clicked the lipstick closed and smiled at me, her lips slick. 'Ready?'

I swallowed, trying to squash down the uneasiness. 'Sure.'

Dallas beamed at Miranda when we returned. He and Lachlan were standing together. Miranda went straight up to Dallas and wrapped her arms tightly around him. I stared at the space beside Lachlan, heart quickening. I could just walk up beside him, über casual. Like it was no big deal. Stand next to him for the entire gig – the warmth of his arm near mine in the dark, our fingers almost touching.

'Olive!' Miranda said impatiently. 'What are you doing standing over there?' She pulled me over, away from Lachlan. I glanced at him – I don't know why. Maybe I was hoping he'd say or do something to intervene. But he didn't. *Admit it, Olive,* I told myself. *He's over you.*

As the band came on stage, Miranda flung one arm around me and the other around Dallas, pulling us in tightly towards her and away from Lachlan, who was left standing on his own. 'I am so glad we've found each other,' she said. 'The three of us are going to have *so* much fun together. I can just feel it.'

TWENTY-ONE

That night was the start of it, I guess – that crazy, weird, scary time. It began fairly slowly – every few nights I'd wait until Mum and Toby had gone to bed and then I'd sneak out my window to find a taxi or Dallas's car waiting around the corner. I'd climb in and we'd head off. Me, Dallas and Miranda, ready for anything.

Dallas always seemed pleased to see me and never made me feel like I was in the way. In the early days he and I would chat a lot – about music mostly – but as the weeks passed our conversations became shorter and shorter. Although she never actually said anything, it was clear Miranda didn't like it when Dallas and I talked too much to each other. We became like 'dive buddies' then, me and Dallas. Not speaking, but waving occasionally, or giving each other the thumbs-up. We each had our roles – I was Best Friend, Dallas was Boyfriend – and we were both working towards the same thing: keeping Miranda happy.

In the beginning, we'd just go to one place per night – always in town – specifically to see gigs. But soon we started going to more and more places each night, every night, and we seemed to travel for longer distances each time. The venues changed, but certain things about those nights were always the same. I'd lend Miranda clothes, which she'd change into in the car and forget to return. Door men, ticket girls and bouncers waved us through unquestioningly – sometimes, it seemed, unseeingly. Bar staff handed over drinks, which we never seemed to pay for, and although I only drank soft drinks I often felt dizzy, stumbling and tripping over nothing.

Miranda's energy was endless. 'Come *on!*' she'd say, sometimes only minutes after arriving somewhere. 'It's dead here.' *Dead, dead, dead.*

At first I felt like a little kid on a massive sugar high at a fun park. I wanted it to go on forever. But after a few months I started to droop. Sometimes, as we sped from one venue to the next I would nod off in the taxi.

Miranda always shook me awake. 'Don't sleep,' she'd say. 'You'll miss out.' But she never explained exactly *what* I was missing out on.

By the time I arrived home I would be shattered, but sleep was hard to get. There were mornings when I crawled in through my window moments before Mum called me for breakfast.

During the day I felt like a zombie, struggling through my classes, constantly fighting fatigue. Sometimes I'd get the feeling in class that Lachlan was looking over at me. But I felt too tired to think about what this meant. Besides, I didn't want Miranda to catch me looking at him.

I limped through my evenings at the Mercury or, when I just couldn't face working, I'd call in sick and tell Mum my shift had been cancelled. But the moment I climbed into Dallas's car or the taxi again, I'd have a sudden, sharp surge of energy that would keep me going – for a little while at least.

Sometimes we went to parties that Miranda claimed she'd been invited to, and often people did come up and greet her warmly. But they almost always called her by the wrong name. I didn't like the party nights much. Miranda and Dallas would disappear off into some dark corner together and I would be left, awkwardly alone in a room full of strangers acting like maniacs. When Dallas and Miranda returned their eyes would look different and they'd giggle together about private jokes as if I wasn't there at all.

It was at these parties that I most often found myself thinking about Lachlan. I'd even fantasise about him turning up out of the blue – walking in and giving me the hugest, goofiest grin. *Hey, Olive! You're here too.* Sometimes while I was doing this, I'd spot someone through the crowd that looked like him. But then he'd be gone. Lachlan hadn't been out with us since that first time, and I knew Miranda had made it clear to Dallas that his brother wasn't welcome.

One night at a party I sat alone on a saggy couch. The urge to sleep was overwhelming – and even though I knew I'd be in big trouble if Miranda caught me, I started to nod off. I was almost asleep when I felt the couch sink a little further. Someone had sat down beside me. This sometimes happened – a stranger would take pity on me sitting alone or even try to chat me up. But this time my sleep-dazed eyes tricked me into thinking that it was Lachlan sitting there.

'Hey, Olive.'

I sat up, my tiredness evaporating instantly. It *was* Lachlan – smiling, but also looking a little strained.

'What are you doing here?' I asked.

'I followed you,' Lachlan admitted. 'In a taxi. I've done it a couple of times, actually. You know – since you three started going out all the time.' He rubbed his chin. 'That sounds pretty creepy, doesn't it?'

'That depends,' I said, 'on why you're doing it.' My heart was jumping around like a loon, but I managed to keep my voice calm.

Lachlan leant forward in the couch. 'I'm worried about Dallas,' he said. 'Really worried.'

'Oh,' I said. *Don't you dare feel disappointed, Olive.* 'Why?'

'He's a mess,' said Lachlan. 'Going hard every night, staying in bed during the day. Not eating. I don't even know what's happening with Luxe.' Lachlan shook his head. 'He reckons he's working on some songs, but I don't think he is.'

I hadn't known that.

Someone turned up the music then, and even more people crowded into the space in front of the couch. Lachlan inched a little closer to me. 'Dallas says he's in love with Miranda. And he thinks she's in love with him.' Lachlan was looking at me intently. 'Do *you* think she is?'

It seemed like a crazy question – of *course* Miranda was in love with Dallas. But then I found myself thinking about the way she talked about him. What an amazing catch he was. How lucky she was, and how many girls wished they were her. And how whenever Miranda flung her arms around Dallas and smothered him with kisses, she always seemed to have one eye on me waiting for my reaction.

'Sometimes –' I stopped, feeling stupid. Arrogant. But I couldn't back out now, so I shut my eyes and let it blurt out. 'Sometimes it's like she's just pretending to be in love with him to make me jealous.'

Lachlan didn't laugh, or look at me like I was a nut. Instead he nodded grimly. 'Exactly.' He looked angry then – the angriest I'd ever seen him – hunched over, fists clenched. When he looked at me again he was calm, but I could tell the rage was still simmering not far below. 'I promised myself I wouldn't interfere with your life, Olive,' he said. 'I know that you've got stuff going on, and I've tried to leave you alone. But I can't stop watching out for you, even though I've tried.' He gave a half-laugh. 'I've really, really tried.'

It made me ache to hear that. And it was confusing too. 'Why are you watching out for me?'

Lachlan looked at me strangely. Like the reason should've been obvious. 'Olive. Haven't you noticed what's happening to you?'

'What are you talking about?' I said, genuinely startled. 'I'm a little tired, but everything is fine otherwise.' I was having fun, wasn't I? Getting tired was part of that.

Lachlan was quiet for a moment. Then he got up. 'Follow me,' he said. 'I want to show you something.'

He pushed past the drunken dancers, leading me to a bathroom. Lachlan flicked on the light – stark and bright. There, on the wall opposite, was a full-length mirror. Reflected in it was someone I didn't recognise. Someone thin and pale, with lank hair, sunken cheeks and dark smudges under her eyes. My reflection and I stared at each other and we both inhaled sharply. *No.*

'I'll call a taxi,' said Lachlan, pulling out his phone. 'You should go. Now.'

Before Miranda finds us. He didn't say it, but I knew it was what he meant. And I realised that this was my only chance to speak. Maybe the only one I'd get.

I turned away from my reflection and towards him. 'You know what I said before, about Miranda trying to make me jealous?' I spoke quickly, before I could change my mind. 'By constantly trying to show me how she and Dallas are in love?'

Lachlan flinched. 'Yes.'

'Well, it doesn't work on me,' I said. 'It can't.'

'Why not?' said Lachlan cautiously.

'Because I'm not in love with Dallas,' I said, the words tumbling out. 'And I haven't been since that gig at the Rainbow.'

We just kind of stared at each other then, Lachlan looking

like he wasn't quite sure what I'd said and me not quite sure if I'd actually said it. And then, before either of us could say anything else, the door swung open and Miranda barged in, her face creased with irritation.

'What are you doing in here?' she snapped, and without waiting for an answer she pushed past Lachlan and muscled her way over to me.

'Olive's going home,' said Lachlan, trying to block her way. 'She needs to sleep.'

Miranda looked like she might bite him. 'No, she doesn't. She just needs you to piss off.'

'That's up to Olive to say, not you,' replied Lachlan steadily.

Both of them turned to me then, but I was too exhausted to deal with the situation. All I wanted was to crawl into my bed and sleep.

Miranda took my silence as a victory. 'Let's go,' she said, grabbing my arm. 'Dallas is already waiting in the taxi outside. This party is dead.'

As she marched me out of the room, I glanced back at Lachlan. I had no idea if he understood what I'd been trying to tell him before Miranda barged in. Or if he believed me. But when Lachlan caught my eye there was something in his face – underneath the worry and stress – that gave me a flicker of hope.

Maybe he hasn't given up on me after all.

o

'God, what a *loser*,' seethed Miranda. She still had me tightly in her grip and I kept stumbling over shrubs and rocks as she pulled me across the front lawn to the waiting taxi. 'Those sporty types are all the same, assuming everyone is adoring them from the sidelines, cheering them on.'

I didn't reply and Miranda suddenly stopped, her eyes boring into me. 'You *don't* care what he thinks, do you?'

I remember Dad explaining to me once that sometimes the body moves instinctively – without you having to think about it – to protect itself from harm. A reflex. Like ducking when a rock's been thrown at your head, or pulling away from something hot. I felt my head shake from side to side. 'No,' I said. 'Of course I don't.'

'Good,' said Miranda. 'A guy like that is totally wrong for you. You get that, don't you? It would never, ever work.'

'You're right,' I said, hoping that I sounded like I meant it. 'Of course it wouldn't work.'

TWENTY-TWO

I spent most of the next day, Saturday, in bed, and when I woke up around 3 p.m. I knew there was no way I could go out that night. I could barely move. But when I went to text Miranda, my phone was missing. I could've called from the phone in the kitchen but there were two problems with that. There was a good chance Mum would overhear me, for one thing. And it also involved me getting up. As the day passed, I felt a creeping sense of panic as I tried to figure out what to do. Just not show up and explain I was sick when I saw her next? Most people would accept that. But not Miranda. It was totally possible that she would march up to our front door and demand to know where I was. Gradually it dawned on me. I would have to go out.

So just before 10 p.m. I dragged myself out of bed, threw on some clothes and headed out the window as usual. But when I turned the corner there was no taxi waiting. Just Miranda standing alone, straight and still under the streetlight.

'I'm not in the mood for crowds tonight,' she said. 'Let's walk instead.'

She started heading off down the street before I even had a chance to reply. But of course it hadn't been a question.

We walked through the quiet suburban streets, not speaking. Occasionally there'd be the barking of a dog in someone's yard, or I'd glimpse the flicker of a TV but otherwise there was little sign of life. Miranda's silence was fine by me. I didn't feel much like talking. I ambled along a few steps behind her, not really paying attention, letting her lead the way. It was only when we came to the main road that I understood where we were going. To the forest.

Miranda's quietness became even denser once we were surrounded by trees. I almost forgot she was there and when she did finally speak it made me jump. She'd stopped just up ahead, near where the path forked into two. The wider trail led through the woods and eventually back to the main road – I'd walked Ralph along it heaps of times. The other one was narrower and more overgrown and it headed up the hill. It was this path Miranda pointed to.

'This leads up to the back of Oona's place,' she said. 'If we go this way she won't spot us.'

'But why are we going there?' My voice seemed so tiny in that big forest.

Miranda smiled. 'There's a game I want to teach you.'

o

The path began tilting steeply and soon narrowed to the point where we had to walk single file to fit – Miranda in the front. When did I get so unfit? Invisible creatures whirred past my ears and I felt – even if I couldn't actually see – nocturnal eyes watching us. *Leave,* I told myself, my pulse quickening. *Get away from here.* But I wasn't sure I'd be able to find my way back in the dark. And there was no way I wanted to be stuck out here alone.

Finally we came to a fence made of thick iron posts. Oona's fence.

'Climb through,' said Miranda.

'Where?'

She pointed to a gap where some posts had been pushed apart. Miranda waited for me to go first, then slipped through herself. 'If you follow me, the security lights won't activate.'

Up ahead was the house, hunched into the hill. But we didn't head towards it. Instead, Miranda led the way through Oona's yard, sticking as close to the fence as possible, until we came to the carport.

'How did she get permission to build this thing?' I said, trying to sound jokey. The carport had been constructed at the end of the very steep driveway and looked like it could tumble over at any minute. Oona's car was parked beneath it, its front bumper touching the fence. Beyond the railings the ground dropped away steeply.

'She didn't get permission,' Miranda said.

I stepped back and of course Miranda noticed. 'You're not scared of heights, are you?'

'No,' I said. *Just depths.*

'Oh good.' Miranda was much more cheerful now. Chatty and excited like she used to be. 'You'll love this game then.' She went over to the fence and used it for a lift up one of the poles. Once she was on the roof, she leant over the edge, her hand stretched down to me. 'I'll help you up.'

'No, thanks. It's easier if I do it myself.' I felt the pole wobble as I began climbing. But I knew there was no backing out. I scrambled onto the roof and sat very still as if that might stop the whole structure from collapsing. Miranda didn't seem worried. She sprang up and sauntered over to the very edge and I noticed something then that I hadn't seen from the ground. The carport roof actually stuck out *over* the fence. Sharp rocks jutted up where the ground dropped away below. I drew in my breath sharply as Miranda took a step forward. Her toes were over the edge.

'Miranda! Stop!'

Miranda laughed. 'You big baby,' she said scornfully. 'This is the whole point. It's a nerve test. We stand here with our eyes closed until one of us chickens out and steps back. Or falls off.'

'I'm not playing that. It's stupid. And dangerous.'

'Aw, sweetie. Don't be scared,' crooned Miranda. 'What's the worst thing that could happen?'

I gritted my teeth. 'We could die?'

Miranda sighed and stepped away from the edge. I felt relieved, until she came over to where I was standing and put an arm around my neck. It was too tight to be called a hug. It was more of a tackle. 'It's just a *game*, Olive,' she said. 'Please show me you're not a coward. I can't stand cowards.'

I found myself being led forward, step by step, until we were both standing balanced on the edge of the carport. I kept my eyes straight ahead, my body stiff.

Miranda stood beside me, her arm still wrapped around my neck. 'Imagine how incredible it'd feel if we jumped,' she said. 'Flying through the air.'

'Imagine how incredible it would feel being smashed to bits on the rocks.' I spoke loudly, cynically. Trying to mask my fear.

But it was like Miranda had heard me say something completely different. 'Shall we do it then?' she said, like she was inviting me to another gig. Another party. 'Together?'

I prised her fingers from my arm. '*No.*'

Miranda didn't even look around as I backed away from the edge and climbed down, my arms and legs trembling. I looked up to see that she remained exactly where she was, silhouetted against the blackness, her arms stretched out to the sides.

'It would be amazing,' she sighed. 'Just imagine – no more being held back by your past. No more guilt about what you did to your family. No more aching for dead best friends.' Miranda sounded blissful. 'Don't tell me that you're not tempted, Olive.'

'Jumping off won't fix anything,' I said stonily.

'Yes, it will. Of course it will.'

I watched her, feeling useless. If I'd had my phone I could've called someone. The police. Maybe if I yelled loud enough Oona would hear us – but that seemed unlikely. I considered climbing up again and pulling her back to safety. But what if she threw her weight forward and we spilled like a waterfall over the edge? The thought made me prickle all over.

'Come on, Miranda,' I pleaded. 'Come down from there. You win, OK? You've got the most nerve.'

I didn't really think she would listen, so it was a shock when she sprang back, ran lightly across the roof and swung herself over the edge. The *safe* edge.

'How great was that?' said Miranda, all twinkly-eyed with excitement.

I couldn't look at her. Now that we were both on the ground again, the panic was being rapidly replaced by fury. 'No, it wasn't *great.*'

Miranda rolled her eyes. 'God, Olive,' she said. 'I never meant for us to actually *do* it.' She shook her head, pouting at me. 'You used to have a sense of humour. I don't know what's happened to it recently.'

'I'm going home,' I said, not even bothering to disguise my revulsion and anger. Walking back alone in the dark was pretty unappealing, but staying was worse. I headed off, and was a few metres away when Miranda came running up behind me.

'Is this yours?' she said. 'I found it in the taxi the other night.' She was holding out my phone. When I took it from her I did something I hadn't done for a long time. I avoided touching her skin.

I shoved the phone in my pocket and walked away without a word.

o

I couldn't bring myself to take the shortcut through the forest. Once I was through the hole in Oona's fence I followed it around to the main road and walked along that instead. By the time I arrived home it was past midnight – early by my recent standards – but my evening didn't usually involve late-night hikes or near-death experiences on shaky carports. I was ready to drop. Perhaps this was why I didn't notice the kitchen light was on. So I almost had a heart attack when the backdoor swung open and I saw Mum standing there, her arms folded.

'Get inside,' she said. 'We need to talk.'

I walked past her, through to the kitchen, then over to the sink where I poured myself some water and drank it very slowly. 'I'm stuffed,' I said, putting the glass down. 'Let's talk tomorrow.'

'No,' said Mum. She sat at the kitchen table and pushed out one of the other chairs with her foot. I was used to her looking worried, but the anger was new. 'I want to know what you've been up to.'

'Well, during the day I'm at school,' I said. 'You know – the one you made me go back to even though I'm a total outcast there? And then some nights I'm here, looking after Toby because you're *working*. And on the other nights I'm slaving away at the Mercury, which I have to do because it's not like I get any pocket money and –'

'Don't be smart, Olive,' said Mum tightly. 'You know what I'm talking about.' Her fingers thunked on the tabletop.

'Sneaking out in the middle of the night is unacceptable, as is lying about it. So let me ask you again. What have you been up to *tonight*?'

Crumbs were spread across the tablecloth like a toast-coloured rash. I pressed hard on one with my thumb, feeling it dig in and then crumble. 'I've been hanging out with Miranda.'

'You were at her house?' said Mum, looking relieved. Like somehow this was good news.

'Yes.'

'Was Oona there?'

I nodded. Oona probably had been there, somewhere. My chair scraped across the tiles. 'Is that it? Can I go to bed now?'

'No,' said Mum. 'I'm glad you've made a new friend, Olive. Truly I am. And I'm happy for you to spend time with Miranda. But I want you to promise me there'll be no more sneaking out.'

To be honest it was kind of a relief to be ordered to take a break from the craziness of the last few months. Especially after what I'd been through that night. But I wasn't about to let Mum know that.

'OK,' I said, sighing deeply. 'I promise. No more sneaking out.'

'I also want to have a family day,' added Mum. 'You, me and Tobes.'

I knew exactly what that *family day* would involve. Mum would make one of the same horrible cakes she always made and we would watch the same selection of boring movies we'd been watching for years.

'That sounds great,' I said.

'Really?' Mum looked like she wanted to believe me so much that it hurt my heart.

I nodded. 'Really.' And as I said it I found myself thinking that maybe it wouldn't be so bad after all. Slothing around with Mum and Toby was pretty appealing just then.

'Sure. I'm working Friday night – tonight – but I'll stay home the rest of the weekend. I promise.'

Mum hugged me then – so tightly that it was actually kind of hard to inhale. 'I'm so pleased,' she said. 'What type of cake should I make? Zucchini and poppyseed?'

'Mmm,' I said. 'I can taste it already.'

o

I'd only just walked through the school gates on Friday morning when Miranda bounded up, acting like everything was fine. Like she hadn't recently tried to convince me to jump off a roof. 'I've got the *best* news,' she said.

'What?' The sensation of her fingers on my arm was giving me the creeps.

'Oona's going away!' gloated Miranda. 'Some *friend* is going to pick her up this afternoon and whisk her off for the whole weekend. Can you imagine Oona having friends?'

I couldn't.

'Here's the best bit,' Miranda continued. 'I'm going to have a party. A super-exclusive one – starting straight after school. Oona will be gone by then.'

'I'm working tonight,' I said coolly.

Miranda's face pinched the way it always did when someone was irritating her. 'So call in sick,' she said. 'Seriously. You can't miss this. It's going to be *incroyable*.'

'I've called in sick a lot recently,' I said. 'Noah won't be happy.'

Miranda's forehead creased. 'Are you being deliberately stupid?' she said. 'I mean, more than usual? Come *after* work then. The party will be going all night. Probably all Saturday too.'

'No.' I'd been so petrified of saying this to Miranda. But now that I was doing it, I was almost enjoying it. 'I promised my mum I'd spend Saturday at home,' I said. 'We're making a cake and watching movies.'

Miranda sniggered. 'You're *not* serious.'

'Actually yeah, I am,' I said.

'You're really not coming?'

I shook my head. 'Sorry.' Although I wasn't.

Miranda's fingers curled up. So did her face. 'You *bitch*.'

The word flew at me like a fist and I knew it was meant to knock me out, or at least wind me. But I didn't feel a thing.

'You can't just ditch me like this,' she said. 'I won't let you.' Then she turned and stalked off.

TWENTY-THREE

Miranda didn't speak to me or look at me for the rest of the day. It was supposed to be a punishment, of course, but it was actually a relief – like taking off a pair of too-tight jeans. I breathed out. Relaxed, just a little. When I arrived home, Mum and Toby were outside. Mum had on thick, way-too-big gardening gloves and was pulling ivy off the front of the house, leaving behind a wall covered in tiny claw-like marks. Ralph was racing around with a long strand of ivy in his mouth, shaking it and growling.

'But I *like* the ivy,' Toby was saying.

'I do too,' said Mum. 'It just needs controlling. It's getting into the guttering.'

This used to be Dad's job. The gloves were his, too. I wandered over, enjoying the feeling of the sun on my face. 'Hi.'

Mum smiled. 'Hey, sweetie,' she said. 'Oh, before I forget – Noah called. He said it's going to be quiet tonight so he won't need you.'

'Really?'

'Are you pleased? It means our family weekend can start right away.' Mum grinned cheekily. 'Maybe it can start with you helping me with this ivy?'

I nodded. 'Sure. I'll just go and change.'

When I opened my wardrobe all the empty coathangers rattled and clanked together. Still, I found what I needed – my old trackpants and a faded jumper with a hole at the collar. They were baggy, but comfortable at least.

I was just about to go back outside when my phone rang. Miranda's name appeared on the screen.

You don't have to answer it. She won't know. But in the end I answered it anyway. I figured she'd have to apologise for calling me a bitch and I relished the chance to hear it.

'Hey, Olive.' Miranda sounded subdued. A little nervous. 'I'm just ringing to say sorry about being a total wonk today. I guess I was just really upset about you refusing to come to the party, especially as I arranged the whole thing just for you.'

I knew the best way to deal with this was to just ignore it. So why was it so hard to do that with Miranda? 'I wasn't being rude,' I said. 'I –'

'Apology accepted,' said Miranda. Then with a heavy sigh she added, 'I'd better let you go. I guess you've got to get ready for work.'

'Actually my shift was cancelled,' I said, and immediately regretted it.

'Really? Fantastic!' said Miranda brightly. 'That means you

can come over tonight after all.'

'No, it doesn't,' I said, horrified by how quickly I was losing control of this conversation. 'I'm staying home. I'm wrecked.'

For a moment I thought she'd hung up. Then I heard a faint sound – somewhere between a sigh and a snicker.

'Miranda?'

'Sorry,' she said. 'I was just wondering what everyone at school would say if they knew.' She spoke in this very casual, careless way and I could picture her examining her nails as she was speaking.

'Knew what?'

'About Ami, of course. I bet they'd all be interested to hear about her. And the kids at your brother's school.' She laughed lightly. 'You have to admit, Olive. It makes a pretty funny story. And they'd probably be fascinated to hear about how you tried to top yourself.'

My body went ice-cold. When I spoke my tongue felt thick and swollen.

'You promised you wouldn't. You said you wouldn't tell anyone about Ami.'

'No, I didn't.' Miranda said sharply. 'I said I *hadn't* told anyone. I never said I *wouldn't*. That would be a stupid thing to promise. Because, you see Olive, I've never fallen for that *I'm so tough* act of yours. I've always known what you really are. Spineless. And I also knew that one day you'd need a bit of ... *encouragement* to do what I wanted you to do.'

The room was beginning to tip and spin around me. Ami

wouldn't have let Miranda do this – threaten me like this. But I'd never been as resilient as Ami.

'OK,' I said. My voice was a whisper. 'I'm coming.'

'Great,' said Miranda. 'See you soon, then.'

Slowly I took off my trackpants and old jumper and turned back to my wardrobe.

o

Mum and Toby were drinking water in the kitchen when I walked in. 'You look like you're dressed for going out,' said Mum, a catch in her voice. 'Not for ivy-removal.'

'I'm going to Miranda's,' I said.

Toby's face fell. 'No!'

'Olive,' said Mum. 'I'd like you to stay home tonight.'

My teeth clenched. 'I'll stay home tomorrow.'

'Please don't go,' said Toby.

I couldn't look at him. I was wishing with all my heart that there was some way to tell him I had no choice.

'Tomorrow,' I said, struggling to stop my voice breaking. 'I promise. I have to go out tonight.'

'No,' said Mum. '*No*. I'm putting my foot down about this. You're forbidden to leave the house. I want you to wait here with Toby while I go to the shops. Then I'll cook something really del-'

'*Wait here with Toby*,' I said, mimicking my mother's voice. 'That's what this is really about, isn't it? Me minding Toby.'

'No,' said Mum. 'That's not it at all.'

'Yes, it is. Admit it.'

Mum stepped back, knocking a pile of dusty travel brochures off the bench. They slithered to the floor.

My chest felt tight. Constricted. All that sea air and I couldn't seem to get it into my lungs. When had I last taken my meds? *Not for days*, I realised. *Maybe weeks.*

'Livvy, what's wrong?' Mum was standing right there in front of me but she may as well have been on the other side of the universe. 'Tell me what's wrong!'

'You take advantage of me,' I said hoarsely. 'Because you know I feel so guilty about what I did to you and Dad.'

Mum's face was creased with confusion. 'What do you *mean*? What exactly do you feel guilty about?'

She wanted me to say it? Fine then, I would. The words scraped along my tongue and burned my lips, but I pushed them out anyway. 'I'm the reason Dad left.'

Mum's arms lifted up, like she was about to embrace me, but then she let them fall again. 'Sweetheart. Oh love. Your dad didn't leave because of you.'

'Don't lie,' I said angrily. 'He left because I was too hard to deal with. I was *awful*. He was ashamed of me and sick of me and all my – *issues*.'

Toby started to whimper, *Stop it, stop it.* I expected Mum to go over to him, but she stayed where she was. 'That's not true. You mustn't ever think that. There were so *many* problems ...'

'Like what?' I said.

Mum started crying too. 'Oh god, where should I start?

259

His inability to deal with things aging. The car. Himself. *Me.*' Mum shook her head, her crying becoming indignant. 'Mid-life bloody crisis. Such a cliché.'

None of this made sense. If only my head would stop spiralling I could sort out my thoughts. 'If I'm not the reason he left,' I found myself yelling, 'then why didn't he visit me in the clinic?'

Mum pulled out a tissue and wiped her nose. She seemed to be avoiding looking at me. 'I should have told you this, Livvy,' she said. 'Ages ago. He did try to see you. A number of times.'

For a moment I felt so light, like I might lift up off the floor. *He does still care.* But the lightness vanished as something dawned on me. I faced Mum. 'You *stopped* him.'

The gardening gloves had slipped off Mum's hands and were lying at her feet. Toby had shoved his fingers in his ears and was making a loud tuneless noise to block out our voices.

'You were so unwell,' said Mum. 'You needed stability.'

'Don't try to make it sound like you kept him away to *protect* me,' I snarled. 'You were punishing him! For leaving. You want to control everything – what I say, what I eat, who I see. Living here is like ...' I groped around, trying to think of the way to describe it, then remembered the perfect expression. 'It's like trying to breathe with a pillow held over my face.'

'No. *No.*' Mum's face was stricken and ugly.

'It's *your* fault he left,' I said. The words were pouring from me, unstoppable, pushed out by my rage.

Toby was huddled up in a tiny ball on the ground. Finally

Mum seemed to break from her stupor and crouched down beside him, stroking his back. When she looked up at me her face was a mess of tears. 'Please, Livvy. Let's all calm down. Talk about this properly.'

I knew I should be feeling something then. There was my mum and my brother – both of them so upset, because of me. But something hard and heavy had pushed up against the entrance of my heart, preventing it from opening. Mum reached out to me, but I didn't take her hand. Her mouth kept opening and shutting and I knew there were words coming out but they dissolved before they reached my ears.

When I began to walk – turning away from Mum and Toby and heading outside – I couldn't feel the ground beneath my feet. The only thing I felt was the vibration of the door as it slammed shut behind me.

I began to run.

o

At first I just ran blind and fast, hoping the wind rushing over me might clear everything away. When I couldn't run anymore, I walked – slower and slower until I was too exhausted to take another step and I sank down onto the curb. A horrible noise started coming out of my mouth – something in between crying and gasping.

I had nothing with me – no money, no phone. *What the hell do I do now?*

I couldn't go to Miranda's place. Not while I was such a mess.

I looked around to see where I'd ended up. On the Esplanade, not far from the Mercury.

Money, I thought. Money was something real. If I had some I might feel less like I was hurtling through space. I stood up. A clear-ish path had formed through the jungle in my head. I would go and ask Noah to give me an advance on my pay.

There was a long queue outside the Mercury. Strange. Hadn't Noah told my mum it was going to be quiet? I squeezed into the foyer and looked around. Standing in the snack bar was a girl I didn't know, scooping popcorn, serving drinks. I strode over to the ticket office and pushed my way to the front of the queue. 'What's going on, Noah? Why is someone else doing my job?'

Noah kept selling tickets. He didn't even look at me. 'What did you expect?' he said. 'You left me in the lurch tonight. Again. It was lucky that Polly was available.'

A hum started up – high and insistent. Polly must have turned on the ice-cream light.

'What are you *talking* about?' I said. 'You rang my mum and told me not to come in!'

'No, I didn't. And I tried to call your phone – about twenty times – to find out where you were.' Noah shook his head. 'Dad is not happy, Olive. He says you've become totally unreliable.'

'There must be something wrong with my phone,' I muttered. 'I didn't hear it ring once.'

'Yeah?' said Noah, looking at me for the first time since I'd arrived. 'Well, maybe you'll hear this then. Olive, you no longer work here. Now, please get out of the way so I can do my job.'

I stood there, fighting to keep myself together. Noah looked at me warily, then sighed and put up the *back in five minutes* sign.

'Come on,' he said, coming out of his ticket office and pulling me over to a bench in the corner. His face was grave. 'Is it true? What everyone's saying about you?'

I frowned. 'What are they saying?'

'That you're on drugs.'

'No!' I said, my throat aching. 'Why would anyone say something so awful?'

'Probably because you *look* like you're on drugs,' said Noah. 'You're so thin. And pale.'

'Noah,' I pleaded, 'it isn't true. And I'm sorry that you think I stood you up tonight, but you have to believe me, that's not what happened.'

Noah crossed his arms. 'So what *did* happen? Someone rang your mum, pretending to be me?'

I didn't answer.

'Are you selling any more tickets or what?' someone called impatiently from the queue.

Noah stood up. 'I have to go,' he muttered. 'Good luck, Olive. I really hope you sort yourself out.'

I pushed my way back outside, the world blurring into tear-mirages around me. Everything twinkled. It was almost beautiful. A calmness came over me then – a foggyish, murky one. Like I wasn't completely awake.

And, almost like I had no say in it, like something was pulling me there, I turned and started heading for the ocean.

I expected to feel the old panic lifting up inside me the moment my shoes hit the sand. The last time I'd been on the beach was the night Lachlan and I were searching for Katie. Although I'd been nervous then, it wasn't hard to block out the ocean – probably because it was dark and I had a task to focus on. I wasn't alone, either. But this time the sky was still glowing from the setting sun, so the water – the waves – were bright, sparkly. There was no task, and no other person, to distract me.

Still, the calmness stayed and I walked along the sand until it stopped being powdery dry and began to squelch beneath my shoes. That's where I stopped. I couldn't seem to move – forward or backwards. So I just stood there, watching and listening.

A woman jogged past with her dog. The dog's paws were kicking up great chunks of sand as it galloped along and it looked at me as it passed, smiling in that crazy-happy way that dogs do. And I started laughing. I mean, how can you *not* laugh at a dog running on the beach? But I was also kind of crying, too. Laughing and crying simultaneously hurts. It hurts and it's confusing.

I turned to watch the dog run off down the beach. That was when I saw Lachlan, walking towards me in that casual, unhurried way of his, a towel slung over his shoulders, hands in his pockets and his hair gently blowing in the breeze.

If he was surprised to see me there he didn't let it show. Instead he just lifted his hand and waved, happy to see me. *Me.*

The girl who was standing there on her own with a blotchy face.

'Hey,' he said. 'How are things?'

'Right now things are a little rough,' I admitted, knowing that my eyes must have looked like cherry tomatoes.

'What's wrong?'

'Just … nothing. Really,' I said.

Of course I longed to tell him everything. I wished I could just bury my head into his chest and let it all out. But I didn't. *People don't want to hear that stuff.*

Lachlan looked at me, but didn't push it. 'Come for a stroll?' he said after a moment.

The answer blurted out of me. '*Yes.*'

Lachlan smiled. 'I like the way you made that yes sound *exactly* like a yes.'

o

To anyone watching we probably looked very peaceful, walking along like that in silence. And I suppose I did feel peaceful, but it was an exhausted kind of peace. The sort that comes from being so empty that you can't feel anything at all.

'You promised me something,' said Lachlan after we'd been walking for a while.

'What?' I said, thinking back over our conversations. 'I didn't promise anything.'

'Well, it was almost a promise,' said Lachlan. 'You said you'd swim with me in the ocean one day. So how about it?'

'You're joking, right?' I said.

'Nope.' Lachlan held out his hand. 'Come on.'

'I can't.' My voice had begun to rise. 'I can't.'

If I went into the water all those horrible feelings would swirl up from below, pulling me down, pulling me back to where I began. I was supposed to be taking *baby steps*, not great big freakin giant leaps into the deep end.

'Nothing will happen to you,' said Lachlan, those brown eyes looking at me steadily. 'I won't let it.'

'No bathers,' I croaked.

Wordlessly, Lachlan put his towel on the ground. He unzipped his jacket, kicked off his shoes and started striding towards the ocean.

'Lachlan!' I was laughing then, but it was a nervous kind of laugh. 'Stop!'

But Lachlan kept going – fully clothed, just like I had that morning after Dad left. It was only when he was waist-high in the water that he finally stopped and turned around. He cupped his hands around his mouth. 'Come on, Olive,' he called. 'Come and keep me company out here.'

The ocean is not to be trusted. It's dark and cold with a treacherous current that pulls you whichever way it wants. It can drown you or it can refuse to drown you. I looked out at Lachlan as he reached his hand towards me. You'd feel pretty safe, I decided, having those hands holding onto yours. I unlaced my shoes and I began to walk towards the water, one tiny step after another.

When I knew I was nearing the edge I kept my eyes up.

The water was cold and as I kept going I felt it seep into my jeans, making them as heavy as cement. The sand began to sink away beneath my feet. Lachlan didn't say anything, but kept his eyes on me, nodding, his arm still outstretched. When I finally reached the spot where Lachlan was standing I seized hold of his hand. And even though he'd been standing all that time in this freezing water, his hand was still warm.

'So glad you could make it,' he said, bowing his head and smiling like we were at some glamorous party instead of standing fully dressed in the middle of the ocean.

The water rose and pushed, nearly making me lose my balance. 'OK, I'm getting out now,' I said nervously, and pulled away from Lachlan. But his fingers curled around my wrist, holding me tight. My heart hammered. 'What are you doing?'

'Now's not a good time to go,' he said quietly. 'There's a wave coming.'

I turned my head to see a wave swelling in the distance – a really *big* wave – rising up like something from a horror movie. I felt the current begin to pull us out and towards it. 'Let me go!'

But Lachlan held on. 'You can't outswim it,' he said. 'We'll have to ride it out. Together.'

'Ride it out?' I said hysterically. 'This is not a *horse*, Lachlan. It's a freakin huge wave.' One that was looming up, larger and closer.

Lachlan wrapped one arm and then the other around me, pressing my chest tightly against his and holding me there. I was so surprised that for a moment I forgot my panic. Forgot to struggle. And when he spoke again I could not only hear his words but feel them, passing from his body directly into mine. 'When I say *now*, I want you to close your eyes and hold your breath. And then just trust me, OK?'

'I really don't –'

But Lachlan's arms pulled me in even more securely. *'Now.'* Then together we plunged down into the water and under the wave. Me and Lachlan.

I kept my eyes screwed tightly closed, feeling the water dragging at my hair and clothes. Strange thoughts darted around my head.

Are we sinking or rising?

Maybe we were suspended in the same spot, going nowhere at all.

I'm drowning.

Maybe I was dead already.

Things slowed down. My fingers uncurled and my pulse steadied. Bubbles tickled my skin like the nibbling of tiny fish and I became aware of a sound – slow and rhythmic. Lachlan's heart, beating against my chest.

Then Lachlan started kicking and we began moving up, up, up.

o

We broke the surface and I gasped. The air felt strange as it filled my lungs, like it was my first ever breath. I gazed around, amazed at how different everything looked. I mean, the sand

and the car park and the houses that lined the beach road – they were all still there, exactly as they had been just a minute ago. But they looked different somehow. Brighter, and cleaner. My head felt like this too, like someone had opened it up and scrubbed off the barnacles. I started to laugh.

Lachlan still had his arms around me, even though the wave had gone and we'd been carried almost to the shore. 'Are you OK?'

'I'm fine,' I said.

But *fine* didn't begin to describe it. I looked up at Lachlan, grinning like an imbecile. 'It's probably safe to let go of me now.'

Lachlan's eyebrows lifted. 'Now why would I go and throw away an opportunity like this?'

And he leant in and kissed me.

As we stood there, chest high in water, I felt like I was in the middle of my own romance novel. Those amazingly beautiful arms of his wrapped around me, those hands pressed against my sides. His lips were ridiculously soft and delicious, and I even felt fluttering butterflies, all wonderful and tingly. Another massive wave could have dragged me all the way to the South Pole and I wouldn't have noticed.

Lachlan pulled back and looked at me, head tilted, smiling a little nervously. 'Was that OK?' he said. 'I mean, was it OK for me to do that?'

'Yes,' I said. 'That was very OK.'

I rested my head against his chest and listened to the rhythm of his heart beating in his chest – that strong, unwavering pulse.

Then I felt the rumble of laughter.

'What?' I said, looking up at him.

'I just can't believe it,' he said. 'I mean, I finally got near you without you-know-who jumping out and stopping me.'

'You mean Miranda?'

'She's like a bodyguard,' said Lachlan darkly. 'Except that she's not trying to protect you.'

Overhead, seagulls screamed and wheeled. I nodded. For the first time in weeks, my head felt clear and unmuddled. 'Miranda's trying to hurt me,' I said. 'The way she hurt Katie.'

'Yes,' said Lachlan quietly. 'She is.'

The words hung there for a while.

'Do you believe that weird things can happen?' I said. 'You know – the kind of things that you shouldn't really believe in if you're a normal, sensible person?' I was speaking quickly, before I could change my mind.

The water lapped around us as Lachlan mulled this over. 'I guess I believe in grey,' he said eventually.

'What does that mean?'

'It's something my grandpa used to say,' said Lachlan. 'Some things aren't straightforward. Not everything is true or false, real or imaginary, black or white. It's not that simple.' He looked at me, a shy smile on his face. 'Does that make any sense at all?'

'It makes a lot of sense to me,' I told him.

Then Lachlan kissed me for the second time and the butterflies were set in motion all over again – looping, swirling, twirling.

When we stopped Lachlan held me a little way away from him, his face serious. 'Olive, I need you to promise me something.'

My heart jumped. 'What?'

'That from now on you let me help you. Don't go doing anything about Miranda without me. Don't even go near her. Whatever we do we'll do together, OK?'

I squinted up at him. 'Are you ever off-duty, Mr Lifesaver Guy?' I said, smiling.

Lachlan shook his head. 'Not when I'm around you,' he said.

This time it was *me* who kissed Lachlan.

When we finally got cold and began to walk back to shore, I felt like a superhero – strong and invincible – ready to save the entire world.

o

On the beach we dried off as much as we could with only one towel and sodden clothes. I didn't even feel cold but Lachlan insisted that I take his hoodie. When I slipped it on I felt like his arms were still around me, holding me close.

'What are you doing now?' he asked, reaching over and brushing the hair from my face. 'Want to go get some pizza or something?'

I did, of course, more than anything, but I remembered the mess I'd left behind at my house. 'I've got to sort something out first,' I said, and seeing the look of concern on his face, I added hastily, 'A family thing. I'll just go fix that up and meet you after.'

Funny. I really thought it would all be that simple.

Lachlan hesitated and I could see him struggling with his lifesaver instincts, but finally he nodded. 'OK. Don't forget what you promised me, though. Stay away from Miranda.'

I hugged him, barely believing how amazing his body felt next to mine. 'Don't worry,' I said. 'I won't go anywhere near her.'

I embedded Lachlan's phone number in my head then watched him sprint off down the beach until he was just a tiny dot in the distance – a very, very beautiful dot. Finally I managed to drag my eyes off him and headed for the steps that led back up to the road, replaying in my head what had happened, trying to commit every tiny detail to memory. The way his leg had brushed against mine as we'd floated underwater together. How he'd looked at me as we resurfaced. The tiny freckle I'd noticed by his ear as his hair swirled around his face. The rise and fall of his breath against my chest.

I suppose I was in a bit of a trance, floating along and not paying attention to anything around me. I was vaguely aware that it was getting dark by then and that I was the only person on the beach – the joggers and die-hard all-year-round surfers had all left. And I knew that it was cold, although it didn't seem to be affecting me.

It wasn't until I actually reached the stairs that I saw Miranda standing there. She'd positioned herself halfway up, one hand holding each handrail, completely blocking the way. I scanned her face, trying to guess what was going on inside her head, how much she had seen. But as usual that was impossible.

The only thing that I knew for sure was that she was angry. Extremely angry.

'Olive,' she said. 'What the hell have you been doing?'

TWENTY-FOUR

'I've been swimming,' I said.

Miranda looked over my sodden form with distaste. 'Obviously. But why were you swimming when you were supposed to be at my place? I've been searching for you. For hours.'

I listened to her talking, wondering why I felt so strange. Something was missing. Something had changed. 'Sorry. I got distracted.'

I saw her eyes fix on Lachlan's hoodie and my heart leapt, wondering if she'd recognise it.

'That's your dad's, isn't it?' she said. 'It's pretty tragic that you're wearing it. You need to forget about him, you know. He's not coming back.'

I bit back my grin. *She didn't see us. She doesn't know.* That was when I realised what was missing. My fear.

'Come on,' said Miranda brusquely. 'We've got to go. I've

wasted a lot of time looking for you. The party should've started ages ago.'

'I'm not coming,' I said, starting to walk away. There was another set of stairs further down the beach. I'd go that way instead.

'So you *want* me to tell the whole world about Ami?'

I was a few metres away by then but it sounded like Miranda was right beside me, speaking straight into my ear.

'You want everyone to know how pathetic you are?'

Up along the beach road the lights had begun flicking on. *Don't stop walking. Just keep going.* That's what Ami would've told me to do. But I had this sudden urge to show Miranda that she couldn't control me anymore. That I'd broken free of her.

'You know what?' I said, pushing a few strands of wet hair off my forehead. 'I've been thinking about that. And I've realised something. Ami wouldn't have wanted to be used as blackmail. So go ahead. Tell everyone. Put in on the school blog if you want. Let the whole freakin world know.'

It felt good to fling Miranda's threats back at her, even though I knew there were risks – the biggest one being how Lachlan would react when he heard. I hoped that Ami would fit into Lachlan's *grey* category. But I didn't know for sure. All those butterflies I'd felt – I might never get to feel them again. But as I feasted on the shock and disbelief on Miranda's face, it was worth it.

That should have been the moment when I turned and walked away forever, leaving Miranda standing there alone. But

Miranda's expression shifted and there was something that made me stay where I was.

'It's time,' she said quietly. 'Time to tell you what's really going on.'

The wind blew across my face, making me shiver.

'Tonight isn't just a party, you see,' said Miranda, flicking her hair. 'It's a launch – for Dal's new album. But if you don't want to come ...' She shrugged and began walking up the stairs. 'It's a pity though,' she murmured over her shoulder, 'considering they're the last tracks he'll ever record.'

'*What?*' I heard myself call sharply. '*What* did you say?'

Miranda turned back around, with this faintly puzzled expression. 'I said, it's a launch party.'

'Not that bit,' I growled. 'Why are these the last tracks Dallas will record?' I was having trouble speaking. My chest heaved like I'd been running.

Miranda sighed deeply. 'You must have noticed what a state he's in, Olive,' she said softly. 'He doesn't look after himself. Doesn't eat. Drinks way too much and does too many drugs. He's ...' her voice sounded choked up, full of emotion, but her eyes were steady, and they were watching me carefully. 'He's not going to be with us much longer. I thought you might want to see him one last time – especially considering how you've always felt about him.'

All the moisture instantly vanished from my mouth. My legs, which had felt so strong just before, now threatened to fold up beneath me. *It's just a threat.* Another attempt to bend me to her will. Maybe. But if there was one thing I knew for sure about Miranda it was that she was capable of carrying through with threats.

'OK,' I said. 'I'll come.'

Miranda smiled. 'Of course you will,' she said. 'You won't regret it. Wait till you hear the songs, Olive. They'll blow you away.'

o

Up on the beach road I saw Oona's car parked illegally on the footpath. I stared at it dumbly. 'Oona's back?'

'Of course not.' Miranda's voice was withering. From her pocket she produced an ancient set of keys, worn thin and smooth from use, and flicked them around her finger. 'I just borrowed her car.' She walked over and opened the passenger side. The smell of disinfectant swung out at me like a punch. 'Hurry up. Get in.'

Don't do it. But what choice did I have? By the time I'd found a phone and called Lachlan – the only other person who was likely to believe my story – it might be too late for Dallas.

I'd already let Katie down. I wasn't going to let that happen again.

The passenger seat made a crackling, scrunching noise as I sat down. I soon saw why. The car's interior was completely covered in plastic – even the steering wheel and the gear stick. I hadn't even found the seatbelt when Miranda took off, the wheels screeching so loudly that I gave a yelp.

'Was that a bit scary for you?' said Miranda. 'Sorry. You seem kind of *jumpy* at the moment. Not quite yourself.' She took her eyes off the road and looked at me intently. 'Has anything happened, Olive? Anything I should know about?'

I dug my fingernails into the seat and kept looking straight ahead as if I could force the car to stay on the road through sheer will. 'No,' I muttered.

Miranda stared at me for a few more moments, then finally returned her attention to the road. The rest of the trip passed in total, deathly silence.

o

Oona's house wasn't the sort of place I thought I'd ever be glad to see. Window grilles and a massive KEEP OUT sign on the gate aren't exactly welcoming. But that evening, as we rounded the final twist on the curvy hill road and I saw it, I was flooded with relief. Miranda's silence in the car had given me a chance to form some kind of plan. My first task was to find Dallas. Then I would call Lachlan and together we'd get Dallas out.

Miranda dug out a remote control from the glove box – the only glove box I'd ever seen that was actually full of gloves – and the metal gates swung open.

She parked the car out the front, near the swimming pool, and was soon unlocking the front door. 'Are you coming in or what?' she called impatiently.

Strange. In all the time I'd spent with Miranda I hadn't once been into her house. In primary school we used to say that

Oona's place was an old prison. It certainly looked like one. *And Dallas is the prisoner*, I thought as I began walking up the steps towards Miranda.

'I'm coming,' I said. I said it extra-loud, hoping that Dallas might hear me and know help was on the way.

'Welcome to the inside of Oona's head,' said Miranda, pushing open the door for me. I stepped inside and she followed, closing the door behind her.

The air inside the house had the same strong smell of disinfectant as Oona's car. To the left was a hand basin, standing in the hall like a short, shiny butler. 'If Oona were here she would've made you wash your hands about fifty million times,' said Miranda. 'Except she wouldn't have let you in at all, of course.' She leant over and coughed on each tap, then smiled spitefully before sauntering off down the hallway.

The hallway was full of obstacles. Vacuum cleaners, rubber gloves still in their packaging, dusting mittens. A box of disposable paper slippers spilled out of a cardboard box, rustling like leaves as we walked past. Halfway down the corridor was a miniature army of hand-sanitiser bottles.

Miranda picked up a spray can of disinfectant. 'She uses half a can on the door handles every time she goes in or out of a room,' she said. Miranda seemed to be enjoying herself, like she wanted me to be as unnerved as possible. 'That's as well as the gloves.'

In the gloom I stepped on something and almost tripped. Lying in front of a closed door was another spraycan, crushed in the middle like someone had stamped on it viciously, over and over again.

'That's Oona's room,' said Miranda, pulling me away roughly. 'My room is over here.'

o

For a moment I stood in her doorway, trying to work out what was going on. Because I was looking into my own bedroom. Or an exact copy of it. Red velvet curtains hung from the ceiling, the curtains tied back with the same thick gold cords that I used on my fortune-teller's tent at home. Identical cushions were scattered around, and the rug was in exactly the same position as my own rug. Even the pattern matched.

Miranda stepped in. 'Sorry about the mess,' she said lightly, as if that was the only thing that might trouble me about her room.

'Miranda! You're back.' Dallas was lying on the bed, as crumpled and grey as an unwashed sheet. He gazed at Miranda with the same look of delight that Ralph gave me when I arrived home from school – but Ralph never looked like he'd been boozing solidly while I'd been away. Dallas managed to smile at me too. 'Hey there, little Ol. Let me pour you a drink.'

Dallas leant over the edge of the bed and produced a jug of something viciously blue. His arm muscles strained as he tipped the blue liquid into two paper cups and held them out to us.

'Not for me thanks, Dal,' I said, trying to sound jokey. 'Blue is nature's warning colour.'

'Olive is being a total wet blanket,' said Miranda. 'She's forgotten how to have fun.'

Dallas considered this and then fished out a little bottle of something red from his pocket. He shook a few drops of it into my cup and handed it to me.

'Now it's purple,' he said, beaming like this somehow solved everything. 'Nature *loves* purple. And so will you, little Ol, once you've tried this.'

I took the cup. Even the smell burned. 'What *is* it?'

'Zombie juice,' Dallas said. 'It could wake the dead.'

Just what we need here, I thought. *Drunk undead people*. When he wasn't looking I hid the cup in a corner.

Miranda clapped her hands. 'Time for us to launch Luxe's new album.'

'It can't be a launch,' I said. 'Vinnie and Pearl aren't here.' *Or anyone else, for that matter.*

Miranda was fiddling with her iPod – Katie's iPod – which was plugged into a small set of speakers on the floor. 'Why should they be here?' she said. 'They're not even in the band anymore.'

I gaped at her.

'Luxe has outgrown them,' said Miranda, like it should've been obvious. Then the music started up.

First there was just a single guitar, strummed by an uncertain hand. Then Dallas's voice joined in. I would've known his voice anywhere, even sounding as weak and quavery as this. And then there was another voice, female this time. She sang very softly to begin with, hovering in the background and harmonising with Dallas. But as the song progressed the female voice took on the main melody. It was only then that I could make out the lyrics. They were about a girl – a beautiful, incredible, overwhelming girl. The sort that you'd die for.

'That's you, isn't it?' I said to Miranda. 'Singing.'

Miranda clapped her hands in delight. 'I wanted to surprise you. Are you surprised?'

I shouldn't have been – Miranda had taken so much by then. Of course she'd try to take Luxe from me too.

Dallas had somehow managed to drag himself to an almost standing position. 'I command that we dance,' he said, beckoning to Miranda. 'Come over here, you slinky thing you,' he said.

Dallas stumbled, almost falling over but managing to recover. He was crooning but seemed unsure of the words to his own song. Then he almost fell again. I couldn't watch, but Miranda didn't seem bothered. She giggled and began twirling around him, like it was all part of some complicated routine they were doing together.

I could see then that extracting Dallas was not going to be easy. There was no way he would just come with me – even if I told him he was in danger. Dallas liked me, but it would only take a few words from Miranda and he'd turn against me in a flash. And then he'd be lost for good.

I stared at the ground, seeing something pink and faded shoved under the bed. It was the T-shirt I'd worn during my suicide attempt. Ever since then it had been tucked in my bundle of Proof in my room. At least, that's where I'd thought it was. When I picked the T-shirt up, three glittery silver things slipped from its folds. My old charm bracelet. Miss Falippi's locket. A small silver key – the sort that was meant to keep a diary secure.

My hands started to shake, but I picked up the bracelet and looked at it. It had been my favourite thing once. After a moment's hesitation I slipped it on, the charms making their familiar jingling noise. I dropped the locket and the key into the pocket of Lachlan's hoodie. I felt better. I'd started reclaiming a few things.

I looked up to see Miranda watching me with the same searching look she'd had on the drive here. Trying to work out what had changed. She unpeeled Dallas from around her and immediately he sagged into the nearest chair. *Miranda is his backbone now*, I thought, chilled.

Miranda walked over to his jug of zombie juice and picked it up. 'I wish you'd cheer up, Olive,' she said. 'You're bringing us all down.'

I kept my face expressionless. Miranda poured out a fresh cup of zombie juice and held it out to me.

'No, thanks.'

Miranda's eyes glinted. 'Take it.'

My dad had always been good at games and he liked teaching me winning strategies. I'd blocked them out since he left, but one of them came to me anyway. *Pet, sometimes pretending that you're losing is the best way of winning.*

I took the cup. It was made of soft plastic and the slightest pressure of my fingers made the blue liquid rise until it nearly spilled over the edge.

'Go on,' said Miranda. 'Drink it.'

I opened my mouth and poured the contents down my throat in one steady stream. Dallas whistled and cheered. Miranda refilled my cup and when I drank that she filled the cup again. As I drained the final drop the room began to turn. I staggered a little as the zombie juice took hold.

'You look so funny,' Miranda tittered. 'Especially in that hoodie. Not like you at all. You used to have such interesting taste. Well, *different* at least. Now you just look the same as everyone else. But deep inside that's what you are anyway, aren't you? Boring and mainstream.'

A new track began to play. A Luxe cover band – that's what this music sounded like. I was having trouble standing up now and I stretched out my arms, trying to find something to steady myself on.

'*I* know what's wrong with you tonight,' Miranda announced triumphantly. 'It's these new songs, isn't it? Because they're all about me – about how Dallas loves me more than anything else in the world. Poor Olive. It must eat you up.'

The whirling, woozy feeling in my head was speeding up. I tried to slow it down by focusing on a single spot on the wall. Miranda stepped closer. 'So does it?' she whispered. 'Eat you up inside?'

Don't let anyone see your cards, Pet. Especially when you've got a winner's hand.

'Lots of girls would kill to be in your position,' I said. 'And have what you have.'

'But what about *you*?' hissed Miranda. 'Would *you* kill to be in my position? Do you want to be me and have everything I have?'

I should've just nodded meekly. Or just said nothing at all. Lulled Miranda into believing everything was OK so that I could work on a way of getting Dallas out of there. But frankly I was sick of these games, and I wanted Miranda to know just how much she'd misjudged me.

'No,' I said, looking straight at her. 'I wouldn't kill to be you.'

Miranda's eyes were like two letterboxes. 'Why not?'

'Because I'm not in love with Dallas,' I said simply.

Miranda's mouth fell open.

'What are you two girlies talking about over there?' Dallas slurred from his chair. 'Come back and dance. The three of us.'

Miranda was still staring at me. 'You *are* in love with him,' she insisted – like a teacher trying to drill facts into a stubborn, stupid student. 'That's why we saw Luxe in the first place.'

I put my finger on my chin, pretending to consider this. 'No,' I said after a moment. 'No, I'm definitely not in love with him.' Then I smiled. 'Here's something you might find funny. It was at the Rainbow gig that I figured out I wasn't crushing on Dallas. It was his *music* I loved. So I owe you. If you hadn't talked me into going that night, I never would've figured out who I was really in love with.'

Sheiss. Me and my big, fat blurty mouth …

Miranda was leaning in so close that her face was practically touching mine. 'Who? Who are you in love with then?'

'No-one,' I said, my hands and face clammy all of a sudden. 'I was joking.'

'Olive?' Dallas's voice was surprisingly strong, and when I turned to him his eyes had lost their murkiness. 'Why are you wearing Lachlan's hoodie?'

At first Miranda didn't register what he'd said – she was too busy glaring at me. But then I saw Dallas's words sink in and her eyes fix on the hoodie. By the time she looked at my face again, she'd started sniggering. The sniggering bloomed into laughter until she was practically hysterical.

'I'm sorry,' she said, when she'd recovered enough to speak. 'I'm just trying to imagine you and Lachlan as a couple. It's too funny.'

I remembered how Lachlan's arms had felt around me. I remembered his warm mouth against mine. 'I don't think it's funny,' I said.

Miranda wiped her eyes. 'Oh come off it, Olive,' she said. 'I mean, I kind of admire you saying that you don't care if everyone found out about Ami and your little *incident*. But that was just a bluff, right? Do you think a guy like Lachlan – someone who could have anyone he wanted – is going to stick around once he finds out the truth about you?'

I didn't bother replying. There was no point. Just like there was no point in me staying here. I was done with Miranda. And Dallas wasn't going to come with me.

'Where do you think you're going?' she said.

'Away,' I said. 'Far away from you.'

It was Dallas who stopped me. He lurched from his chair and draped his arms around Miranda and me. 'Hey, no fighting,' he said. 'This is a *party*. We all love each other here.'

'Get off!' Miranda yelled at him, shoving him away. 'You're always *pawing* at me. I'm sick of it.'

If I'm logical about it – rational – I know that it was the way Miranda shoved Dallas that caused him to fall, to slip on the rug and knock his head on the table. He was so shaky and unstable anyway. But to me it seemed like it was what Miranda said to him that caused it, and the look of absolute hatred she flashed him.

When he hit the ground, his eyes closed.

'Dallas!' I leapt over to him, knelt down and rolled him onto his back. There was blood on his forehead, and a sudden purple swelling underneath it. I patted his face. Gently at first, then more firmly. 'Dallas?'

He made a vague noise but his eyes stayed closed.

I stood up. 'Give me your phone,' I said to Miranda. 'We have to call an ambulance.'

Miranda looked down at Dallas as if she wasn't sure who he was or how he'd ended up on her floor. Like he was something boring.

I wanted to shake her. 'He's hurt!'

Miranda rolled her eyes. 'He's just drunk. As usual. Let him sleep it off.'

I shouldn't have been shocked, of course. I'd suspected for a long time that her interest in Dallas was just a way of getting at me. So it made perfect sense that she'd give up the pretence the moment she realised I had no feelings for Dallas. No *romantic* feelings, that is. I did still care for him. A lot.

I felt the anger rush up through me as I headed for the bedroom door. Clearly Miranda wasn't about to hand over her phone. I'd have to track down the landline. 'God, Miranda. Why are you *like* this?'

I wasn't expecting an answer.

'You know why I'm like this.' Miranda sounded calm. 'You've always known. You just let everyone convince you that you were wrong.'

I stood there, hand poised over the door handle as Miranda walked up and stopped beside me. I found myself looking at her mouth, knowing exactly what she was going to say even as her lips were forming the words.

'I'm a shapeshifter.'

o

There was this time – I was just a kid – when I'd known something that no-one else had known. It was one of those silly bits of information that you grab onto as a kid. *Flies take off backwards.* I'd taken my interesting fact to school and told everyone during show-and-tell. No-one had believed me – not even the teacher – and by the end of the day I'd started to doubt it myself.

But the next morning the teacher stood up the front of the class and made an announcement. 'Olive was correct,' she said. 'I checked, and flies do take off backwards.' Then she apologised for not believing me, and made everyone else apologise too.

When Miranda said that she was a shapeshifter I had the same feeling of triumph. I wanted to call Dr Richter. *See? I was right. Now apologise.*

. But the feeling passed almost immediately. Was Miranda telling the truth? Maybe. Maybe not. Because after all these months of hanging out with Miranda, there were only two things I knew for sure. Two things that threw everything else into doubt.

'You,' I said, 'are a liar. And a manipulative bitch.'

I knew that Miranda wasn't likely to let that pass by. But when she hit me, her hand cracking like a whip on my face, I was shocked.

'You're the liar!' she spat. 'You tricked me into thinking you liked Dallas!'

I watched her face, how her anger twisted it. I heard how pathetic she sounded, and felt amazed that she'd ever had any power over me. I reached out for the door handle again, and this time I turned it, pushing the door open. My face was tingling from the slap and I imagined the marks of her fingers glowing on my face. 'I'm going to find a phone,' I said. 'Dallas needs an ambulance.'

The hallway was pitch-black and I felt a sudden wave of hopelessness. The phone could be anywhere. That's if germ freaks even *had* phones.

'Wait. Please, Olive. My phone's not in here. I'll take you to it.'

Maybe I turned back because something in her voice had changed. Softened. Or maybe I turned because I didn't know what else to do.

Miranda glided past me, out of her room and into the hallway. 'This way.'

o

We went upstairs. It was hard to imagine it could've been darker than down below but somehow it was. Stuffier too. I peered around in the gloom but couldn't see a phone anywhere. Miranda reached up her hand and pulled a chain that was dangling from the roof. A square of grey appeared in the roof above us – a trapdoor. There was a clunking sound and then a set of stairs slid out, leading up into the roof.

'Up *there?*' I said. Why did my voice have to squeak like that? I told myself I was just worried about Dallas.

Without bothering to reply Miranda began climbing the ladder. I watched her climb, feeling the cold air from the attic fall and settle across me.

The thing that always bothered me about scary movies was how stupid the victims always seem, and how they never act on their instincts. They might say something like *I've got a bad feeling about this*, while they dither about opening the cellar door. When we showed movies like that at the Mercury, someone in the audience would occasionally call out a warning. But of course the characters always opened the door or pushed the button.

If anyone had been watching me, hesitating at the bottom of a ladder that led up into a dark roof, they would've yelled, 'Don't do it!'

But I did it anyway.

o

The attic was the only place in Oona's house that didn't reek of disinfectant, and after my eyes adjusted I saw why. The two small attic windows – the only windows in the entire place without grilles – had been pushed open. A breeze was blowing and I could smell the sea mixed with a whiff of chlorine from the pool down below. Miranda was standing in front of one of the windows, a dark, still shape. Can you radiate darkness? She seemed to. There was a pause. And then the dark figure disappeared through the window frame.

'Miranda?' I called, moving as quickly as I could across the uneven floor, stepping over the roof beams and around the taped-up boxes. I felt unstable and foggy-brained. When I got to the window I looked down. There was the swimming pool, glimmering way down below. But I couldn't see Miranda. There was a noise on the roof, to my left. Hunched there, close to the edge, was a dark shape.

'Funny place to keep a phone,' I muttered.

'We need to talk,' Miranda said. 'You're so strange now, Olive. Heartless.'

I was heartless? Dallas was lying on the floor of her bedroom, unconscious, and she didn't seem the slightest bit concerned.

'I don't want to talk,' I said. The floorboards creaked beneath my feet and maybe Miranda thought I was about to walk away because she quickly pulled something out of her pocket. Her phone.

'Here,' she said, holding it up. 'I've got it here. Join me – just for a moment? There's something I want to show you. After that, you can call a thousand ambulances and whoever else you want.'

The smell of the pool wafted up. Off in the distance I heard cars. *I could just run out to the street*, I thought. *Flag someone down.* But that would mean leaving Dallas here alone with Miranda. I looked at her again, sitting on the roof, hand outstretched. Maybe if I just went out for a moment. And then I'd take the phone. It wasn't like her words had any sway over me now.

That's what I was thinking. I guess it sounds stupid.

'OK, OK,' I muttered. 'I'm coming.' The zombie juice rumbled and rolled in my stomach.

I climbed out of the narrow window and into the orchestra of night noises. The whirr of insects. The ocean. The distant traffic. The loudest sound of all was my own breathing. *Don't look down.* Once I'd made it onto the roof, I shuffled across the sloping surface on my bum, inch by inch. Miranda was only a metre away but it seemed to take forever to get to her.

I finally stopped, panting and clammy, at what I felt was a safe distance away from her.

'What did you want to show me?'

Miranda had placed the phone down on the other side of

her, away from me. She pointed out into the night. 'That,' she said. 'All that darkness, stretching on forever. Doesn't it make you feel small? Like a worthless little speck?'

'It's not so dark,' I said, partly because I felt like disagreeing with everything Miranda said – but also because it was true. Maybe it looked dark at first, but if you waited a little bit, then you started to notice things. The stars. The moon. The glow of the city. Headlights working their way up the hill. The longer I sat there the more light there seemed to be.

The moonlight on Miranda's face had turned her skin and hair silvery-white. 'We've got a lot in common,' she said. 'And I know you've had fun hanging out with me. Admit it.'

Far away there was the sound of a car alarm going off.

I shrugged. 'Sure,' I said. 'It was fun. At first.'

Miranda looked at me, eyes shining. 'We can still have fun, you know,' she said. She sounded excited. Hopeful. 'How about we make a deal? I won't tell anyone about Ami or your "history" if you don't leave me.'

'I'd rather have no friends than agree to that,' I retorted. 'You really have no idea, do you?'

And then I saw that this was true. Miranda knew how to manipulate and twist people, how to drive them to the edge – even over the edge – but she knew nothing about being a friend.

It was a long time before Miranda spoke again, and when she did her voice was subdued. 'I don't belong around here.' She laughed flatly. 'That's stating the obvious, huh? But let's be honest. I'll never belong anywhere.'

293

She hunched over herself, arms tucked under her legs, chin resting on her knees. The breeze was blowing her hair into her eyes and mouth. 'You don't know how exhausting it is,' she said. 'Being me. I'm so tired of it.' Miranda rose to her feet. 'I'm going,' she said, stretching her arms out theatrically. 'Out there.'

'I've had enough of these stupid nerve tests,' I said, furious that she was trying this again. 'Get away from there.'

She looked at me, a strange sad smile on her mouth. 'Would you be sad if I jumped?' she asked softly. 'Or relieved?'

'I'd be pissed off,' I snapped, 'because I'd be the one left behind to deal with the mess.'

Miranda's smile vanished. I never saw it again. She took a step closer to the edge.

'Miranda!'

I don't remember stretching out my arm towards her but I must have, because quick as a flash, Miranda took hold of my wrist. Her fingers dug into my flesh.

'Come with me then,' she said unevenly. 'We can merge with the darkness. Together.'

She shuffled up next to me, her grip strengthening, until she was right beside me, her voice in my ear, making the buzz in my head return. Or maybe it had never gone.

'Be honest with yourself, Olive. People like us are too much hard work. We wear everyone down. We'd be doing everyone a favour by ending it all.' Her words stabbed into me. 'What difference does it make if you die tonight or in a few years?' she said. 'It's not like your dad will care. Your brother's just a kid –

he'll forget you pretty quickly. Your mum? Maybe. But you've caused her plenty of grief already. She might be less cut up than you think.'

'That's not true,' I said, teeth gritted.

'So who does that leave?' said Miranda, as though I hadn't spoken. 'Lachlan?' She snorted. 'He won't grieve for long.'

If I shook my head hard enough, maybe I could keep the words out. 'No.'

Miranda's face darkened. 'I'm tired of you saying no to me, Olive. If you won't do it on your own then I'll *make* you jump.'

She stood, yanking me up so that I too was standing. I was right on the edge of the roof now, and Miranda positioned herself behind me. We must have triggered one of Oona's security lights because suddenly everything down below was dazzlingly bright. The grass shimmered. The trees pulsed. The swimming pool was the biggest, bluest eye you ever saw, staring right at me. *This is it.* The only thing I could hope for was to land in the pool and not on the concrete. I tensed up, waiting for the push. But it didn't come. Miranda started to make this strange, choking noise, and a moment later she let go of my wrist.

I stepped back from the edge, turning towards her. Her shoulders were shuddering.

'Miranda? Are you *crying*?'

Even though I was desperate to get away from her and the edge of that roof, I felt a tiny twinge of something. I knew about being sad and alone and how much it could wreck your life. Watching her, I felt a weird mess of things churning inside me.

Anger and hate, of course. Fear. But something else too.

'Poor Miranda. You're so screwed up, aren't you?' I said.

Instantly she turned on me, wild with fury. 'Don't you dare say that! Not *ever!*' she snarled, her arm sticking out blindly to push me away.

At first I had the strange sensation that the roof was tilting away from me. Then I realised what was happening.

Falling.

I was falling.

Grabbing hold of something as you fall is an automatic response. Another one of those reflexes. But when I grabbed onto Miranda as I fell off the roof, it felt way more deliberate.

Like I was thinking, *If I fall, then you're coming too.*

TWENTY-FIVE

Did either of us scream? I'm not sure. Maybe there wasn't time. Then the surface of the pool slammed against us, resisting us for only a moment before we plunged through.

Cold. It was so cold in there. But the moment I was in the water, I felt all the tightness in my body dissolve. I can remember how Miranda looked, I think. Her hair swirling, the bubbles streaming from her nose. The wide, fearful eyes. But how could I have seen so much detail? It was crazy and chaotic in the water. I do remember one thing for sure, though – the feeling of Miranda's fingers curled like tentacles around my neck.

Kick. The sudden strength came from nowhere and I kept kicking until I'd struggled up to the surface, Miranda still hanging from my neck. I grabbed a gulp of air, maybe two, before her panicked thrashing dragged us both down again.

One kick, then another kick, then another. Up up up. There was barely time for a gasp of air before she dragged me back under. *Get away from her or you'll both drown.* While there was still air in my lungs, I took hold of Miranda's hands from around my neck and pulled them away. I expected her to fight me of course, to cling on with everything she had. But she didn't. Miranda let me untangle myself and suddenly I was free of her. I began swimming up. Up, up and away.

At first all I could think about was breathing again. I surfaced and gulped the sweet, incredible air, my weak arms clutching the pebbled edge of the pool. When I could, I looked around, expecting to see Miranda nearby, drinking in the air like I was. But she wasn't. I worked up the courage to dunk my head into the water again, and saw a dark shape drifting just below me.

I guess there are people who would've climbed out of the pool and left Miranda where she was. There are probably people who would've said things were better off that way. But that didn't even cross my mind, and I'm glad of it. Because if I'd left her there, what kind of a person would that make me? Someone just as bad as Miranda. Worse, maybe. Or at least that's how I see it.

So I filled my lungs and dived down towards the dark shape. I hooked my arms under hers and tried to pull her up. It was difficult, so much harder than I'd thought, and I was about to go back up for air when someone dived into the pool and glided towards us. A sleek shape – fast and strong. For the second time that evening, Lachlan's arm encircled me. He held me and I held Miranda and together we made it to the surface.

Lachlan took Miranda from me and lifted her from the pool

as I struggled out. I flung myself on the ground. How *good* it felt. How solid. I rolled over and watched as Lachlan turned Miranda on her side and cleared the water out of her lungs. She coughed and gasped and her eyes opened for a moment. Then she closed them again.

'Is she OK?' I asked.

'She's breathing, at least,' said Lachlan. 'The ambulance should be here soon. I called one the moment I saw you two in the pool.'

I remembered something. 'Dallas!'

Lachlan nodded. 'I found him. Had to kick in the back door to get inside. He's messed up but I reckon he'll be OK.'

I nodded, suddenly feeling tearful. 'I'm so glad you're here,' I said, my nose going all kind of weird and snuffly. 'Although I've no idea how you knew where I was.'

Lachlan gave a little laugh. 'I know you better than you think, Olive Corbett,' he said. 'When I got home I started daydreaming, *what would she be doing right now?* And then I realised that you were probably off trying to rescue Dallas.'

Miranda's eyes had opened again. She was watching us. Something inside me leapt.

'She's awake.'

Lachlan crouched down beside her. 'Miranda? Can you hear me?'

She looked at him and her eyes were more serene than I'd ever seen them. 'She's not right in the head, you know,' she said softly. 'Your little *girlfriend.*'

Lachlan frowned and leant in closer. 'Pardon?'

When she spoke again, her voice was stronger. 'Olive tried to drown herself. Didn't you know that? And then she got herself an imaginary friend. *Ami*. Olive mutters to her all day long, like a *freak*.'

Insects buzzed and whirred around us as Lachlan's eyes met mine, filled with confusion. He didn't say anything, but I could see the question on his lips. *Is it true?*

For a moment I couldn't speak. And then I felt the fury rise. Rise and spill right over the top. I leant over Miranda so that my face was right above hers.

'It's lucky for you Ami's not around anymore, Miranda Vaile,' I said. 'Because I know exactly what she'd say right now. She'd tell me to push you back into that pool.'

Lachlan's expression changed then. The doubt receded just a little, and a smile appeared. That same smile that I'd once thought was mocking. How did I ever make such a stupid mistake?

'Who was this Ami?' he asked, like he was scared of the answer.

'She was just me,' I said, and made my same old joke. 'But with better hair.'

Lachlan reached out and touched my face, my sodden hair, so tenderly I could have cried. He left his hand there in a way that gave me a sudden rush of hope. There was a whole lot of stuff I had to tell him. Obviously. But I felt that at least he would listen.

'Well, it wouldn't be hard to have better hair than you right now,' he said teasingly, and I knew everything would be OK.

There were sirens then, coming up the hill towards us. Lachlan stood up. 'I'd better go and work out how to open the gate.' He looked at me. 'Want to come?'

I nodded and together we walked towards the gate, leaving Miranda lying by the pool.

o

Miranda wasn't at school on Monday. She wasn't there the day after either. Two whole weeks passed before I finally allowed myself to believe she wasn't coming back. It wasn't that surprising, I suppose. After all, it had always been just a matter of time before Oona got sick of Miranda and shunted her off to another relative.

No-one spoke about Miranda's sudden disappearance from school, or even mentioned her name. It was like they'd forgotten she was there in the first place.

It was almost a month before Oona's body was found. One of her regular delivery guys became suspicious about the uncollected mail spewing from her letterbox. He scaled the fence, opened the unlocked front door and found Oona dead on her bedroom floor – gloves on, clutching a can of disinfectant. Died of natural causes, the local paper reported. Heart attack.

When I heard that, I'd instantly pictured Oona returning early from the trip and dropping dead in horror when she realised germ-encrusted strangers had been in her house. And it was all too easy to imagine Miranda driving off coolly in Oona's car, the one that only I seemed to have noticed was missing. But one afternoon, I suddenly remembered Oona's closed bedroom door the night of the party. I found myself wondering, my skin pimpling up, if she'd been lying there dead the whole time. Just as quickly, I made myself push the thought away. There were more important things to focus on, like sorting out stuff with my family. Miranda had taken up enough of my life.

o

Fixing things with Mum and Toby began with some hardcore apologising – which wasn't so difficult because I felt pretty terrible about the things I'd said. And then I had to spend a *lot* of time at home watching boring movies and eating bad cake. It was all worth it though, because things really changed after that. For instance, Mum said that after our fight she'd realised she *had* been taking me for granted, and now she pays me for babysitting. I still cook a lot, but that's mostly because I want to protect Toby and me from tofu schnitzels.

Sorting out things with Dad is taking a bit longer. I realised I was really, *really* mad at him for leaving us so suddenly, and without saying goodbye. When I told him that on the phone the other day, he said he felt he had to go or he'd explode. 'It wasn't anyone's fault, Pet,' he said. 'It was just one of those things.' That sounds like a dumb excuse to me. I'm still mad at him, but at least I don't feel like it's my fault he left, and I've decided that I will see him again. Eventually. Maybe it'll be easier to talk about this stuff when we meet up.

It was because of Lachlan that I started to make more of an effort with people at school. You know, talking to them, and not just avoiding them because they might think I'm weird. I *am* weird, and you know what? That's OK. So are most interesting people. Lachlan seems to get that, and I like the way he sometimes makes gags about imaginary friends. Like it's just something quirky. I can laugh now, even if I do still miss Ami.

Lachlan and I have been spending a lot of time with Dallas, getting him back on track. Lachlan helped Dallas patch things up with Vinnie and Pearl, and he's even been working on finishing the album with them. There's a new edge to their music these days. A good one.

But mostly it's just the two of us, me and Lachlan. Unless you count those thousand butterflies launching inside me every time we kiss. Sometimes I meet him down at the beach in the morning and we'll go for a swim or stretch out on the sand, listening to music.

For the first few days it was mostly me talking – telling him about everything that had happened, and about Ami. Why I needed her around. Why I don't anymore. But now we talk about other stuff too – like what we might do when school finishes. It changes all the time of course, but the latest plan is to head overseas and buy a van, then drive around the world. We'll stop at beaches during the day and go to gigs at night.

So there hasn't been much time to think about Miranda. But just occasionally I find myself wondering what she's up to these days. Where she is. That's the thing – she could be anywhere, doing anything. It'll sound strange but I feel like there's still a bond between us. Maybe I miss her, just a bit. I know that's kind of crazy, but I can't deny it.

Last week, with a thumping heart, I typed Miranda's name into Google. Nothing came up. But that doesn't mean she'll never reappear. I'm pretty sure she will, actually. Somewhere. One day.

ACKNOWLEDGEMENTS

This book owes a huge debt to the amazing people at Hardie Grant Egmont; in particular the incomparable Hilary Rogers for liking the idea from the start and for helping so much with the early drafts. Thanks to the wondrous Marisa Pintado for her excellent editing and manuscript advice, the early morning Skype sessions and the virtual arm-patting. I am enormously grateful to Charlotte Bodman for all the work she's done for this book at the markets, as well as to the HGE marketing team for their promotional support. I feel very lucky to have such a fantastic cover too, designed by Astred Hicks of Design Cherry – she managed to hit the perfect note of creepy versus pretty.

Vielen Dank to the staff at the Langen Flugsicherung Biblioteque and to all librarians in general – especially my personal favourites, Jim and Julie Badger.

Thanks to Kylie Boyd for the Interesting Fact. A big cuddly squeeze to Mads for letting me use Bim-Bim and Spanner's names in this book.

And finally enormous, heartfelt thanks to Matt Wallace for your endless, unwavering support. This book would never have been finished without your help.

Em Bailey is an Australian living in Germany where, despite having been a vegetarian for many years, she now enjoys the occasional Wurst. Em used to be a new-media designer for a children's television production house and is now a full-time author. *Shift* is her first YA novel, although she has written a number of books for children under a different name.

When she's not writing, Em is generally getting lost, losing stuff, reading, hanging out with her friends and family, and listening to Radiolab podcasts. Like Olive, she doesn't like leggings that look like jeans, but has no problem with tofu schnitzels.